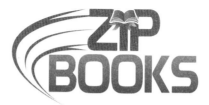

This item was purchased for the Library
through Zip Books, a statewide project of
the NorthNet Library System, funded by
the California State Library.

KIMBERLY KREY

Reese's Cowboy Kiss
Witness Protection ~ Rancher Style

Sweet Montana Bride Series
Book One

KIMBERLY KREY

Reese's Cowboy Kiss

Witness Protection ~ Rancher Style

Sweet Montana Bride Series
Book One

The Sweet Montana Bride Series

(Complete collection on Amazon, Barnes & Noble, and CreateSpace now)

by KIMBERLY KREY

Reese's Cowboy Kiss

Blake's Story

Jade's Cowboy Crush

Gavin's Story

Cassie's Cowboy Crave

Shane's Story

Second Chances Series:

by KIMBERLY KREY

Rough Edges

Allie's Story

Mending Hearts

Logan's Story

Fresh Starts

Bree's Story

See Amazon, Barnes & Noble, and or
CreateSpace.com for availability

DEDICATION

To my beautiful BayLee girl:
You lend light and laughter
with your wit and charm, and
I absolutely adore you. May you
always see the wonderful things
about yourself, and never be
afraid to share them.

Table Talk questions found on Six Sister's Stuff website @ http://www.sixsistersstuff.com/2013/03/50-family-dinner-conversation-starters.html

ACKNOWLEDGMENTS

A big thanks goes to my husband and kids for their patience, support, and love.

And to my critique partner, Jamie, who's continued to be a support through the (quite beautiful) life-changing events in her life – thank you!

Thank you beta readers; I sincerely appreciate the time you've taken to provide your ever-helpful feedback.

And lastly, to the wonderful Writing Group of Joy and Awesomeness: Chantele Sedgwick, Christine Houston, Donna Nolan, Erin Summerill, Jamie Thompson, Jeigh Meredith, Jessie Humphries, Julie Donaldson, Katie Dodge, Peggy Eddleman, Ruth Josse, Sandy Panton, Shelly Brown, and Taffy Lovell. I love and adore you all and feel so blessed to have you in my life! Thank you for the support, the good times, and the fabulous food at our writing retreats. Here's to many, many more!

CHAPTER ONE

Reese glanced over the large crowd of dancing bodies as she caught her breath. It hadn't been easy to keep up with the fast-paced line dance in a gown and high heels, but she'd be lying if she said it hadn't been fun. Still, it was almost time to pass off her crown to this year's winner, and she needed to freshen up.

With a shallow sigh, she searched the crowd once more, glad when she failed to see the man with the unyielding gaze. The gawking stranger had set her on edge since she'd arrived. Perhaps he'd gone home, she decided, feeling hopeful at the mere thought.

The rowdy song came to an end while she moved along the outskirts of the dance floor. A warm Texas breeze wafted over her skin just as the band started a new tune – a slow and easy number. The kind that had her picturing warm days at the lake. Or romantic strolls on a moonlit night. She smiled as a young couple among the group caught her attention. Their intimate contact seeming to reach into that longing place in her heart. Reese's glance shifted to the man's hand, clenched around the woman's waist as he kissed her, passion oozing from his every move. Never had she been kissed in such a manner. Or even known a man she wished would kiss her that way.

"Some folks just don't know when to get a room," a familiar voice spoke.

Reese spun around to see her younger brother, CJ, standing close by. Her face flushed with heat as her gaze fell back to the couple. "Yeah," she agreed with a sigh. "I guess you're right."

"Why ain't you dancin' with nobody?" CJ asked. "Too big of a snob?"

She slapped his arm. "You know I'd never turn anyone down. I'm just looking for Mama, is all. She's got my makeup bag."

"Well, wish I could help ya, but I'm off to find a pretty little thing to dance with." He flashed her a mischievous grin, rolling his shoulders back.

"You enjoy yourself," she said. "And don't you go makin' out on the dance floor."

Her brother cocked one eyebrow, gave her a wink, and then disappeared into the crowd. Reese's gaze wandered to the auction tables along the stage. And there was her mom, frantically scribbling on a tattered notepad.

The lights on the stage were bright against the night, causing Reese to squint as she moved. She'd made it only part-way up the steps when a wiry hand clamped around her wrist.

"Would you like to dance?"

Reese spun around, knowing who'd asked before even seeing the man. She forced a polite smile as her fears were confirmed. It was him – the man who'd burned holes straight through her body with his steely glare alone. He was fairly thin, but his features were soft and round; from the outline of his clean-shaven jaw, to his small nose and bulbous cheeks. He blinked a few times, his bright green eyes watering from the blaring stage lights.

"I'd love to," she lied, guessing the makeup would have to wait. Her peace of mind would be put on hold too, but it was just one dance. She could get through it.

His clammy fingers skidded down her wrist to where he took hold of her hand, pulling her deep into the crowd before settling on a spot. Reese grimaced, suddenly feeling like a giant. With the help of her three-inch heels, she was half-a-head taller than the guy.

He glanced up at her, the intensity she'd seen in his eyes replaced by something entirely different. Reese tilted her head; she'd made a habit of looking for the inner light in folks – that unique spark that made each person shine. She could usually sense it quickly enough. A humble kindness or confident gleam. A determined spirit or forgiving heart. Surely this guy was no exception.

Or was he? She furrowed her brows as she looked at him further, unable to get past the odd shifting of his eyes. The strange way he evaded her gaze.

He was simply shy, Reese decided, as he stepped closer and wrapped his arms around her back. She rested her hands on his shoulders in return, unnerved by his tense and rigid form. Her skin objected to him too. The very feel of him against her was all wrong.

There was an obvious rhythm to the slow song playing, but the guy barely lifted a foot. Reese had danced with several men that evening. Everything from true Texas gentlemen to cocky, bull riding brutes. But none of them had made her feel the way this guy did. On edge. Almost ... afraid. She pulled in a deep breath, counting down the seconds, dying for the song to end. She felt guilty for being so turned off by the man; he was obviously nervous. Most likely he'd simply been working up the nerve to ask her to dance as he'd stared throughout the evening. Why couldn't she be endeared to him instead?

The answer stood in the energy surrounding him; it felt off. Eager. Intense. And as much as she wanted to make polite conversation to ease the discomfort of it all, she couldn't think of a word to say. He'd just have to be the one to speak up first.

Yet as the band played on, the odd stranger never uttered a word. And as ugly as it felt, staying silent as they danced, Reese did just that.

At last the music began to fade as a deep voice blared from the stage – Corbin Carmichael, the host of the annual event. "One last song, folks," he announced, "and then our Pearland Rose and our new title holder will take the stage for the passing of the crown." Hoots, hollers, and cat calls sounded from the crowd. "Now let's hear one more round of applause for our rip roaring band for the night, the Texan Blasters. I wanna see all y'all on the dance floor for this one. Time to get those boots a stompin'!"

Reese cleared her throat and backed away from the awkward man, causing him to drop his arms at last. "Thanks for the dance," she said, turning away from him. She was anxious to be free from the man, to find her mom, and to get freshened up before passing on her crown.

It was that tight and sudden grip around her wrist that stopped her short, a repeat of what he'd done the first time. His palm felt cool and wet. "Guess it's time to finally give up your title," the young man said. "I'm really going to miss seeing you in that crown."

Reese's gaze had been set on the grip he had on her. She glanced over to the bodies stepping to the line dance before looking into the man's face. Beads of sweat coated his forehead and upper lip. The surface of his cheeks looked red and swollen. "I hardly ever wore the thing," she said.

"You wore it to all your public appearances." His fingers loosened the slightest bit. The corner of his lip twitched.

Reese nodded, his intrusive gaze causing her to shift; the striking green of his eyes becoming oddly familiar. "Do I know you from somewhere?" she asked.

"High school," he explained. "I'm Donald Turnsbro. We were in Mr. Li's biology class together."

"That's right," she said. Only she couldn't actually place him. It'd been five years since high school after all. The crowd started to move in on them, forcing their bodies close once more. "Well, thanks again for the dance," Reese said. "I better go freshen up." She darted toward the stage, barely dodging a collision with the dancers on the floor. She folded her arms over her chest as she sped up the stairs, recalling the way he'd reached for her wrist; the recollection making her shiver.

She spotted her mom next to the auction table, arranging paper slips next to each item sold. "Mama?"

A large smile spread over her face as she spun around. "Hi, darlin'. You're going to be up in just a bit."

Reese remained motionless as she adjusted the hair around her crown. "Is it a mess?" she asked.

"Nah, I've seen worse. But here, you'll be wanting this." She spun around and began scrounging under the picnic table at the edge of the stage, the curtain barely covering the mess of tote bags, Tupperware, and boxes. "Here." She handed over her makeup bag. "Doesn't look like there's a line to the ladies room. Why don't you sneak on in there."

A deep sigh made its way through Reese's chest as she tucked the small bag under her arm. "Thank you."

"What's a matter, baby? Sad about giving up your crown?"

Reese shrugged, looking over the crowd for the strange man. "Maybe a little."

Her mom placed her hands on Reese's cheeks, waited until her gaze settled back on her. "Well there's a bright side to it, ya know? Close your eyes and take a whiff."

Reese looked back at her warily.

"Trust me, baby. Just do it."

While releasing another sigh, Reese closed her

eyes. Her mom's hands moved to Reese's upper arms. "Now," she said, "inhale a nice, deep breath."

Reese inhaled until her chest rose.

"What do you smell?" she asked her.

"I don't know."

A chuckle escaped her mom's lips. "Boy, you *have* been dieting for a while. Haven't ya? Try again."

Reese focused as she breathed in, noting the incredible aroma, thick on the evening air. Rich and smoky, tangy and sweet. "Barbeque," she said. "Smells just like Grandma Dee's."

"That's right. And you don't have to worry about fitting into these gowns or keeping trim for any special events. Soon as you hand over that crown, let the new girl count calories and you go get some *real* food."

Reese gasped. "Mama," she said with a chuckle. "I can't believe my ears."

"What? I ain't suggesting you let yourself go completely. But you need to take advantage of the perks of *not* being Miss Pearland's Rose."

Reese smiled. "Yeah, maybe you're right." Her mouth watered at the thought.

"That-a girl. Now skedaddle on outta here and go freshen up." Her mom had managed to distract her from the disturbing encounter with the strange man; Reese was grateful for it. She always did know how to make things right.

Feeling a bit more at ease, Reese sped toward the restrooms behind the stage. She gripped hold of the thick, black curtain along the sidewall, knowing the bathroom doors were entirely hidden by the thing, and spotted a man among the hefty cloth.

Her heart jumped.

She tilted her head, anxious to get a better look at his face, when he disappeared into the fabric folds. With renewed force, Reese shoved the curtain aside once more, wondering if her mind was playing tricks on her. She might not have gotten a solid look at him, but the man she'd seen looked just like Donald Turnsbro; she was sure of it.

Her hands trembled slightly as she tugged the curtain back one last time, knowing she was in the right place. And there it was, the sign she'd been looking for, the letters carved right into the bathroom door: *Senoritas.*

Anxious thumps pressed their way through her chest as she pried open the heavy oak door, desperate to get into the quiet space and grip hold of her rampant thoughts.

The music died down as the door closed behind her, the soft glow of light a welcoming change. She skipped the mirror altogether and sped straight for the only stall. Reese had the door partway closed before she noticed a young woman standing at the sink. She tilted her head to catch eye contact with her through the mirror. Blonde hair, a sash over her shoulder, and a dress that matched the color of Reese's gown.

"Howdy," Reese offered with a shaky voice.

The girl blinked her lashes through a wand of mascara before glancing at her. "Can't wait to get my hands on that crown," she said. "Are you sad about giving it up?"

Reese shook her head. "Only a little. I mean, it's been a great year, and you're going to enjoy every minute of it I'm sure, but I think I'm about ready to be done with it and move on. You know?"

The girl reached into her makeup bag before twisting a small lid off a tube of lip gloss. She smothered it over her top lip as she spoke. "I don't know," she said, moving to the bottom lip. "I'm not gonna stop here. I plan to go onto Brazoria County, Miss Texas, Miss America. I want it all."

Reese smiled, charmed by the young woman's ambition. There was quite a difference in their ages. Pearland's new rose had won at the young age of eighteen, while Reese had taken the crown at the maximum age of twenty-three. "Well, good for you. I'll be cheering ya on from the sidelines," she said before closing the stall door. The latch to lock the metal door was old and rusty. Nearly impossible to slide. She tightened her grip around the dull knob and shoved, the loud 'pop' filling the quiet space. "Sorry," Reese said. "Stubborn lock."

Her gaze fell to the small tiles on the floor as she folded her arms over her chest, wishing she could skip the ceremony altogether, slip out the back door and go home. Her interaction with the man on the dance floor had her feeling nervous. Afraid, though she knew it was foolish. The guy couldn't possibly mean her harm. He'd only been awkward was all. Not dangerous. She nodded to herself, convinced to shake it off.

With a wave of assurance urging her forward, Reese reached for the latch to unlock the stall. Just as she shoved the stubborn thing into place, an ear-splitting explosion rocked the room. Reese pressed her hands to her ears and ducked down, cringing as the deafening blast echoed throughout the small space.

A gunshot? Had somebody just shot a gun? Her heart thudded against her chest, the pressing rhythm making it hard to breathe. A sharp ringing pierced her ears as she lifted her chin, and then straightened to a stand altogether. Through the crack of the stall frame, a view of the mirror came into sight. Only she didn't see the girl. Instead Reese saw a man reflected there – his green eyes wild. And then he was gone, lost in the black fabric folds.

The door creaked to a close. The shrill ringing only intensified as she yanked open the flimsy stall door. Blood. A dark, oozing pool of it soaked the satin banner across the young girl's chest. A hand flew to Reese's mouth as she screamed, a horrid realization coming to mind: The man in the mirror – it had been him. The one who'd sent her rushing to the restroom in fear. He was dangerous after all. And though it hurt to think it, Reese was certain the bullet in the girl's chest had been meant for her.

CHAPTER TWO

The field was quieter than usual. Oddly quiet. Blake brought Tucker to a slow trot, knowing it'd be dark soon. He used to like this time of day – the sun beyond his view, the temperature cooling with each passing breeze. But lately something about the twilight hour felt ominous and bleak. Or perhaps it was just his recent outlook. How could he keep a handle on the cattle ranch with just three ranch hands this summer? There was too much to be done. He could employ two full-time hands for the hay fields alone. Forget about the fence that needed mending. The swather that was out of commission. And the demon calf who was hell-bent on busting out to gorge on the neighboring greens. There was simply too much to be done.

A burst of static broke through the CB at his belt. "You there, Blake?" It was Tom, his timid voice sounding more anxious than usual.

Blake brought the box to his mouth. "Yep."

"The guys are about to leave, but I told them we better check your location first. Make sure you weren't planning to join us."

Blake didn't have to ask where they were headed; the ranch hands had talked of nothing but the entire week: the big country swing. With the push of the small button beneath his thumb, Blake replied, "You go on ahead, Tom. I'm not interested."

"Yeah, but…" The kid proceeded to spout off a list of reasons he should join in on the fun while Blake rolled his eyes. That was the annoying thing about walkie-talkies – no interrupting someone when they got off on a pointless, rambling jag.

"I appreciate all that," Blake said once Tom was through, "but I've got no time for that kinda stuff right now. You go on. Have fun." He turned off the CB, unwilling to hear another word. He'd meant what he'd said. The last few times Blake had gone to the country swing, he'd met gals who were barely old enough to drive. And there he was, almost ten years older, politely declining their invitations to dance. He was a grown man after all, and he was looking for a grown woman, not some wild teenager.

Tucker picked up speed at his command, seeming to sense Blake's irritation. As if getting him home quickly could lighten his mood. Blake shook his head, wishing it were only that easy.

CHAPTER THREE

Reese ran the smooth surface of her thumbnail over her lower lip, back and forth, her eyes fixed on a spot beyond the windshield. Her parents sat on either side. Her mom cradling one hand. Her dad resting a comforting arm along the seat behind her head. Sheriff Finn – a close family friend – drove the car while Lloyd, another officer, sat up front.

There were four people in the vehicle with her. Two of which were emotionally closer to her than anyone, save CJ, of course. A solid shield of protection, love, and comfort surrounded her, yet in that moment Reese had never felt so vulnerable. So afraid. They hadn't been able to find Donald Turnsbro that night. In fact, according to Sheriff Finn, he'd left his home nearly a month ago. Donald's sister – the one who'd been raising him since their parents died – had been more than cooperative. Let them into the home to look around, and said she would contact them if she heard any word. But with a cleared-out closet, empty dressers, and a job he'd quit months ago, the officers weren't holding their breath.

"There are some kind folks on the ranch you're headed to. Should make you feel right at home," Sheriff Finn said. "They sounded pleased as puddin' about having you out there. Said they could let you help out on the ranch – earn a decent salary while you're there if you'd like."

Reese nodded blankly. "Sounds nice." Though she hadn't registered a word he'd spoken.

"Montana's a beautiful place, baby," her mom said. "Just beautiful."

"Will I be back in time for football?" Reese asked, snapping out of her trance. "I can't miss any of CJ's games."

"You won't, honey," her dad promised. "We've still got two months before the first game starts."

She glanced up to the sheriff for confirmation. He didn't look so sure. "I uh, reckon you will be, darlin', but I don't wanna go makin' any promises."

Reese swallowed the swarm of remaining questions buzzing through her head. They'd already been answered – most of them more than once – but hardly any to her satisfaction. What did it matter? Life had taken a turn. Had things gone differently this night, she'd have been shot like the poor, unsuspecting girl who'd taken her bullet. What right did she have to complain?

"I sure am glad that gal survived," Reese said, recalling the hollow reflection in the girl's eyes. "She looked gone to me."

"Yep," Sheriff Finn said. "She's real lucky, that one."

Her mom spoke something in reply. Her dad joined in next, and soon Lloyd was part of the conversation as well. All of it was background noise to the sounds in Reese's head. The young girl's voice. Her aspiring words. The sound of the rickety lock – loud, yet nothing compared to the gun blast. The ripping noise that tore through the air like a rocket, its massive echo crashing against the bare bathroom walls.

The visions seeped in next, a stream of broken images. Crimson blood soaking white satin, oozing across the gold letters on the sash – a title Reese had held for the last year of her life.

She closed her eyes against the sight, a stream of fresh tears sliding down her cheeks. Reese was headed to an airport, ready to be shipped to the safe harbor prepared for her. But the other girl was left fighting for her life, and she couldn't help but feel as if she was to blame.

CHAPTER FOUR

Blake rolled down his truck window as he neared the airport, inhaling the fresh Montana air. Sure it might be only six in the morning, but he knew it would be a great day. The sun was up, the weather was fine, and he was about to get the ranch help he so badly needed. Uncle Earl had called just as Blake was about to post the ad, letting him know the good news – they had a witness who needed protection. One with ranch experience, no less. Talk about luck.

After bringing the truck to a stop, he reached an arm out the window and yanked the ticket stub from the small machine. The yellow bar raised, allowing him to enter. He'd been told the witness would have an escort. An officer, from what he gathered. So when Blake saw a man dressed in uniform standing under the specified airline gate, he allowed for a pleased smile. "That was easy," he said under his breath. But where was Reese? The guy he'd be taking back to Emerson

Ranch?

His brow furrowed as he noticed a woman standing next to the cop. Not just any woman, he realized, running an appreciative gaze over her figure. Tall, blonde, and curvy in all the right places, she was the sort that could stop traffic with her appearance alone.

Blake pulled to the side of the curb a few gates away to check the text once more, making sure he had the gate name correct. "Hmm." He tapped out a quick message to let the officer know he'd arrived:

I'm here, he typed. *In a black pickup truck.*

He looked up to the pretty woman while waiting for a reply. A snug pair of Levi's. A fancy-looking top, and a pair of bright red cowgirl boots that belonged more in a shopping mall than an actual field. The cop next to her pulled out his phone, lifted his chin, and motioned for Blake to pull forward.

"What's going on?" He shifted the gear into first. If he didn't know better, he'd say the cop was the very man who'd just received his text. But it couldn't be; he didn't have Reese with him. Still, Blake obeyed, rolling up to the curbside where they stood.

The cop motioned for him to roll down his window. "Are you Mr. Emerson?" the man in uniform asked as the window slid down.

"Yes." Blake glanced at the girl behind the man. She was hunching down to grab her luggage.

"Well if you'd kindly exit your vehicle I can

introduce y'all properly, have you leave your John Hancock in a few places, and you two will be on your way."

Blake's eyes widened. *Who two?* What was he missing?

The officer cleared his throat, reminding Blake he was supposed to exit the vehicle. "Oh," he said, shutting off the engine. "Let me just..." He climbed out of the truck, lifted the hat off his head, and ran a hand through his unruly hair. It was impossible not to look at the beauty next to the cop. In addition to being stunning beyond all reason she was the subject of the strange mystery at hand. Who was she and why was she there instead of the guy he'd planned to take home?

"You brought ID, I assume," the cop said. "I just need to verify that you're Earl's nephew 'fore we proceed."

Blake tore his eyes off the woman, pulled out his wallet, and handed the man his driver's license. After a thorough look at the thing, the officer handed it back.

"I guess we're good to get down to business then." He motioned to Blake first. "This here is Mr. Blake Emerson, your new escort. And Blake," the man continued, motioning to the blonde beside him, "this here is Reese."

What? Was he kidding? Blake had known a kid named Reese back in the third grade. A little towheaded know-it-all who ran his mouth all the time. He'd expected a towheaded boy. Man. Guy. Not a tall, boot-wearing blonde. An inner part of him misbehaved – the stupid, hadn't-been-close-to-a-woman-in-years part.

The larger, much smarter part took over with a vengeance. What in tarnation was he supposed to do with this woman? And how could she possibly help on the ranch?

"Howdy." She rested her bag to extend an arm his way.

Blake worked to snap out of his stupor. He looked down at her dainty hand before shaking it in return. "Hi." The beauty gave him a wide smile, her hazel eyes warm, friendly, and set right on him. His belly warmed in response, giving life to that weak side of him once more.

"Well then," the officer said. "Let's get you signed up and squared away." He patted at his chest before looking to Reese. "Do you have them papers?"

Blake followed the officer's gaze.

"Yes," the woman said. "I just tucked 'em in here after I signed 'em." She handed the stack directly to Blake, before digging into her bag once more. "Here's the pen."

Blake hadn't known he was such a sucker for the sound of a woman's southern accent. Turns out he was. "Thanks." His mind was blank as he thumbed through the stapled pages, his fingers clumsy and numb.

"Your part's the latter section of the document," the officer said. "Just uh... sign at the double X's there. 'Course I'm supposed to encourage you to read through it first, but it basically states that you'll help protect the gal, won't disclose any of her information, stuff along those lines."

Blake nodded before glancing at the woman once

more. *That* was Reese? He couldn't get over it. He whipped past the pages she'd already signed, noting how lovely her signature was. The truck served as a table top while he scribbled his name at two different places before handing the stack to the officer. "Sorry about the dirt," he said, wiping the back of the page. He suddenly wished he'd run the thing through a carwash.

"Aw, a little dirt never hurt no one," the officer said. He reached out to shake Blake's hand. "I've got a plane to catch." He turned to the woman next. "I've always wanted to say that."

She smiled and tilted her head, a soft laugh trickling from her lips. "Thanks for all your help, Lloyd," she said, throwing her arms around the man. "I know my family ain't supposed to contact me, but I'm just dying to know how the girl's recovery goes. Think y'all could sneak me a few updates somehow? Maybe by mail or somethin'?"

"I'll see what I can do, Reese. Just assume that no news is good news. 'Sides, Doc Halloway says she'll recover just fine." He turned to Blake. "You take good care of this gal. She's one special lady."

"Will do," Blake assured. After a bout of awkward silence he spoke up again. "Let me get your things for you."

As he loaded her items into the back seat of his truck, Blake tried sifting through the new thoughts running through his head like a mean stampede. Just a few minutes ago he'd been certain his prayers were answered. Getting a new guy on the ranch. One with experience, no less, like Earl had suggested. Instead he'd been handed another job to take care of. A rather attractive one, he'd admit. But talk about distractions. How was he supposed to keep on top of things while caring for some high maintenance, sweet smelling, smooth-handed woman from Texas whose accent alone could melt every good sense he had?

After loading her luggage, Blake held out a hand, assisting her onto the running board. She offered him another one of those smiles as she stepped up. It wasn't until she'd pulled the seatbelt across her lap that Blake realized he was staring. He tore his gaze away while stepping back and closed her door.

He shook his head as he strode around the back of the truck. Heaven help him. He was more distracted than a rooster in a hen house. How would the guys respond back home? He'd gotten them all up, shared the good news about the new ranch hand who'd replied to his help-wanted ad (as he'd told them) and now he'd bring home a woman – one the guys would be whistling at, drooling over, and hitting on. His protective nature roared up. Blake would do what he could to shelter the pretty thing from all their crass remarks and pick up lines. He only felt bad that she'd been sentenced to such a fate.

But how had the mistake been made in the first place? Uncle Earl had never had such a thing happen before. And now... he paused before opening his side of the truck, a thought occurring to him. Earl sure had been harassing him over staying single for so long. 'Course twenty-four was still young, way Blake saw it. But still, was it possible his uncle had done this on purpose? Allowed the woman to come to the ranch in hopes that his hard-working nephew would find love? *No,* he decided. It'd been an innocent mistake, was all. And though it might not be what he wanted – or needed – as far as the ranch was concerned, Blake would shelter this woman the best he could. So long as she could take it. Poor woman didn't know what she was in for.

CHAPTER FIVE

Reese let out a long, slow sigh as she took in the lay of the land. Beyond her side of the truck, a spread of tall green grass stretched clear to the massive mountain scape in the distance. Clusters of bright yellow flowers were scattered throughout, hovering just above the tall blades. The mountains beyond were a sight all their own. From their great height and broad scape, to the beautiful shades of purple and grey. She was certain it was well enough into summer that snow couldn't remain in a place so warm. But along the jagged tips of several pointed tops, stood evidence of the wintery frost, a nearly glowing white.

"They say everything's bigger in Texas," Reese said, her gaze wandering up to the sky. "But lookin' at the scenery here, I have to wonder if those folks have ever been to Montana." The striking layout of sky seemed larger than life. Something about the wide, open view had her breathing more deeply, wanting to fill her lungs with the beauty of it all. She had the restless urge to run through the meadow while grazing her fingers over the velvety petals.

She hadn't dared look too closely out the other side. Mostly because the view of the quiet cowboy did something to her insides. Her mom always said Reese had been flirtin' with the boys since she was born. And Reese never did deny it; with their easy manner and playful banter, the opposite sex was some of the finest company there was. She didn't discriminate either; was never easily affected by the appearance of folks. But Blake Emerson looked like no one she'd ever seen. In person, anyway. She let her gaze veer toward him, only slightly, as he removed his hat and ran a large hand through his gorgeous brown hair. It wasn't long by any means; just long enough to hold a thick, gentle wave as it tousled between his fingers. His finely trimmed facial hair matched, framing his well-defined jaw and perfectly sculpted lips. Yet it was those eyes that had captured her from the moment he'd stepped out of the truck. The warm brown color – all mystery and allure – was a compliment to the silent strength she'd detected in them.

She ran the smooth surface of her thumbnail over her bottom lip while trying to figure the guy out. He wasn't real talkative, that much was sure. It wasn't as if what she'd said had called for a reply, but an acknowledgement would have been nice. She crossed one leg over the other, draped her hands over one knee, and turned to look at him. "So how exactly did you get roped into doing this witness protection thing?" she asked.

He'd set his cowboy hat back on his head, the shade of it adding new depth to his now dark and slightly guarded eyes. He shrugged. "My uncle is a retired marshal. Still takes in witnesses every now and again. A while back he got a kid – close to ranching age – who ended up being one of his best hands." The cowboy – Blake, she reminded herself – paused to glance briefly at her. "My uncle does cattle ranching as well. Anyway, my own father said he'd be willing to take in witnesses from time to time too. Especially if they were a decent fit for ranching. It'd give the witness a place to hide and a nice wage at the same time. Of course, it's more like a safe house at our place, you know. No marshal on duty or anything."

Blake stopped there, causing Reese's mind to race with questions. "I certainly wouldn't want anyone paying me at all. I just plan to help out wherever I can. Earn my keep, as they say. But uh … have y'all taken in a girl before?"

His grip on the steering wheel tightened. He glanced over to her once more, his gaze shifting quickly from where her hands rested on her knees to her face. "Nope. You're the first."

A dart of tingling heat warmed her chest. Something about the sound of his deep voice – smooth and scratchy all at once. She wanted to hear more of it. "So what made you decide to try a girl?" She studied his face, glad to have reason to as she waited for his response.

A world of unspoken words seemed to stir in the depths of his eyes. To her surprise, a hint of a dimple appeared in his cheek, giving evidence of a smile threatening to form. But then it vanished. "Just uh, well, Earl mentioned something about you having a bit of experience," he said. "Did you grow up on a ranch in Texas?"

Reese shook her head. "Oh, no. My daddy's an accountant for several major companies. He specializes in businesses founded right there in the home state," she said proudly.

Blake cleared his throat, shifting in his seat. "So you don't have ranch experience?"

"Oh no, I do. I mean, I worked on a dude ranch the summer after my senior year. I'd earned a scholarship to a local college, but I wanted to earn some extra cash, get a bit of experience before I immersed myself in books."

"What exactly did you do on this... *dude* ranch?" He put emphasis on the word as if it was poison on his tongue.

"Oh, you know, washing, cleaning, cooking. That type of thing."

"So you didn't work with the horses. Cattle. Any of that?"

She shook her head once more. "Uh-uh."

His brow furrowed as he kept his gaze on the road. It seemed as if his shoulders had slumped too.

Disappointment, she realized. "Is somethin' wrong?"

"I'm just thinking of the best way to keep you safe.

My family knows you're under protection, and one of the ranch hands, too. The others believe I've just hired you on to help. I figured I'd have you do what you did at the ranch, seein' that they told me you had experience, but–"

"That's perfect," she blurted. "Only, like I said, I wouldn't have y'all paying me. I just want to earn my keep, is all."

"And you don't mind that you'll be staying with a bunch of men? I mean, we might be able to arrange for you to stay at my folks' place. It'd be a heck of a lot quieter."

"I can't imagine I'd be real helpful there," she said. "If it's all the same to you, I'd like to be where I can contribute most. And no, I don't mind being with a bunch of men. I'm sure y'all are kind and gentlemanly."

"Not all of us," he muttered under his breath.

"Hmm." She couldn't help but wonder what made this guy so somber. And was he always like this, or did it have something to do with bringing her onto the ranch? She didn't like that idea at all. "So what do you do for fun, Mr. Emerson?"

"Blake," he said. "Uh, the guys went to a country swing last night. I stayed behind." He glanced over at her, and though the look was brief, her ridiculous heart thumped out of beat. "I'm getting a little old for those things," he mumbled.

"Okay," she said. "Now that I know what the ranch hands do for fun – at least one of the things – what about you?"

That dimple threatened to show once more. "I ride

bulls. Scored first place at the last town rodeo." His voice lacked in pride or interest.

"Alright," she said. "I dated a bull rider once." She broke off there, realizing she'd be better off not to share that tidbit.

"Why do I get the impression it wasn't such a good experience?" he asked.

Reese glanced at him in surprise. Bright rays of sun played across his face as he drove, lighting the fresh spark of curiosity showing there. "He was definitely … interesting."

"Don't sugar coat it for my sake. Not all bull riders are the same. What was wrong with the guy?"

"I'm not one for baggin' on folks," she said, "but he was real self-absorbed, you know? Thought my whole world should revolve around him and his rodeos. Spent a lot of time bragging about himself at family functions. Rarely took any interest in others. And he wouldn't stop smackin' my butt in public."

When he didn't respond right away, Reese turned to see him lift a brow. "So you didn't mind the butt-smacking. Only the fact that it was in public?" There was that hint of the dimple again.

She laughed. "Pretty much."

"Sounds like my experience with pageant girls," he said.

That took the smile off her face. "What's wrong with pageant girls?"

"They always spank my butt in public," he said. "Naw. I dated one for a while. She was self-centered too. Only cared about the pageant. Dresses. Manicures.

Shoes. Her, her, her."

"Hmm."

"What? Don't tell me you're a pageant girl?" He looked worried.

"As a matter of fact I am. Well, I was about to pass on my crown last night. But I..." She wasn't ready to talk about it yet. So she ended it there.

Blake cleared his throat. "Sounds like we have a bit of rectifying to do."

"What do you mean?"

"I've got to change your impression of bull riders. And you can see about changing my opinion of pageant girls."

"You mean women," she said.

A hint of red snuck over his face as he eyed her. "Women," he repeated. "Sound like a deal?"

Reese nodded. "Deal." Though already Blake Emerson had shown he was worlds away from the man she'd dated. Now she'd work on changing his impression of pageant women. Something about the prospect brightened her mood already.

CHAPTER SIX

The drive *to* the airport had felt like a lifetime. Blake had been anxious to get the witness, bring him home, and get to work on the list of things that needed to be done. The ride back was a different story. He worried about getting back too soon. Not giving Tom and the guys any time to make the proper adjustments. He needed to let them know that Reese wasn't what they'd been expecting.

He shook his head while glancing over. Her lips were curved into a pleased grin as she eyed the scenery. He didn't have the heart to tell her he'd been expecting a guy. Hadn't known what to say when she'd mentioned doing laundry and cooking and cleaning. Hell, he hated the idea of the guys having their own, personal maid. They were sloppy enough as it was. But what else could she do to create a cover? And did she really think he'd allow her to do all those things around the place without getting paid? He'd put money aside for her whether she took it or not. And send it home with her if he had to once it was all said and done.

She'd clammed up when she spoke about her evening last night, and though he was curious to hear about what she'd been through, he'd decided not to pry. Not yet, anyway.

"You hungry?" he asked. The small town shops were fast approaching, and it would be their last chance to stop before reaching the ranch.

Reese nodded. "A little," she said.

"Me too. How about we put off home for a bit and grab a bite to eat? There's a place up here that serves pancakes bigger than your plate."

She laughed. "Sounds good to me."

Sounded good to him too. It'd give him a chance to warn the ranch hands, while giving them enough time to make a few adjustments.

"So you ride bulls, dodge pageant girls, and harbor witnesses from time to time. Tell me something else about you. How many siblings do you have?"

"Just two brothers. I'm the oldest, so I run the ranch and keep track of the ranch hands. Gavin – he's a few years younger than me – he has sort of a wild streak in him. Had a falling out with my old man a couple years back. He took off to Vegas. Hasn't returned since, but I'm hoping one day he will."

"How awful," she said, concern thick in that sweet, southern tone. "I hope he does too. And the other one?

How old is he?"

"Shane's just sixteen, but he's strong for his age. Should've been a wrestler, that one. I'm telling you he can tackle a man twice his size, which is why he's always been so good with the cattle. Helps hold down the calves during immunizations and all that. He has a pretty good knack for roping them too." He nodded as he thought on it. "He's a good kid." Blake glanced over at Reese. He wasn't one for small talk, but was anxious to get the focus off himself.

"So... you're from Texas, you steer clear of bull riders, and like red boots," he said, eyeing the spiffed up pair on her feet. "What's your family like? You got brothers, sisters?"

"One little brother," she said. "He's gonna be a football star one day, I just know it."

"Hmm," Blake murmured. "How old is he?"

"Seventeen. But coach let him play on varsity his sophomore year. He's already attracted the interest of several colleges from across the country."

"You don't say. Well, I'll have to keep an eye out for him, then." He liked the idea; knew it'd make the game all the more interesting to have some inside link to one of the players.

Reese rummaged through a small hand bag on her lap. Blake watched as she flipped down the visor, began spreading some sort of gloss over her lips. Nothing too bright or bold. Just a subtle shine that drew his eyes to that pretty mouth. A deep burning warmed his belly as he wondered what it might feel like to kiss those lips. Instantly he forced the thought from his mind and his eyes from her face. She'd have enough men chasing after her back at the ranch. He needed to be her protector. Not her pursuer, for crying out loud.

Reese primped for a bit more, adjusting the blonde locks of her hair before slumping back into the seat. It seemed as if her temperament had changed. The expression on her face almost solemn.

The thought made him question – once more – just what she'd been through. If there was one thing he'd learned during his history with women it was that they liked to talk about their thoughts and their feelings and everything else under the sun. Perhaps he should give her the chance to share her experience.

He cleared his throat, wondering if she'd open up to him. "My uncle didn't exactly tell me what brought you here," he said. "To the protection program, I mean."

Reese's gaze was set on a distant spot out the window. "What was that?" she asked, turning to look at him.

Whoa. Those eyes of hers. Wide, innocent, and welcoming. "Just wondering what uh... brought you here, if you don't mind my asking."

Her long lashes fluttered as she tore her gaze from his. "Oh, I don't mind. I was at this celebration..." She paused there. "Man, I can't believe that was just last night. It was one of those outdoor things. Barbeque by day with an auction for desserts, a dance by night with a live band and all, and the annual passing of the crown for Miss Pearland's Rose."

"Rose – as in the flower?" He fought back a smile. "And that was you?"

She nodded. "Yes. I won last year and was set to pass off the crown to this year's winner. A real doll, actually. So ambitious where pageant life's concerned. Anyhow, this guy had been leering at me the whole night long. And just as the evening's about to wrap up, he asked me to dance. I couldn't really get a grip on him. His personality, I mean. His eyes were all shifty. His palms sweaty." She shook her head absently. "They say women are too quick to shrug off their instincts. They want to trust when they shouldn't. Stay though they feel they should run. Lloyd – the officer who brought me here – he used to complain an awful lot about women who put themselves in stupid situations, and how they ended up hurt."

Immediately Blake's mind wandered. He pictured the officer, curious to know if the two had dated. Or had they only been friends? When he looked back at Reese, her forehead was creased with concern.

"I don't know what I could've done differently. I mean I danced with him, but only with a large crowd surroundin' us. I hadn't led him on in the least. Trust me when I say I can be a real flirt, but I did nothin' of the sort. I took off as soon as we were done and went to freshen up." She brought her thumb up to her mouth, bit at her nail for a bit. "I said just a few words to the new girl – the one who'd be wearing the crown next. She was touching up her makeup at the mirror. And shortly after I closed the bathroom stall, there was a big ol' blast." Her chin quivered. A stream of tears slid down her cheek.

Blake had the urge to pull over. Wrap his arms

around the woman. Instead he drove on. Took his voice down to a whisper. "The bullet," he said. "It hit the other gal?"

She nodded while wiping back tears. "I saw him through the mirror. His round face and bright, green eyes. He looked crazy. And the worst part is that the girl was wearing a gown a lot like mine and so I have to wonder if he meant to shoot her or if he meant to shoot me."

The statement made him recall the conversation he'd overheard between her and the officer. "The police mentioned that the girl would recover, according to the doctor. Is that right?"

"Yeah," she sniffed. "But when I saw her, I could have sworn she was dead. I was so relieved when I felt a pulse at her wrist. And just ... desperate to fix it all. To fix her. I just kept telling her I was sorry. The whole time the medics worked on her, got her hooked up to tubes and carried into the ambulance. I couldn't stop apologizin'."

Blake frowned. "But it wasn't your fault."

Reese sucked in a loud, jagged breath. "Yeah, but what if I could have done things differently. Maybe went to find Lloyd or Sheriff Finn. Told them how uncomfortable the man made me feel."

A lump of irritation formed deep in Blake's throat. He didn't like seeing this woman blaming herself. "They wouldn't have been able to do anything," he assured.

She shrugged. "We'll never know."

He should let it drop. He knew he should, but he couldn't. "Maybe if you'd have said something, things could have gone worse. What if he would have killed somebody? The officer who decided to follow him after you'd pointed him out. What if the guy started to feel threatened and decided to shoot into the crowd? Or held you at gunpoint and dragged you away?" When no response came, he continued. "Sounds to me like things ended up pretty good, all things considered. Only one person was shot. And she – according to doctors – will make a full recovery."

Reese turned her face toward the window, wiping at her cheeks once more. "I just would rather it was me who took the shot. Not that poor girl. And now they have an attempted murder suspect on the run. Someone they fear may strike again."

"They haven't caught the guy?" he asked.

She shook her head.

"Hmm. Usually they catch 'em, he makes bail, and they hide the witness to ensure they make it to the trial in one piece. How'd this jackass get away, anyhow?"

Again she did nothing but shake her head, as if she was baffled by the question herself.

Blake hadn't realized it, but his muscles had tightened into knots. His shoulders and arms were stiff and achy. And his palms – he'd been clenching the steering wheel so hard they'd broken into a sweat. Everything about the story disturbed him. From the way the creep had been staring at her, to the fact that he'd asked her to dance just before. And worse – that he'd gotten away with it – to this point, anyway. "So you're thinking he was trying to shoot you."

Reese shrugged. "That's the tricky part. They don't

know whether he wanted to kill me – being, I don't know, weirdly obsessed with me in some way – which I hate. Or if he wanted to stop the next girl from taking my crown so he tried killing her – which I hate even more."

He considered that. "They have no clue where he could be?"

"None." She straightened up once more, shifting in her seat to face him. "And here's the part I'm not supposed to say anything about." She'd taken her voice down to a whisper. Her pretty eyes were wide with worry.

"Okay," Blake said.

"My daddy's the best of friends with the sheriff. He has been for years or I'd have had none of this inside information. I mean, he could get into real trouble if –"

"I won't say anything," Blake assured. Just who in tarnation did she think he'd tell?

She nodded, looking only somewhat satisfied. "Well, they found pictures of me in his room."

A frigid chill pricked his skin. "Pictures?"

"Yes. Stuff from the pageant, newspaper clippings. Things he'd printed off the internet. And worse, he'd defaced some of them. Had them stuck all over the back of his closet door like some sick..."

"Shrine," he finished for her. The information felt like a low punch to the gut. What kind of twisted SOB were they dealing with, anyhow?

"This is all stuff that'll be brought to a jury as evidence, if they ever get that far." She inched closer to him, as much as the seatbelt would allow, lessening the gap between them. He'd be damned if he didn't like the feel of her near. "When the officers went to the guy's house, his sister answered the door. She said he'd moved out of the place like a month ago. Guess it's just been him and his sister for years now. Their parents were killed in a car accident years back, so she took care of him. 'Course he's a grown man now."

"Hmm," he managed.

"It's strange, all of it. I just hope they hurry and find the guy so they can put him away."

Blake nodded. "Yeah. So do I."

He continued to muse on things as he pulled into the tiny lot of the diner. Of how frightening it would be to experience what she had. And to hear that somebody was so obsessed with her as this pervert was. It was a wonder she had an appetite at all.

"I'll get your door for you," he said before exiting the truck.

Reese didn't argue, simply placed her small hand in his, allowing him to help her down. As she brushed past him, Blake inhaled the lovely scent of her. He'd noticed it earlier as well, only this time he recognized the fragrance: rose. She smelled exactly like the roses he used to pick for Grandma Emerson out front. One of his favorite scents. He cleared his throat and redirected his scattered thoughts. He needed to get her seated, make a quick escape, and call back to the house.

The waitress was all smiles as she led them to a cozy booth at the far end of the room. Reese took no time ordering her food. Blake was pleased that she'd ordered an actual meal; not some poor excuse for one like toast and fruit.

"I'll be back in a jiffy with your food," the waitress said. "Just holler if you need anything."

Blake came to a stand. "Excuse me while I step out to make a phone call," he said, nodding to Reese.

She smiled at him, a warm and genuine smile that threatened to weaken him in ways he could hardly fathom. "Go right ahead."

Though he'd been outside only moments ago, the sun seemed nearly blinding. The brightness a great contrast to the dim lighting in the diner. He pulled his phone from his pocket, started to call Tom, but thought better of it. He didn't need him asking a slew of questions about Reese's age, height, and hair color. No need to get the men all excited. He only needed to warn them so their shock wouldn't show when he arrived with Reese the woman, not Reese the guy and ranch-hand-that-might-save-their-hides-this-season.

He shook his head while typing out a text, hardly able to believe the twist of events. He wanted to be more upset over his misfortune, but two things made that impossible: The first was easy – comparison. After what Reese had been through, he had no right to complain. Her life had been threatened, a gal shot before her eyes, and then she'd been ripped from her home and loved ones. His problem looked like a glass of spilled milk next to the flood of difficulties she faced. The next wasn't so easy – to admit, anyway. But he sorta liked Reese. She was hard not to like. That sweet-sounding accent, killer smile, and eyes that seemed to see more than he was willing to show. Which made him worry all the more. The woman didn't need a bunch of hormone-driven men hounding and harassing her at every corner. And it was up to Blake – him being the foreman – to set the tone. He'd sworn to protect her, not chase her 'til her legs gave out, he reminded himself for the hundredth time.

He looked down at the small screen on his phone and read over the text before sending it to Tom:

New ranch hand is NOT a guy. Not sure what we'll do with her, but we'll figure something out. Get the place cleaned up and we'll give her the other room. Be there in a few hours.

Satisfied with the message, Blake hit send and stepped back inside the cozy restaurant. Reese was toying with the stack of sugar packets when he came back. The pretty tips of her fingers grazing over the thin, paper edges. He sat down in silence, watching the perplexed expression on her face.

"This is really a lot of trouble for you, isn't it?" she asked.

Blake shook his head, wondering where the comment had come from. "No," he lied. "Not at all. I was just making sure they were getting things ready. House full of men, place isn't always in the best shape if you know what I mean." He shifted his gaze to the table, tore the strip of paper from around his napkin and silverware, and began twisting the thing around one finger. He didn't want her to think she was a burden, which only added to his growing list of worries where she was concerned:

Give her something to do.

Keep her safe.

Make sure the guys didn't hit on her.

Make sure *he* didn't hit on her.

And now... make sure she didn't feel like a burden to everyone at the ranch.

A deep sigh pushed its way through his mouth; he hoped she hadn't sensed what had caused it.

"Here you go," the waitress chimed in from behind. He remained quiet as the woman placed their food on the table. Steaming hotcakes, scrambled eggs, and hash browns. His eyes followed the series of bottles she slid onto the table next. Ketchup, hot sauce, and maple syrup. "Anything else I can get ya?" the waitress asked.

He looked to Reese. "Need anything else, babe?" The word slipped off his tongue like oil on an ice sheet. He rapped his knuckles on the table while a rush of heat burst out his ears.

Reese shook her head, smiling first at him, and then at the waitress. "This looks delicious. Thank you."

The waitress grinned. "You two enjoy your meal."

Blake reached for the hot sauce, wanting to drown in the stuff after using the pet name for Reese. "I was thinking about the duties you wanted to take care of," he said. "I figure if you cook a couple nights a week that should be plenty. My folks feed everyone on Sundays. You can take a few evenings beyond that and we can fend for ourselves the rest of the time." He watched for her reaction, hoping she'd forget that he'd called her *babe* only seconds ago.

"A few nights a week sounds good. What about breakfast? Lunch?"

"No need," he said. "The guys downstairs have their own kitchen. We usually just do our own thing. Grab a bite for breakfast. Make a quick sandwich to bring along. Besides, the ranch hands are like stray dogs. You don't want to go feeding them too often or they'll wind up at your door for every meal."

That earned a laugh from her. "I plan to do the laundry too," she announced, "and I won't have you arguing over it either."

When he failed to come up with a rebuttal in time, she spoke up again, looking like she'd just won her first war. "Well, I guess we should dig in." She stuck her fork beneath the melting pat of butter on her hotcakes and discarded the blob onto a napkin. She grabbed the knife next, used it and the fork to cut the stack down the center, and then looked at Blake. "You want these?"

Blake shrugged. "Sure."

With quick movements, she transported half of her pancakes to his plate and then set back to work. "This looks like more than two eggs to me. And there's no way I'll be able to eat all these hash browns." And there she was with the knife and fork, separating her food once more. "Want these too?" she asked.

He tilted his head. "I guess so."

Once she'd dumped the extra food onto his plate, she reached for a small container of jam. Her face scrunched up as she inspected it.

Blake shook his head as he grabbed the maple syrup, pouring it amply over his hotcakes. "What are you reading there?" he asked.

"Calories. They didn't have any light options on the menu and I was kind of thinking it didn't matter much because it's not like I have to fit into my gowns any time soon but then when I looked at all this I sort of panicked." Her slow, southern tone had picked up pace, the words coming out in a female frenzy.

"You're panicking now," he said.

Her wide eyes met his. "I am?"

"You are. Now if you're trying to change my impression of pageant girls, I have to tell you, this isn't helping."

The statement earned him a glare. "Oh, *really?*"

"Really," Blake said with a nod. "When was the last time you had yourself a nice breakfast like this? Without splitting things in half and counting calories."

She shrugged. "I can't say."

He couldn't imagine being bound by those types of restrictions. The thought led him to another question. "And exactly what is it that's stopping you from smothering that stack in maple syrup and enjoying every last bite?"

Reese tilted her head. "What is this, some sort of challenge?"

"Maybe." Blake rested his elbows on the table, leaned into her, and fixed his gaze on her face.

"What? You don't think I would *dare* eat all this food? Is that what you're saying?"

He wasn't so sure what he'd been saying, but he liked the fire he saw in her eyes. "Yep."

She lifted her chin and laughed. "I can eat," she

assured him.

"Then do it."

"I will. And if I pork out like some… gargantuan blimp then you'll have no one but yourself to blame."

He covered a grin. "Fair enough."

With a bit of angst in the action, she yanked the warmed syrup from his hand and began pouring it freely over her half-stack.

"Oh, what about…" Blake pointed at the abandon butter blob.

Her lips tightened as she snatched up the napkin, scooped the butter onto her knife, and spread it over her pancakes, creating a caramel-looking drizzle that oozed down the sides and onto her plate. "Happy?"

Blake folded his arms. "Not as happy as you're going to be once you take a bite."

Reese rolled her eyes and grabbed her fork. "Yeah, right." She lifted the bite toward her mouth, eyeing the food like it was poison. Instead of closing her lips around the fork, she slid her teeth over it, the scraping sound making Blake cringe.

His eyes narrowed as she chewed the bite. "Hmm," she said, cutting another helping away with her fork.

He smiled. "Good, right?"

She shrugged indifferently. "It tastes fine."

Blake watched her take another bite, an amused grin pasted on his lips.

"You gonna sit there and watch me the whole time or what?" she snapped.

He chuckled, readied a bite for himself and brought it to his mouth. This girl had a bit of fire in her, that was sure, and he was glad to see it. Things had gotten rather dull back at the house. This Texan bombshell might not be much for helping to carry the load, but one thing was certain – she was sure to liven things up. And perhaps that was just what he needed.

CHAPTER SEVEN

"Admit it," Blake said to Reese as she gazed out the window. The scenery had changed as they neared the ranch. From distant mountains, nearby rivers, and great, green valleys, to long stretches of flat land, patches of gold and green. And the cattle. She'd never seen so many in one place.

"Well?" Blake's voice came again. "I'm waiting..."

"For what?" She worked to keep a straight face as she glanced at him, but a slight smile tugged at the corner of her lip.

"Don't give me that. You *know* what. The meal?"

Reese pulled her gaze away from him. "I told you it was nice. I offered to pay for it and thanked you when you—"

"Oh, come on. You go who-knows-how-long without eating a decent meal, least you could do is tell me I was right."

She glanced back at him again. At the expectant spark in his alluring brown eyes. "Tell me. Was it one of the best things you ever tasted?"

Reese smiled. And then laughed. "Yes," she finally

admitted.

"Serious?" he asked.

Her smile widened as she unleashed what she'd been holding back since her very first bite. "That stack of hot cakes was one of the most scrumptious things I've ever eaten in my entire life."

Blake nodded proudly, a satisfied grin on his face. "I knew it."

"I've had pancakes with syrup before. But I tell you," she turned in her seat and placed a hand on his arm, reverencing her tone, "that butter... I can't remember the last time I allowed myself to indulge so much. It was like heaven on my tongue."

Blake glanced at her, raising a brow. "Like a good kiss?" he said, giving her a flirtatious wink.

A mass of heat seemed to burst through her chest at his words. And that wink. She pulled her hand off his arm. "What was that?" Oh, she'd heard him alright, but she wanted to hear it again.

"Heaven on your tongue. A good kiss should feel that way."

There went that thrill again. Bathing over her skin in a live and tingling motion. Never had she considered those words with a kiss before. But in that moment, all she could picture was him – kissing her – and how it might be that very thing: heaven. Quickly she turned away from him, began fanning her face with her hand. The sound of him chuckling deep in his throat made her blush.

"What are you laughing about?" she asked, refusing to show how affected she was.

"You."

She stopped fanning her face. "What about me?"

"You clammed up when I said that about the kiss. Makes me wonder if you've ever been kissed right, is all."

She gasped. "I have been kissed plenty of times, thank you very much."

"*Plenty?*" The emphasis he'd put on the word made her scowl.

"A normal amount," she assured.

He kept his gaze on her, causing her face to warm even more. "Well then you should know just what I mean."

She turned away from him. "Of course I do." Only she didn't. She'd had some decent kisses before. Some horrible ones too. But nothing that had ever caused her to walk on clouds. "So, tell me what's going on up here. These houses and barns and all."

Blake shifted his gaze, seeming to buy into her attempt at distraction. He pressed on the brake and spun around. "Oh, I meant to point out the property my old man gave me. Each of us sons were given a piece of land to build on once we're ready. See that lonely old tree out there about a mile back?"

Reese scanned the rustic-looking field, spotting a single tree that looked out of place. "Yeah."

"That's my acre." He nodded up ahead. "Now this here, where the road goes from paved to dirt at the turn off, that's my folks' place. Names are Betty and Grant. You'll meet them soon. That's where I grew up. Shane still lives there, being sixteen and all, but if you look further down, past the barn..." Blake pointed over the land as he approached the turnoff at a slow crawl. "That's my Gramps' place. 'Course he's no longer living but it'll always be his place to us. That's where we'll be staying."

She took in the area as he pulled onto the dirt road. First at the house he'd grown up in, which faced the paved road they'd been on. A nice-sized home, with white siding, lots of windows, and a welcoming glow. A large tree grew mighty and tall out front, shading nearly half the yard with its leafy branches. A wraparound porch led to the backyard. Behind that was the weathered barn. Rusty machinery lay scattered in tall grass lining the distant yard. Yet the immediate area surrounding the home was well kept. Freshly cut grass complimented the yard while flowers in lovely pots lined the porch railing and showed a woman's touch.

"I used to climb up that tree until I reached the roof," Blake said. "And then I'd walk over the pitch, hunch down at the edge, and jump right onto that trampoline out back."

"You are kidding," Reese said. "My mama would have paddled my behind had I done a thing like that."

"That was just the beginning of the mischief we got into around here. But boy, did we have some good times."

She grinned, picturing it in her mind. Three rowdy boys growing up on a ranch. Causing their mama all sorts of grief. "So those are your horses then?" she asked, eyeing the corral. Two beautiful horses raced about the area. A few more stood clustered near the distant fence.

"Yep. Mine's the brown one, his name's Tucker. He's a loyal horse, that one." Blake slowed down as they approached the second home. This one faced the dirt road, and looked older than the other. Charming. Like a square-shaped log cabin with an oversized porch. Matching logs created a railing, giving the place a nice country feel. There wasn't much in way of flowers, like those she'd seen outside Betty and Grant's place. But there against the porch, a tall rose bush grew, thick with green leaves, red buds, and bright flowers.

"Home sweet home," Blake said, shutting off the engine.

He had her door open before she could gather her thoughts. Reese rested her hand in his as he helped her from the truck. She gripped her tote bag with the other, wondering what the men inside would be like.

The wood creaked noisily beneath her boots as she climbed up the stairs. She'd been excited about meeting everybody only moments ago, but now she was a bucket of nerves.

Blake propped the screen door for her, pushed open the main door next, and motioned for her to enter. She peeked into the small front room, complete with a couch, love seat, and coffee table. Sun streamed through the large, front window, lighting an old rug that lay across the hardwood floors. She took a step inside.

"I'll be right back with the rest of your things. Then I'll show you to your room."

Reese nodded in return, stepping further inside to look at the art on the wall – colorful paintings of the

Montana scenery. She smiled, happily recognizing traits of the landscape she'd appreciated on her way there. Deep blue skies, thick pines, and endless fields. One frame held an image of what looked like the old barn out back. As she leaned in for a closer look, a loud rumble sounded from the other room, followed by voices.

"... or you better believe Blake will–" The voice broke off. Someone whistled a long, slow cat call. Reese glanced to the open walkway, spotting two men standing there.

"That ain't her, is it?" the blond kid said. His light, bushy eyebrows seemed to be glued on an inch too high.

"Of course it's her," the bulky redhead replied. "I'm Stockton. You must be Reese."

Reese walked toward the doorway and shook Stockton's hand with a smile. She made a quick mental note of his stocky build, knowing that'd help her remember his name.

"Howdy." She turned to the thin blond kid next. "And what's this fine man's name?"

"Oh. I'm uh..."

"He's Tom," the one named Stockton said with a laugh.

"Yeah," he confirmed. "I'm Tom. Come on down here and uh, we'll show you to your room."

"Why, thank you, gentlemen. Aren't you sweet?" Reese felt the tension ease from her shoulders as she followed them into the bright kitchen. A mop leaned against the counter, and spray bottles and scrubbers were piled on the cabinet, their scent strong in the air.

Despite their obvious efforts, streaks of dirt remained on the tiled floor. She bit at her lip; there'd be plenty of time to give things a thorough scrubbing soon enough.

The dining area, adjacent to the kitchen, was small but clean. Beyond that was the laundry room, which led to the basement stairs. The shy one, Tom, had already raced ahead of them. Stockton paused at the top and flashed her a grin. "After you," he said.

The stairwell was narrow but bright. Reese pulled her bag in front of her as she went, overhearing Tom speaking to someone in the other room.

"No way," a voice spat in a whisper.

"Serious, dude. Go look. You're gonna crap yourself."

Reese bit on her lip to keep back the awkward laughter threatening to embarrass them all. She worked to tune out the rest of the conversation, but their heavy whispers seemed to bounce off the walls.

"Wait, put your shirt on," was the last thing she heard before a massive guy walked toward the base of the stairs. The shirt part had been disregarded, she realized, as she took in his broad chest and bulging biceps. Stockton was stocky, but this guy was huge. All muscle, mass, and wagging eyebrows.

"I'm Rowdy," the man said. "You'll be staying down here with me and Stockton."

"Hi there, Rowdy." Reese moved to extend her hand but was stopped short when a voice boomed from the top of the stairs.

"The hell she will." It was loud. Angry. And unmistakably Blake's. "Tom, what were you thinking?"

Blake barreled down the stairs, brushed past Reese, and sped down the hall. "Where is that kid?"

Rowdy threw a thumb over his massive shoulder.

Reese kept her gaze on Blake as he stopped in front of the doorway. "Exactly what room did you prepare for this woman?" he demanded.

Her eyes darted to Rowdy, and then Stockton in the quiet moment. Each had their gaze pasted on her.

Tom sounded frantic. "I just figured that we'd put her in the extra room down here and..." Tom's voice died off as Blake crossed his arms over his broad chest, his silence somehow louder than the kid and all his babbling.

"Or... I guess I could move down here and let her move up there," Tom finally said. "Yeah. That's what we should have done."

"Gee," Blake said. "You think?" He shook his head in disgust as he marched by, not meeting Reese's gaze in return.

"Sheesh," Rowdy said. "*He's* in a good mood."

"Get up here and help Tom move his stuff out," Blake boomed from the top of the stairs. "Hurry, boys. I thought you already took care of this."

In a mad dash, Tom scurried past them and rushed up the stairs. Rowdy and Stockton motioned for her to go ahead. "After you," Stockton said again, running a hand over his buzzed hair. Here, it looked more auburn than red.

Reese grasped onto the railing, rolling her eyes at the whispered remarks made behind her. She paused to speak over one shoulder. "Y'all best be on your good behavior, boys. I'll be cookin' your meals, ya know." She smiled when the chatter stopped cold. Yet soon her mind was musing on another matter. Blake had turned into an entirely different person since coming home. Angry. Domineering. And bossy. He hadn't thrown her so much as a glance as he'd barreled down and then back up the stairs.

Her brows furrowed as she took a seat at the bar in the kitchen, hoping to stay out of the way. Tom and Blake came through first, arms filled with clothes, boxes, and bedding. Soon Stockton and Rowdy came through, each carrying odds and ends. An old baseball bat, a lamp, and a stack of books. Reese felt terrible that Tom was getting kicked out of his room because of her, but after seeing Blake's reaction to the alternative, she thought it best to hush up about the matter. Besides, Blake was doing her a favor, taking her in the way he had, and she'd do what she could to keep the peace.

Still, it seemed Blake was used to maintaining some rather calm waters. And if there was one thing Reese had learned over the years it was this: water wasn't worth swimmin' in if ya couldn't make a splash. From the looks of things, Blake Emerson wasn't used to much splashing.

The sun felt hotter than a branding iron on the back of Blake's neck as he dug, working to loosen the broken post. Time had dragged on slower than molasses on a winter's day and it wasn't hard to guess why.

"....and did you catch a look at her backside?" Rowdy gushed from a few posts down.

"Oh, yeah," Stockton bellowed, howling into the sunlit sky like a moron.

From the corner of his eye, Blake saw one give the other a conspiratorial nudge in the arm. "Blake thinks that trapping her upstairs with him is gonna give him an advantage. But I saw the way she was looking at these pecs." Rowdy broke into his stupid pectoral bounce, as if there was a person alive who wanted to see it.

"Would you guys just shut up about her already? It's like you haven't seen a woman in years."

"Haven't seen one that hot in a long time."

"Wonder which one of us she likes the best," Tom said. He'd remained quiet until then, digging loyally beside him.

Blake spun around slowly . "She doesn't like any of us," he spat.

"Speak for yourself, old man," Rowdy said. "I know she has eyes for me."

Blake rammed his shovel into the dirt and stormed toward the truck. It had been just a few hours since they'd left the house, but already he was itching to know how the Texan beauty was doing. He'd wanted to hold out another hour or so before checking in, but with all the mouths running who could take it?

Once in the truck, he reached for his CB. "You there, Ma?" he asked. During the silent moment, he pictured what the women might have been up to since he'd been gone. Getting the bathroom scrubbed, he decided, since the three stooges had cleaned up the wrong part of the house. Betty had come equipped with fresh bedding and towels, ones with flowers and lace and everything fancy. Boy was she excited that Reese was a girl.

"Ma, you there?" he tried a second time, wondering if he should drive back to the house. Reese had been in danger after all; perhaps it'd been irresponsible to leave her and Betty unprotected. Of course Grant was always close by, and never went on the field without his gun. Blake reached for the key, prepared to crank the thing over when a burst of static broke through the speaker.

"Right here, Blake. What do ya need?"

He eyed the box. "Just checking in on you two. Is Reese nearby?"

"Yep."

"Howdy, Blake," Reese hollered. His name spoken in her sweet southern tone warmed his blood.

In the awkward pause, Blake shook his head, feeling foolish for calling. "I'm just making sure you're getting settled, is all." He may as well address Reese directly, seeing that she was listening in.

"Why, thank you, that is so kind. I'm getting settled right nice with your mama's help." Her voice quieted as she mumbled something he couldn't discern. The two giggled.

"What was that?" he asked.

"Oh, nothing. Betty was just asking me about my grandma's barbeque sauce. We're fixin' to feed y'all a feast the size of Texas tonight."

"Sounds real nice." He looked up in time to see Rowdy spin around, hunch over, and pull down his pants. "I'm getting mooned out here by the one who ain't housebroken yet, so I guess I better go so I can throw some dirt on him."

Reese giggled.

"I'll see you ladies tonight." He eyed the box, wondering if she'd reply.

"Alrighty, then," she returned. "See you soon."

Soon. Hmm. He should be looking forward to the home cooked meal. The gathering with everyone too. But for a reason he couldn't quite grasp he was dreading it instead. With an edge of irritation, he leaned back on the seat and reached for the cooler. Rowdy and Stockton were barreled over in laughter. Tom struggled to keep his hidden. He was smart to hide it; Blake was the one who had their lunches.

He sighed before biting into his sandwich. It wasn't that he didn't know how to laugh with the guys, it was just that ... The silence that filled his mind was puzzling. It seemed as if he didn't hardly know himself anymore. In the last few months, things he used to find joy in were no longer fulfilling. Heck, he'd practically forced himself to compete in the local rodeo this year just to prove he was still alive. Winning had felt great, he'd admit that, but the satisfaction was fleeting. And Blake couldn't help but feel like he was missing out on some greater purpose. He only wished he knew what it might be.

CHAPTER EIGHT

Reese eyed those seated at the large gathering, a sense of gratitude swelling within her. Not more than twenty-four hours ago, a brutal crime had taken place right before her eyes; she'd been certain in those moments that a cloud of darkness bigger than the sky itself had drifted into her life. Yet here she was, surrounded by folks kinder than Christmas, enjoying a feast of barbeque like she hadn't eaten in years. The food had long since been blessed, but Reese took a moment to thank the heavens above for the guiding star that led her to the warm family on Emerson Ranch.

Her gaze wandered Blake's way. She shouldn't have been surprised when he chose to sit at the far corner opposite her, allowing Stockton, Tom, and Rowdy to sit close by. But she was. After all, he'd warmed up to her that very morning. They'd gotten to know each other a bit, even. Yet since the moment they'd stepped foot on the ranch he seemed to avoid her at every turn. Despite that, she'd continued to catch glimpses of him throughout the evening. The few times he met her gaze, Blake looked away before she could offer even the slightest grin.

"Well," Betty said, coming to a stand. "There's a reason we had you all come in from the field a little earlier tonight. And that's cuz we didn't want to keep our new ranch help up late, seeing that she just got here and all. Now, while I serve up dessert you guys can play a bit of Table Talk."

A few of the men groaned.

"Oh, hush," Betty said. She held up a large jar, the words *table talk* printed across it. "Now Shane's going to start, and then we'll pass it on around the table."

Reese rose from her chair, expecting to help Betty with the dessert.

"No, no darlin'. You stay put and play. I've got this guy to help me." She patted Grant's shoulder.

Blake's father – a rather tall man – shook his head and grumbled, his reluctant half-smile reminding Reese of Blake's in an instant. The man eyed Reese and gave her a wink. "Might not be any dessert left once I'm through with it," he said.

She chuckled, musing that might be just fine by her. Reese had eaten more calories in that one day than she'd consumed the entire week before. Who knew what she'd look like by the time she went home.

Blake's brother, Shane, came to a stand. He was young, as Blake had said, but he sure was handsome. Probably already breaking his share of hearts. He cleared his throat before reading the slip of paper in his hand. "If you could eat just one food everyday for a month and nothing else, what would it be?"

Murmurs broke out over the table.

"Pizza," she heard Rowdy say.

"Cheese," Stockton mumbled.

Rowdy smacked Stockton upside the head. "Cheese is *on* pizza." Reese chuckled, her gaze veering over to Blake's end of the table. Her face flashed with heat as she realized his eyes had been set on her. This time she was first to look away.

"Well," Shane said. "I'd have to go with potatoes. Then I could have fries or hash browns or mashed..." He continued to list his options while Tom debated whether or not au gratin potatoes would be available as it called for other ingredients.

Stockton grinned at Reese before coming to a stand. "Let me see this thing," he said, taking the jar from Shane. He laughed while reading it over silently first. "Ha! What's the craziest thing you've ever eaten?" He scratched at the back of his head. "I could go on all night. Let's see, grasshoppers, frog legs, crickets, snakes..."

"Snakes?" Betty hollered from the kitchen counter. "Did you at least cook the thing first?"

"Yeah," Stockton said. "It was pretty good."

"That's nothing," Rowdy blurted. "I've eaten rat poison."

Stockton nodded his head. "Yeah. We figured as much." The table broke into laughter as Stockton handed over the jar. He used both hands to do it, letting his fingers slide along her wrist. "Here you go, Reese."

"Thanks." Reese reached into the jar and pulled out one of the small slips. "If you could stay up all night long, what would you most like to do?" She paused after reading it, catching the words that threatened to spill from her lips. Something about the fact that she nearly *had* stayed up the entire night before. But that would no doubt lead to questions she couldn't answer – stuff about the shooting and all.

Hmm, if she could stay up all night what would she... suddenly Blake's words came to her – *'like a good kiss'* – he'd said. Heaven on her tongue. Her eyes shot to his corner of the table as she considered what a night spent kissing Blake would be like. He returned her gaze, a smoldering heat flaring behind his deep, brown eyes. She licked her lips, searching for something to say, but before she could speak the guys broke out in hoots and hollers.

"Think she's looking at you there, brother," Shane said.

"That's just cuz she doesn't want him getting all angry when she says she'd like to spend the night in my company," Rowdy said.

"You mean *mine*," Stockton interrupted.

A shrieking whistle blasted through the room. The space went silent as all eyes shifted to Betty at the counter.

"Hush up, boys, so the girl can answer the question." She smiled at Reese before setting back to work, cutting strawberries into a large glass bowl.

"I guess I'd have to say read. I can devour novels when I have the time. And it seems lately I haven't had much time at all." She nodded, glad to have found an honest answer. "Yeah. I'd read."

"Darlin'," Betty said. "Have I got the books for you. Don't you leave without taking a stack, you hear?"

Reese nodded, enjoying the idea of cuddling up to a good book. "You want me to draw a slip for you, Betty?" Reese asked.

"No," she replied. "Skip Grant and me and hand it on over to Tom."

Tom took the jar without looking at her, not bothering to stand. "Thanks." He pulled a slip with his thin fingers. "What is the most beautiful place you have ever seen?" he read. "Easy. Riverfront Park, late fall. When the sun's just right for setting and all the bright colors from the trees and shrubs bounce off the water."

"That is a mighty fine view," Grant boomed. "Took the boys fishing there a time or two." Reese couldn't help but appreciate the way the big burly man stood next to his wife in the kitchen. Heaping cream atop the plates one by one.

Rowdy came to a stand as he took the jar. The guy's large hands made it look small in comparison. "Mind doing the honors for me?" he asked Reese. "My hand won't fit."

"Sure." Reese assumed he could've reached the slips easily enough, but she retrieved one of the typed questions for him just the same. He grinned as she handed it to him.

"If you had the attention of the entire world for just ten seconds, what would you say?" Rowdy cleared his throat.

"This oughta be good," Tom said, pulling out his cell phone. He pressed at a few buttons. "I'm going to time you... Go!"

"Good afternoon, ladies and gentleman," Rowdy said in a deep, low voice. "I'd like to thank you all for tuning in. However, this part is just for the ladies. I'm single. And you can reach me at–"

"Time's up," Tom interrupted, jumping to his feet.

The room broke into laughter, Reese's included. "That's a shame," she said. "I was on the edge of my seat waitin' for that number."

Rowdy lowered his head like a shamed puppy, glancing up at her as he sat. "I'll still give it to you if you want."

"Alright, son," Betty said. "You're up."

Blake shook his head, looking irritated as he dug a slip from the jar. "What has been the happiest day of your life and why?" He stared blankly at the question as the room fell silent.

Reese watched in wonder as he thumbed one corner of the slip. He moistened his lips. Cleared his throat. And furrowed his brows.

A sudden ache began to grow in Reese as she watched him struggle over the simple question.

"I can think of one," Rowdy whispered.

Stockton chuckled under his breath. "Me too."

Blake finally shook his head, a defeated expression on his face. "I don't know."

"How 'bout when you scored that eight-second ride?" Shane offered.

"Yeah," Grant added. "Nobody ever stayed on Big

Blue that long and lived to tell about it, that's for sure."

Blake nodded, keeping his eyes cast down. "Yeah. I guess that'd be it."

Grant stepped over to the table, two plates in hand. He gave one to Reese on his way to his seat, and set the other in front of himself. "Well, it's right over there," he said to the others. "I only serve up to pretty ladies." He straightened his shoulders. "Now, if I was gonna answer that question, I'd have to say I had *five* best days. First, the day Betty agreed to marry a rebellious cowboy like myself. Next, the day we wed. And after that, the day each one of my sons was born."

The statement made Reese smile. "Sounds about right to me."

"Well, let's dig in, shall we? But first…" Grant came back to a stand, lifting his glass over his head. "We'll make this to our purdy new ranch help."

The men hoisted their half-empty cups toward the center. Stockton gave her a tap. "You're supposed to join in," he said.

She looked up to see Blake's cup was among them. "Oh, sorry." The rim of her glass caught hints of light as she moved it toward the center. Betty came up and stood behind Shane, leaning over to put hers in the mix as well.

Grant looked at Reese, a smile on his face. "Thanks for coming on out and being a part of the gang."

"Here, here," Rowdy bellowed.

The glasses clinked as Stockton tipped his head back and howled.

"Thank *you*," Reese said, "for making me feel so

welcome. Y'all are some of the kindest folks I've ever met." She took a sip of her drink and lowered herself onto the chair, anxious to try the dessert.

The tangy strawberries, mixed with the soft, sweet cream tasted better than she imagined. Reese moaned in approval with her first bite. "Betty," she said, "this is delectable."

"I'm glad you like it," the kind woman said. "It's Blake's favorite."

A slight dimple showed in Blake's cheek as Reese eyed him. "Tastes like heaven on my tongue," he said, giving her a wink.

She smiled, glad the playful side of him had made a second appearance. Reese may not know what it was that seemed to throw Blake Emerson into bouts of somber reflection, but as she looked at him in that moment – the mischievous spark brewing in his eyes – Reese prayed she would have the chance to find out.

Blake was certain the day had been extended by an hour or two on either end. From sunup to sundown, each minute had been chalk-full of more excitement than he could take. And now it was finally coming to an end. The gang had already gone in through the back door and headed down to the basement, leaving Blake and Reese alone as they climbed up the porch steps.

He cranked open the old screen door, pushed the front door open next, and waited for Reese to step inside. Reese stood there for a blink, peering into the dark room.

"Here," Blake said. "We'll make a habit of leaving this light on for you. You being new and all, I'm guessing you might not know your place in the dark just yet."

Reese giggled. "Not quite yet."

His arm slipped along her waist as he reached for the light switch, and he couldn't help but relish in the warmth of her near.

"Thank you," she said once the light kicked on. She stepped further into the room, but then paused to watch Blake close and lock the door.

The ticking of the clock on the wall picked up where the crickets left off. Blake rocked back on his heels before gesturing toward the hall. "I reckon you've already noticed that the bathroom lies between our rooms. What you can do is just lock the door leading to my room anytime you go in there. That way you won't have me walking in on you. 'Course, you'd probably mind more than I would."

She laughed. "I'm pretty sure I won't forget."

Blake worked to keep his gaze off her backside as she slowed in front of him. He hadn't planned to make small talk. Only to hit the sack and put his mind to rest. Yet as he reached the end of the hall, Reese turned toward him and leaned against her doorframe.

"It's been a long day," she said. "I bet you're battered and beat and ready to drop."

Why the woman was worried about him after what she'd been through he could hardly fathom. "I'm fine," he assured. "But how are you holding up?" The question came out more tender than he'd meant it to. No more than a whisper.

She shrugged. "I'm alright. To be honest, I'm overflowin' with gratitude right now."

Blake furrowed his brows, waiting for her to elaborate.

"I know it sounds odd, but I can't help but count my blessings. The shooting – like you said, that could have been a whole lot worse. And then gettin' shipped away – I could have wound up anywhere. But I was brought to this warm and friendly place filled with kind folks and more beauty than I've seen in a long time. I know Texas is beautiful and all, but I just didn't pause long enough to appreciate it."

He gulped. Being around Reese made him feel like a criminal in more ways than one. Blake had griped more times that day than he could count, and now, as the sweet southern blonde talked of blessings and looking for the good in life, he found his eyes following the trail her hand made along the opening of her blouse. It had been far too long since he'd been in the company of a woman. And he'd been pushed past the level of exhaustion too. Hell, the better part of him had checked out hours ago. Only the rugged rogue in him remained, and as hard as he tried Blake couldn't quite contain it.

He forced his eyes back to her face, suddenly humbled by her lovely features. Skin that seemed to wear the warmth of the sun. A soft pink blush that made her cheeks glow. And hazel eyes that opened up to the world. Opened up to him. He felt his mind begin to shift. "I'm glad you came here," he said, feeling the truth of it.

He didn't like the idea of her going someplace else. She was too kind. Too trusting. Here, he could protect her. Make sure no one took advantage of her. Assure her needs were met. He vowed then and there to do that very thing.

Reese surprised him then by taking one step forward, followed by another. He held motionless as she approached him, wondering what in heaven's name was on her mind. At once she lifted her arms, threw them around him, and tightened her squeeze around his shoulders. "Thank you for taking me in like this." The warmth of her breath grazed his skin. He only hoped she hadn't seen the effects of it in the goose bumps moving over his arms like dominos. Arms he'd wrapped around her in return.

"You're welcome," he managed, his voice low and scratchy. The tempting scent of her seemed to toy with him then. That hint of rose still lingering on her silky skin.

She dropped her arms as she took a step back, her face just inches from his. Blake's eyes drifted to the full and rounded shape of her lips. Plain and simple. Free of lipstick or gloss. Perfect for kissing. Why thoughts like that had to enter his mind he'd never know. Especially after he'd sworn to keep her safe. What she really needed protection from was *him*. "You can have the first shift in the bathroom. I'll shower once you're through."

"Okay. Thanks." She spun around and strode toward her room.

"Just remember to unlock my door once you're done," he added. "You don't want me having to creep through your room at night to find my way there."

She looked over one shoulder. Delivered a coy smile that would have knocked a weaker man on his tail. "Don't I?" She chuckled then. "Goodnight."

A slow breath made its way through his open mouth as he stood there, stunned by her flirtatious words.

"Hey, Blake?" Reese leaned back into the hall. "What do y'all do around here on Sundays? You go to worship?"

Worship. Worship. Why couldn't he identify that word. "*Oh,* yeah," he said. "At noon. Means we get to sleep in." If he could sleep at all with her under the same roof.

"Alrighty. See ya in the morning. Oh, and Blake?" She waited until their eyes met. "I really do appreciate you taking a chance on a girl this time around."

A hint of something warm and pleasant pulsed through his chest as he nodded, forcing the only reply he could muster. "Like I said – happy to do it."

CHAPTER NINE

Bright rays of morning sunlight peered through the kitchen window, casting an inviting glow about the cozy place. Reese looked through the glass, smiling as the horses grazed in the pasture. She was glad it was Sunday; after what she'd been through in the last few days the worship service would do her some good. Perhaps it could somehow manage to vanquish the darkness that had spoiled her sleep the night before.

She sighed, making her way to the fridge. Reese had needed a good night's sleep more than ever last night, had been positive she'd get it with as tired as she'd been. It was a safe place after all. The bed was comfy. The covers soft and warm. Yet it was the inner places that had bothered her. Unreachable images lurking in the dark corners of her mind. Haunting each peaceful thought. The constant stirring and restless dreams had left her feeling as if she'd run miles on a treadmill the entire night long.

No matter, she told herself as she pulled out a carton of eggs. Today was a new day. She'd make the most of it and catch up on sleep tonight.

The sound of a door opening from down the hall drew her thoughts to Blake. She smoothed a hand down the front of her skirt, wishing she'd have been able to check the outfit in a full-length mirror. As it was, she'd resorted to standing on the bathtub ledge to get a look at herself.

"Good morning," his deep, masculine voice sounded from behind.

Reese spun around to see Blake standing in the entryway. A loose-fitting pair of sport shorts hung low on his hips while his chest – the full impressive span of it – boasted muscled contours that made her warm all over. She felt a blush rise to her cheeks in response. "Morning," she offered, hoping it sounded more natural than it felt.

He ran a hand through his dark hair, the loose waves tossing between his fingers. "Slept in a little later than I meant to."

"I'm glad," she said, tearing her gaze from his chest. "I worried that I might wake you while I was showering. It's good to know that you slept through it."

When he didn't say anything in return, Reese glanced over her shoulder once more, forcing herself to keep her eyes on his face this time. But that view was even more stunning. Finely trimmed facial hair accented every chiseled angle of his full jaw and slightly dimpled chin. And those eyes – dark and warm, yet guarded, impossible to read this morning. "I thought I'd make some breakfast for y'all," she managed, reaching for a loaf of bread. "You like french toast?"

"Sure, thanks. But don't worry about the other guys. They don't go to worship service. In fact, they'll probably sleep until we get back."

Reese nodded, recalling what Rowdy had told her just the night before. He'd said he went to worship regularly. And that he planned to attend that very morning as well. Still, she decided to keep that to herself. "Well, this will be done in a bit so…"

Blake nodded. "Sure. I'll go get ready."

It seemed easier to breathe once he was no longer in sight, which was ridiculous, Reese told herself. She wasn't a child, after all. She was a grown woman. One who found herself more drawn to Blake than she wanted to admit.

Similar thoughts occupied her mind as she prepared the meal, scrambling a few eggs to serve up too. She'd been so wrapped up in her thoughts that she hadn't seen Blake step back into the kitchen. The sight of him climbing onto the barstool at the counter surprised her.

"Smells good," he said.

So did he. She ran a quick gaze over him, wondering if she'd ever seen a man wear a shirt and tie so well. He wasn't wearing his hat, but he'd altered his hair a bit, the reckless waves slightly tamer than they'd been a moment ago.

Reese slid a plate across the counter toward him before motioning to the food. "Eggs, french toast. I found the maple syrup, so that's here too." She stopped there. "I hope it's okay. Me makin' myself at home like this."

Blake spooned some eggs onto his plate, reached for the french toast next. "Of course, please. This is your home now, too. I want you to see it as such during your stay." His expression turned thoughtful. "Hey, I know we agreed to have you cook a few evenings a week."

She nodded.

"Well I don't want you to feel obligated to cook for me beyond that, just because we share a kitchen."

Reese shrugged, filling her plate as she spoke. "I don't mind. I mean, only the two of us. Seems silly not to at least cook for you as well. Anyhow, it's no fun eatin' alone."

Blake grinned. "I'll give you that."

His reply had her recalling his somber mood the night before. His hesitation to answer the question he'd drawn. Was it possible the hard working cowboy was lonely?

"So you shower in the morning, and I shower at night," he said. "I'd say we're off to a good start."

"I'd say so too." She reached for the syrup. "You sure are different company from the rest of the guys."

He looked up at her, his brows furrowed. "How so?"

Reese shook her head, nearly regretting the statement already. "It's only been a day, so this might be premature, but it just seems like they're full of innuendos. I don't think they'd be capable of mentioning the shower without – you know – getting all..." A dose of heat spread over her face.

He frowned. "All what?"

"You know how they are. Especially Rowdy and Stockton."

Blake stopped eating, rested his elbows on the counter. "I can talk to them if you'd like," he said. "If their comments bother you or get out of line–"

"No," she interrupted. "Really, I shouldn't have said anything. It doesn't bother me in the least and trust me, if it ever does I won't be quiet about it. I was just pointing out the difference is all. Their minds are constantly going and yours... isn't."

His gaze drifted up until his eyes met hers once more. The corner of his lip turned up, just enough to touch that dimple in his cheek. "I see."

She felt transparent suddenly. As if she'd just revealed something. She replayed her own words in her head, wondering how he'd interpreted them. "I didn't mean that I wanted you to say stuff like them." *Worse.* She was making it so much worse.

"No?" he questioned.

The adamant shake of her head was meant to serve as her reply. But Reese couldn't help but add to it. "Not if you don't..."

"Don't what?" There was that smirk again.

Reese refused to answer. Instead she stabbed a bite of food and brought it to her mouth, lifting her plate off the counter as she did.

"Are you going to stand while you eat?" he asked. "You could come join me, you know. Take a load off." He patted the stool top next to him. "Come on. I promise to only bite my food." He gave her a wink.

Reese chuckled. "Alright." She made her way to the barstool, swearing to regain her composure. The lovely sight out the sliding glass door helped take her mind off Blake and his brazen allure. She focused on it as she thought of something to say. "What do y'all do around here after service?"

"We have a big get-together with everyone. My aunt and uncle usually come over with my cousin, Allie, and her husband and kids. Sometimes he'll bring some of the ranch hands too. We play football, eat, hang out."

She straightened up. "Do the women play too?"

"Football?" He crinkled his nose. "No."

"Why not?"

"Cuz we tackle each other like animals. You've seen football."

"Yeah," she said, "but back at home we play with the boys all the time."

The look he gave her was nearly comical. "What kind?"

"Haven't y'all heard of the kind where you don't tackle?"

His face scrunched up. "Huh?"

"You know. They pull the flags off your belt thing..."

Blake groaned. "Flag football. Allie's been harping on us to play that ever since Terrance injured his collarbone. The guys won't go for it."

Reese bit at her lip, picturing the faces of Rowdy, Stockton, and Tom. "If I tell 'em it's because I want to play along, I think they'll be singing a different tune."

Blake stayed quiet while the look of defeat swept

over his face.

"Do you know if Allie – is that her name?"

He nodded.

"Do you know if she has the gear for it?"

Blake shook his head. "No clue."

"Hmm..." Excitement bubbled within her at the sheer prospect. She eyed the sun-lit tips of grass beyond the porch. The machinery scattered across the distant yard leading to the barn, charmed by the sight. "So how was it growing up on a ranch?" she asked.

"Can't think of a better place," he said. "It's kind of a popular thing for people to whine about their childhood. Blaming their folks for any old trouble they face. But I can honestly say I couldn't have had it better."

She wasn't sure why, but there was something about his statement that intrigued her. The admiration in his voice. The conviction on his face.

"How old were you when you learned to ride?" she asked.

"I was still a babe, really. I rode my first horse in that very corral." He pointed to the distant field. "His name was Blaze. My grandpa was there. It's kind of a family affair, you know? 'Course I didn't start riding on my own until after Gavin was born. But I always did like to ride. Still do. There's something about it. About the connection you make with the animal. And just, being out on the land. Being a part of it, almost. It's nice." He kept his focus out the window for a blink, his expression thoughtful. "You ever ridden a horse?" he asked.

"Few times."

He tilted his head. "Alone or with someone else?"

She smiled. "There was this worker on the dude ranch who taught me how to ride. Before that I'd only been on pony rides at the fair."

"Hmm. Some wannabe cowboy snuggling up to you on a horse, huh?"

Reese gasped. "He was very kind to spend his time off teaching me how to ride," she said. "I didn't get real good at it or anything, but it was fun. I can see what all the fuss is about."

He looked at her for a bit, thoughtful. "Mmm, hmm. So tell me why you wanted to be in pageants," he said. "I just can't imagine why anyone would want to put themselves through something like that."

"I only ever did the one," she said. "It was a lot of fun, honestly. I loved getting to know all the gals in the show. Having the chance to get out there and do my best." She set her fork down and crossed one leg over the other. "There's a lot more to it than swimsuits and gowns. They each vary, of course, but ours had a talent division, an essay question, a scholarship program, which I gifted to the runner-up in my sister's name, since I was just a term away from getting my bachelor's degree."

"Wait. Your sister?" Blake repeated, a confused expression on his face.

Reese nodded, realizing she hadn't told him yet. "Yes. My younger sister, Chelsea. She died in a car accident when she was just thirteen years old."

"I'm sorry to hear that," he said. "How old were you at the time?"

"I was fifteen." She shook her head. "It was

devastating. But you know, she's part of the reason I joined the pageant to begin with. She always looked up to pageant girls. Said she wanted to be queen one day – Pearland's Rose. I decided to try and live that out for her." Reese offered Blake a soft smile as their eyes met once more. She was stunned by the softness she saw there. The once dark depths seemed warmer now. More gentle and less guarded.

"You know what I miss most?" Her voice was barely a whisper.

Blake shook his head. "What?"

"Girl time. Braiding her hair. Getting all dolled up together. She'd only just started wearing makeup, but we'd gone and done more make overs at the mall than was legal, thanks to my mama." Reese felt her smile fade. "I don't know. After Chelsea died, Mama didn't want much to do with it anymore. Not the makeovers or the shopping. Seemed like the pageant days brought that back though. I think it was healin' for the both of us."

Blake remained quiet, yet his eyes continued to search hers in the silence. "My cousin lost his twin last year. Was also a car accident," he said. "Of course, Alex was a lot older than your sister. He'd been helping my uncle run his ranch. Hadn't married or anything. But it sure did seem to block out the sun for a while, I'll tell you that."

Reese knew just what he meant. "Were you close to him?"

Blake sighed. "I was closer to Logan, his brother. Gavin and Alex though – now those two were close. But uh ... we all felt the loss of him. Still do, truth be told."

And there was that energy again. Seeming to dance in the space between them. A pull that made her want to lean closer. Breathe deeper. Reach out to him, even.

Her gaze drifted to Blake's hand as he moved it toward her. She gulped as he ran a solid finger over the side of her arm where it rested on the counter. Up, then back. "I get pretty ornery around here at times, what with the ranch hands going in all directions at once. But I want your stay here to be comfortable. And if I'm acting like a jackass or making things miserable then just say so. You can holler at me, slap me, whatever it takes."

A warm dose of what felt like sugar rushed through her veins at his touch. Sweet and tingly. With the slightest contact he'd nearly managed to seduce her. She pulled in a breath, ran through his words once more. "I have permission to slap you?" she asked with a grin.

He smiled now. "If you must."

A sudden urge took hold of her then – the desire to gently cradle his face in her hand. To feel the solid structure of his cheek against her palm. The coarse feel of his scruff along her skin.

"Anyone home?" A loud ruckus sounded from behind the laundry room door. A knock came next, followed by more hollering. "Hello?"

Reese moved to get the door, but Blake reached out to stop her. "It's unlocked," he said. "Come on in."

The door swung open, revealing a mass of button up shirts. Reese eyed the three men as they strode in, stunned by the fresh new appearance of each man. Stockton wore a pair of faded levis with his dress shirt. Boots and hat in place. Rowdy donned a pair of khakis, and Tom was dressed in a full suit and tie, his light blond hair slicked back to perfection.

Reese stood to greet them. "Goodness me," she said. "Y'all look so handsome I'm startin' to blush. You're shined up brighter than new pennies, you are."

All three men ran a slow gaze over her from head to foot. Stockton let out a low whistle. Rowdy lifted his brows.

The tilted angle of Tom's tie caught Reese's attention. She smoothed a hand over her skirt before striding toward him. Tom froze like an ice statue as she approached. He stayed that way while she adjusted the knot of his tie. "There," she said, patting his face.

"Wish I had a tie," Stockton mumbled. Reese reached out to pat his face next, a broad smile at her lips.

"What has you all up and at 'em this morning, boys?" Blake asked, spinning in his seat.

"Just thought it'd be nice to join you for Sunday service today," Tom said. "You sure look nice, Reese," he added. Stockton and Rowdy mumbled their agreement.

Blake cleared his throat. "I'm surprised you know what time service starts."

Tom shifted from one foot to the next. "Betty told us."

Stockton shoved him in the ribs.

Blake eyed his near empty plate as he came to a stand. "Guess it's about time we get going then."

At the front door, he motioned for the others to proceed him. Reese was last to go, and couldn't help but smile as she saw him shaking his head. He leaned in as she passed him, murmuring just a few short words under his breath. "Them ranch hands are full of crap."

CHAPTER TEN

Reese leaned over the simmering pot, inhaling the tangy aroma of fresh, homemade spaghetti sauce. She closed her eyes, recognizing scents of garlic, basil, and oregano as the steam rose toward her. Fresh meatballs sizzled on the nearby skillet, the salad was chilling in the fridge, and the table had been set for two. All she needed now was Blake.

The sun had taken a slow dip into the horizon that evening, the colors settling over the land in a vibrant display. And while Reese had enjoyed the view, she felt anxious for Blake's return. They'd had a nice moment together Sunday morning, the quiet breakfast with just the two of them. She'd assumed that there'd be several more throughout the week. Turns out she'd been wrong. Blake seemed to get up before the sun did. And while he'd call to check in each day, he hadn't made it home in time for dinner even once. Reese had made the most of it. Kept the soup hot on Monday. Reheated the casserole on Tuesday. On Wednesday she decided to let them all – as Blake suggested – fend for themselves. If it wasn't for Betty and her friendly ways, Reese might have been terribly lonely.

"Hey, Reese," Blake's handsome voice blared from the CB on the counter. "You there?"

Reese tapped the wooden spoon before setting it on the nearby plate. "Right here," she said, securing the small box in her hand.

"I know I said I'd be home by dinnertime, but I'm knee-deep in mud trying to fix a leak here in the ditch."

Her eyes landed on the table setting as she replied. "How much longer will you be?" She could hear the guys rumbling down the stairs as she waited for Blake's reply.

"I'll probably be out here past dark."

"By yourself?" What she really wanted to ask is why he felt the need to work later than everybody else.

"Can't exactly ask the guys to stay out here all night."

"I could come help out," she offered.

Static came from the box.

She pressed the button again. "Hello? Did you hear me?"

Blake came through at last, covering a chuckle on the other end. "No thanks. You go ahead and eat some dinner. I'll be in when I can."

"Fine." Reese turned the small switch to *off*, unwilling to hear anything else he had to say. That man was condescending and rude. Chuckling under his breath at her offer. Like he was too good for it. And leaving her to eat alone – again. She was starting to feel like a neglected housewife.

An idea came to mind as she heard the men razzing one another downstairs. Reese straightened her shoulders, strode through the laundry room, and opened the door leading to their quarters. "Hey, fellas," she hollered down the stairs.

A strained bout of silence proceeded a lone response. "Yes?" Tom's voice came.

"Y'all want to come join me for a spaghetti dinner?"

"Heck yeah," Stockton bellowed.

"Move it," she heard Rowdy say. Reese thought of the table setting for two and dashed into the dining area, quickly stacking the plates and cups before clustering the silverware. She grabbed more plates and utensils as the trio burst through the doorway.

"Smells so good in here," Stockton said, sticking his nose in the air.

Reese smiled. Blake had warned her not to feed the hands too often. He'd also told her not to invite them upstairs, especially when he wasn't there. But she'd had enough of eating alone. And Reese knew full well the boys were harmless as kittens.

"You guys get started on the salad while I boil up the pasta," she said.

"You look mighty purdy in that there apron, Reese," Rowdy said, nudging her arm as she set the salad on the table.

Reese chuckled. "Why, thank you, Rowdy. You look mighty fine yourself this evening. Would you mind searching the fridge for the dressing while I check on the breadsticks? I almost forgot about 'em."

"Sure thing."

Reese had been planning to send some pasta down with the ranch hands along with their clean laundry, which is why she'd made extra from the start, but she liked this idea much better. Let Blake work alone and eat alone and whatever else he wanted to do. She'd had enough time to herself for one week. Having company was a welcome change. One she planned to enjoy whether Blake liked it or not.

Reese had known men to be quiet creatures, especially when food was involved. But dinner with Stockton, Rowdy, and Tom was far from it. They'd shared stories of time spent on the land all through dinner, and while they cleaned up as well, after Tom insisted they help with the dishes. And though Reese was having a nice time, she couldn't help but worry over the late hour. She'd turned the CB back on half-way through dinner, concerned Blake might try to get hold of her, but she still hadn't heard a thing.

"How late does Blake stay out?" she finally asked, noting how dark the sky had become. A lone bulb glowed from the barn out back, its light too small to reach even the horses in the corral nearby.

"Who knows," Stockton said. "He's wound up too tight, if you ask me."

"He didn't used to be," Rowdy said. "Something's bothering the guy is all. But it sure is taking all the fun out of things."

Tom nodded in agreement.

"It's not since I came, is it?" Reese couldn't help but ask. "I mean, it didn't start with me, did it?"

"Oh, no," the men said in unison.

Tom's lips twisted as he considered. "It's been the last few months or so, I'd say."

"Hey, Reese, watch this cool trick." Rowdy came up behind her where she dried her hands at the sink. "Come back here in the open space."

Reese did as he said, stepping closer to him in the center of the kitchen.

"Okay, now put your arms flat against your sides and make fists with your hands," he instructed.

"Oh, I know what you're doing," Stockton said, his tone sounding jaded.

"What?" Reese looked at Stockton. "Should I not do it?"

Stockton shrugged. "Naw, it's fine. But I have something to show you next."

"Okay," Rowdy said. "I'm going to put pressure on your arms like this…" He hunched down and wrapped his giant arms around her, pinning her wrists where they rested against her legs. "Now try to resist me. Keep your fists locked, and try to press your arms away from your body."

She tightened her limbs, fought to move. "I can't," she groaned, relaxing her arms.

"No. Don't stop or it won't work. You're not going to be able to do it, but just keep trying anyway."

"For how long?"

"Just a minute or so."

The sound of the front door creaking open caught

Reese's attention as she waited there in Rowdy's solid bear hug. The slow and distinct sound of Blake's boots on the hardwood floor had Reese picturing the brooding cowboy in all his way-too-handsome glory. She couldn't help but feel a bit of satisfaction when he rounded the corner and eyed the scene with an angry glare.

"What's going on in here?" he barked.

Stockton, Rowdy, and Tom stood there silent and still, like three blind and very frightened mice.

"I invited them up here," Reese announced in a chipper tone.

Blake narrowed his eyes as he looked her up and down, pausing at Rowdy's grip around her waist.

"Rowdy is trying something on Reese," Tom explained.

"Mmm, hmm," Blake mumbled.

Rowdy's grip had loosened in all the commotion, but at once it tightened back up. He began counting aloud. "Three, two, one." Releasing his grip, Rowdy stepped back and watched her expectantly.

Suddenly Reese's arms began floating up at either side. As if helium balloons were strapped to her wrists.

"Do you feel that?" Rowdy smiled. "Cool, right?"

"Yeah," she said. "It's like they're doing it on their own. It feels neat."

"My turn," Stockton blurted. He pushed past Blake's rigid form, proving Reese's comment had put them all at ease.

Blake gave Stockton an icy glare before looking at Reese. "Is there some food somewhere, or should I just..."

"Sure is." Reese said. "I made a plate for you. It's in the fridge."

"Well, it *was* in the fridge," Rowdy said, "right before I ate it."

Blake didn't laugh. Instead he pulled open the fridge, grabbed the plate, and walked it over to the microwave.

"Give me your hand," Stockton said, taking hold of her wrist. He proceeded to show her some trick, a weird exercise that made it feel as if her fingers had been sewn into fists.

"That is bizarre," Reese said, intrigued by the strange sensation. Stockton nudged his forehead against hers, glancing up at her through his lashes.

"I know. It's crazy, huh?"

She hadn't realized how close he'd gotten. Not until that moment. Blake had already removed his food from the microwave, was seated at a barstool up to the counter. In the flirtatious moment, her thoughts drifted to him. So did her gaze. Blake's brown eyes darted to his plate the moment she looked at him.

Reese giggled. "Yeah," she said, resting a hand on Stockton's arm. "It's crazy, alright." She knew it was straight out childish to go flirting with Stockton to get Blake's attention, but the thought was secondary to the ideas rummaging through her mind. Blake had been neglectful the last few days, and Reese felt it was high time he knew she had other options. Ones right close by that weren't so bad to look at either.

"Time for you guys to take the party downstairs," Blake said. "I'm going to hit the sack as soon as I'm finished here."

"Come downstairs with us," Tom said, coming to a stand.

The look Blake gave her in that moment presented a dare. The heat of his angry glare assuring her she'd meet opposition if she accepted.

"Alright," she blurted.

Blake's back straightened. His shoulders raised. "Reese?"

The guys stopped in their tracks. Reese responded as she continued to walk. "Yeah?"

"I wanted to talk to you for a minute," he said.

Reese didn't bother looking back at him. She had wanted to talk to him too. Before he'd spent the entire night away. Again. "I'm sure I won't be too long," Reese finally said. "We can talk when I come back." And with that, she headed down the stairs, three chuckling ranch hands at her heels.

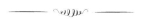

Blake made a mental note to put dirt in the boys' soap downstairs. Or perhaps their beds would be better. He wanted to get even in some way. But for what? For spending time with Reese? And what right did he have to be angry with her? Yet he was. It was just...

He tried to block out the remainder of that sentence while smearing shaving cream over his neck. He cleared the shower mirror next, shaking his head as the steam fogged it up once more. The sentence forming in his head finished out as he scraped the razor along the sides of his throat. It was just that he'd been making such an effort to give the girl her space. To not bombard her with staring and flirting and lame attempts to get close. Only to have the three stooges surface from their quarters and take his place. Times three. Problem was, she seemed to enjoy their company.

His hand tensed, causing the blade to nick his skin just beneath his jaw. Blake muttered a curse as he spotted blood. Nothing major, just enough to irritate him even more. He would take his time in the shower, and while drying off as well, but if Reese wasn't upstairs by the time he was through, Blake planned to go right on down there and get her himself. He wasn't about to let her stay with those guys half the night. Especially when she was under his watch. A hint of guilt crept in at that thought. He'd been gone way too often since she'd come and he knew it. He vowed to come in sooner. End his day's work before the sun went down, and have dinner with the girl every once in a while. It was better than letting the boys have at her, and it was clear she didn't want to be alone.

Blake shut off the water and reached for his towel, patting his face before wrapping it around his waist. The bathroom sure looked different since she'd come. One corner of the counter looked like some sort of beauty salon. Makeup in baskets. Perfume and lotions standing nearby. He reached for a small pink bottle, brought it to his nose, and inhaled the scent – rose. The soft, fragrant smell made him think of her. That lovely heart-shaped face. Her wide, hazel eyes and that flawless smile. He replaced the bottle, a mass of heat surging through his blood. He wasn't sure why, but the thoughts he had about Reese made him feel like a criminal. As if he was targeting some damaged woman in her weakest moment. She may be in a compromising position, but she was far from weak, he knew that. Still...

The sound of her door knob turning silenced his thoughts. He glanced over to see that he hadn't bothered locking it. A set of shocked eyes met his gaze through the mirror as Reese stepped inside.

"Oh my heavens. I'm so sorry." She turned her face from him, her eyes shifting from one place to the next before settling on the floor. "Do you want me to step out real quick?"

Blake glanced down at the towel covering him from the waist down. "Naw, I'm decent."

A shade of pink spread over her cheeks as she glanced back up at him.

"How was your visit with the boys? They show you more fascinating tricks?" He hated the hint of jealousy that clung to his words.

Reese shimmied up to the counter, grabbed her toothbrush, and proceeded to smother it with toothpaste. "Uh-huh," she said. "There's one that's really cool. I can show you if you'd like, but you'll have to lay down somewhere."

"Lay down? Stockton didn't convince you the only place it would work was his bed, did he?" Blake felt a hint of relief wash over him when Reese laughed at the snide comment.

"You mean it would have worked someplace else?"

She rinsed her toothbrush before starting to brush.

He laughed now. "I'm sure it'll only work for me on *my* bed," Blake said with a wink. "If you want, I'll even throw some clothes on. Least some shorts. Unless it works better nude." He chuckled as Reese reached out to shove him with one hand. With the other, she was busy meticulously scrubbing her teeth. "Oh, you didn't answer," he teased. "They didn't convince you to get undressed, did they?"

She shook her head and leaned over the sink, turning on the water to rinse her mouth. "It worked with my clothes on." She dabbed her face with the nearby hand towel. "And while I was flat on the ground, thank you very much."

Blake reached for his toothbrush, enjoying the way her cheeks reddened with the topic. "Well now you've gone and made it sound kinda boring. Not sure if I want to do it anymore."

She reached for a small bottle, squirted a blob onto her hand, and began rubbing it over her arms and neck. The scent was sweet and tempting all at once; like Reese. "Well I forgot to mention that while it worked for me fully clothed, it'll only work on you if you keep your shirt off."

Blake's eyes widened while he looked at her through the mirror. This girl was dangerous. "Just come in my room when you're ready," she said. "I'll show you in there." Correction – very dangerous. Had she seriously just invited him into her room? At night? With her smelling so incredible? He wondered if he could control himself. What if she got too close? Too playful or friendly? He'd worked himself hard all week long, and the excessive labor had him feeling weak in her presence. It seemed counter productive; she was the very reason he'd stayed out so late. Got up so early. This is what he was trying to avoid.

Still, the voice that repeated that very thing in his mind was a whisper compared to the one that urged him forward. It was just a simple trick she was going to show him. And he needed to give Reese more credit. She wouldn't allow him to do anything she didn't want him to. After brushing his teeth, he threw on a pair of sports shorts and tapped on her door, wondering if she'd changed into pajamas of some sort.

"Come on in," she hollered.

Blake hadn't seen the room since she'd moved her things into it. It looked like an entirely different place. All floral and lace. It smelled different too. Smelled like her. She sat on her bed, a novel in her hand, something silky on her body. A matching top and shorts, the satin-like material was caught between yellow and white, and looked terrific next to her tan skin.

"Okay," she said, resting the book on the bed. "Lie down on the floor, facedown with your arms stretched out in front of you. Like you're about to go down a water slide."

A large rug covered most of the hardwood floor. He positioned himself on the rug as she climbed off the bed.

"Now I'm going to … let's see." She took hold of both his wrists and lifted his arms off the ground.

"You want me to get up?" he asked.

"No. Keep your body loose like you're still trying to lay. I'm just going to lift you up like this." She pulled on his arms until his chest came slightly off the floor. He was left with a view of her bare feet and slender ankles.

His eyes wandered up her curvy legs. "This doesn't feel very good but the view is terrific," he said.

Reese giggled. "Good thing I'm not wearing a nighty."

Blake chuckled in return. "Good thing for who?"

"If my hands weren't tied up I'd slap you," she said through a laugh. After a few quiet moments she spoke up again. "I think we're just about there. Are your hands feelin' a little tingly?"

He tried wiggling his fingers. "What hands?"

"Oh, you're definitely ready. Now I want you to close your eyes and turn your head to the side while I rest you back down."

Slowly she started to lower him. Just inches at a time. His chest, and then his head. At last she lowered his arms completely, resting his palms face down on the floor. Yet it felt as if they continued to move down. Further and further still, as if his upper body was sinking into the floor. "Whoa. That's..." he faded off as the motion continued.

Reese broke into a laugh. "Is that the coolest?"

"I feel like I can't move," he said. "Like my body is buried somewhere in the floorboards."

"I know," she cheered. "I love it."

Blake pulled himself onto his elbows. "You do?"

The floor creaked as she dropped to her knees in front of him. "Don't you?"

He shrugged. "I guess." He searched her face, liking the way she'd enjoyed the ranch hands' silly little games. Attempts to get closer to her is what they were. Yet she'd liked them all the same. He glanced over at the bed. "How's the mattress in here? Have you been comfortable? "

Reese nodded. "It's real nice. Probably better than the one I have at home. Wish I could sleep, is all." A small frown puckered her brow.

"You're not sleeping well?" he asked, surprised by the news.

"Well you know when you start off someplace with a bad experience and then it just sort of ruins things for you?"

Bad experience? The idea didn't sit well with him. "No. What do you mean?"

"I mean I love the room and the home and everything. But my first night here I had this terrible nightmare, I'm sure from the whole shooting and everything. But now, since that was so ... impactful, it's like every time I lay down I just start imagining it all over again. I can't stop reliving it each night."

Blake nodded, feeling more disturbed than he wanted to admit. "Have you tried sleep aids or something like that?"

"It's not that I can't fall asleep. It's just that same horrible dream keeps on wakin' me up. It's exhausting."

"Hmm. I remember staying at my cousin's house for a week. We watched a bunch of scary movies in the basement on our first night there. Gave me terrible nightmares. And I remember experiencing just what you're saying. Each time I'd climb under the covers, it'd start back up again 'fore I could even fall asleep." He considered that for a moment, recalling what he'd done to remedy the situation. "I remember turning myself around in the bed. Putting my pillow where my feet had been. And sleeping that way instead."

She tilted her head, biting on her lower lip. "Did it work?"

"Yeah." He pushed himself off the ground and maneuvered his legs enough to sit up. The action put him closer to her face. Their eyes locked. Blake gulped.

"I'll have to try that," Reese said. "I was hoping that doing a little reading would help. Betty lent me some great books. I've been reading each night before I go to bed, you know, take my thoughts to another place. But when I turn the lights out my mind just shifts back."

"What are those novels all about, anyway?" He'd never been one for picking up a book on his spare time. Hadn't really found anything that caught his interest.

Reese rested a hand on the floor, leaning slightly to one side. "The one I'm reading now is about a girl who gets shipped away from her home to stay with her wicked aunt. And while she's there she meets this incredible man who sweeps her off her feet."

"Hmm. Romance."

"Of course," she said. "I love romance. What girl doesn't? I just wish it was enough to keep the nightmares away."

Blake wondered if a little *real life* romance would do the trick. Was tempted to give it a try then and there.

It'd been a wayward thought for the most part, but

as Reese's arm brushed gently across his, he realized she'd scooted closer to him. The warmth of her felt electric next to his skin. And there went that fire – burning low in his belly as his gaze fell to her lips. Boy, did he want her kiss. Anticipation hung heavy in the air as he breathed – the taste of it sweet and alluring.

He leaned in closer, hungry for more. Reese's lids grew heavy as he neared. His pulse felt like rapid thunder, picking up pace with each breath.

Wait. What was he doing? Where would this lead? He was half-naked, sitting on her bedroom floor just inches from her bed. He hadn't even gone on a first date with this woman, yet he was moving in for a kiss? A kiss she probably didn't even want.

As if countering that thought, Reese's gaze drifted to his lips. She wanted it. So why was he chickening out?

"I better let you get to bed," he spoke, hating himself for spoiling the moment.

Reese cleared her throat, hopping to her feet before he spoke another word. "Yeah. I'm going to get back to my novel." She strode over to the side of her bed.

Already Blake wanted to go back in time. Ten seconds was all he needed. He'd go back, forget the stupid thing he'd said and kiss the woman long and hard. As it was, he came to a stand and shuffled toward the door. "See you in the morning."

He made himself a promise as he stepped out of her room. The next time the opportunity came – and he knew darn well it would – he'd kiss Reese Taylor without so much as a second thought. Reese may have been haunted by nightmares of what she'd been through, but Blake was sure to have torment of his own tonight in the form of one torturous question: Why in heaven's name hadn't he just kissed her?

CHAPTER ELEVEN

Reese laced up her gym shoes, a wide smile set on her face. The guys stood on the grass, stretching their limbs as if they were up for the race of their lives.

"You ready?" Allie's blue eyes were wide with excitement.

"I think so. I've been looking forward to this all week, but now I'm feeling nervous suddenly."

Allie reached up to tighten her pony tail, the brown strands coming loose around her pretty face. "Blake and Terrance are refusing to be on our team," she said.

Reese gasped. "You're kidding."

"Nope." Allie shook her head. The two of them scowled over at the men in unison.

"Let's make 'em regret it," Reese hissed.

Allie kept a focused glare at her husband. "Absolutely." The two broke into laughter then. Reese had liked Blake's cousin, Allie, from the start. With the combination of her quick wit and loving nature, the mother of two was simply charming.

"So your girls decided not to play, huh?"

Allie gave her a nod. "Yeah. They said they'd feel safer just watching for now. Though I think Terrance bribed them back at home. Probably offered them money if they sat out the game."

Reese glanced at the two beautiful girls. "You ladies are going to cheer for *our* team, right?"

Jillian, the eleven-year-old, nodded her head, her blonde curls bobbing up and down. "Heck, yeah. We want the girl team to win."

The younger of the two, Paige, nodded in agreement with a wide grin. Allie's daughters were simply beautiful and charming and Reese loved them already. "That's my girls." Reese chuckled, knowing her other teammates– being men and all – wouldn't appreciate being called the girl team. She leaned into Allie. "Doesn't look like they mind too much."

Tom walked over to the porch, squinting from the afternoon sun. He pointed at his posse clustered in the corner. "We've got the teams figured out."

Reese folded her arms. "So who's on ours?"

"Stockton, Rowdy, Shane, Allie and you."

She summed up the opposing team. Blake and Tom would be with Terrance, Allie's husband, and the ranch hands who'd come with him, Quinn and Frank. Although Rowdy had the most muscle of the bunch, Blake wasn't too far behind him in build. He was taller too, which meant he could easily be faster as well. The guys Terrance brought were built more like Stockton. Short and stout, while Terrace was tall and lean. The other team outweighed them where testosterone was concerned, but what mattered in flag football was speed. And thanks to her faithful attendance at the gym back at home, Reese had become quite a fast runner.

"You ladies coming?" Terrance tossed the football in the air, nearly missing it as it came back down.

Reese looked at Allie. "Let's do this." The walk down the porch steps caused knots to twist in her stomach. She glanced up at Blake to see his eyes set on her, a hint of a smile on his seriously too handsome face.

As she reached the base of the stairs, he walked toward her, his thin tee shirt hugging the muscled contours of his broad chest. "You nervous?" he asked. The lively spark that shone in his eye made her smile, despite the fact that she was more nervous than she wanted to admit.

"Nope," she lied. "Are you?"

That earned a laugh from him. "A little," he admitted. "Oh, but not about losing. I'm worried you might hurt yourself trying to outrun me."

She forced a fake-sounding chuckle. "You know, I can't believe you chose to be on the other team."

Blake reached out and gave her waist a squeeze. "That's cuz I'd rather chase you than the guys."

The warmth that pooled into her chest quickly traveled up her neck. She felt the heat of it settling in her cheeks as she bit at her lower lip. She liked this side of him. The playful, non-brooding side that knew how to joke and flirt and have a good time.

"We going to play sometime today or just stand here all night?" Rowdy griped, strapping on his belt.

"Here's yours," Allie said, dangling the gear over her head.

Blake took hold of it before she could. "Here, I'll do it."

"I'm pretty sure I can figure it out myself," Reese said. Though she secretly liked the idea of him snuggling up to her.

Blake took hold of her hips and spun her to face away from him. "I know you can, princess, but we don't want you to wear yourself out before the game's even started."

"Princess?"

"Would you rather I call you my little rosebud?" Suddenly his arms were wrapping around her as he positioned the belt at her waist. She might have countered his snide remark but she was too busy inhaling the masculine scent of his aftershave. "There." He spun her back around to face him, his large hands lingering on her hips. "You're ready to play."

When their eyes met, she cleared her throat, wonderfully distracted by his touch. "Thanks."

The dimple in his cheek showed as he grinned.

"C'mon, guys," Rowdy hollered. "It's time to start."

Allie looped an arm through Reese's, tearing her away from Blake. "Yeah. No more conspiring with the enemy."

They wasted no time getting the game in play. Shane caught the kickoff and sped down the yard, dodging Terrance and Frank along the way. It was Blake who finally caught up to him, but not until he'd made it a good way down the field. The field being Betty and Grant's large stretch of grass.

Reese gave Shane a high five; things were looking

good so far.

"Okay, guys," Stockton hollered, motioning for everyone to join him. "Let's plan this thing out." Once Allie and Reese reached the circle, the men threw their arms around them and ducked their heads. Reese watched as Rowdy traced out the game plan on his palm. It involved Rowdy hiking the ball to Allie while Stockton darted down the field, but Allie would do a trick toss, throwing it to Reese instead. Then, with Rowdy and Shane as her guards, Reese would try to run the remaining distance in one shot.

When it was time to dismiss, Reese got a slap on the butt from the men. Allie didn't. "Let's do this," Shane said. In the outdoor setting, his clothes similar to Blake's, Shane looked more like him than ever. Blake's team was already hunched in position. Terrance and Blake were up front. A bead of sweat ran down the side of Terrance's face.

Adrenaline rushed through every inch of Reese's body. It was hard to hold still when Rowdy hiked the ball. Allie wrenched her arm back, eyes set on Stockton. Tom and Quinn were quick on his trail while Terrance and Blake looked ready to rush.

Suddenly Allie flung the ball in Reese's direction. She barely caught the thing before Blake sped toward her like a charging bull.

"Run," Shane yelled, shielding her from Blake's reaching arms.

Reese ran like her life depended on it, glad Shane had covered so much distance at the kickoff. The muscles in her legs burned as she bolted toward the marked flags at the far end of the yard. It wasn't supposed to be tackle football, but there went Shane and Blake just the same, wrestling a few yards back.

"Go, go," she heard Stockton shout. There were more cheers too. Allie's girls hollering from the deck. Betty and Grant cheered from the patio as well. She swerved to miss Quinn's grabbing fingers as she passed him, smiling as she crossed the posts at last. No second, third, or fourth down – just a touchdown.

Rowdy and Stockton barreled toward her. Stockton got there first, wrapped his arms around her, and lifted her feet off the ground. Through the surprise laughter bubbling in her throat, Reese acknowledged they'd only gotten lucky. Still, they were off to a good start.

As the game continued, Blake's team made three touchdowns while her team managed to make just one more. Terrance and Tom kept calling fouls but nobody would listen; this was each man – or woman- for themselves. Reese was set to hike the ball this time. It was fourth down and their last chance to tie things up. Stockton called an emergency time out and began drawing the final plan on his palm.

"If you guys don't score, the game goes to us," Terrance announced. "If you do, we go into overtime."

"Overtime will have to wait 'til after dinner," Betty hollered. "Cuz it's time to eat."

"It was a big mistake to cut out the field goals," Rowdy groaned.

The teams hunched into place. Reese waited for the prompt, hiked the ball to Rowdy, and then watched as it soared across the yard toward Stockton. Allie and Shane worked to shield him from Terrance and Tom, but in less than a blink they had his flag on the ground, making it official at last – the game was over.

Reese couldn't help but feel the sting of their defeat. She didn't like losing, especially when there'd been so much build up about the women playing. Terrance took the ball from Rowdy and spiked it with a vengeance. Quinn and Tom broke into a lame victory dance while Blake strode toward her. Reese had noticed a burning in his eyes as they'd played. A constant pool of heat brewing beneath his gaze. A gaze that seemed to linger on her several times throughout the game.

"Not bad," he said as he neared, extending an arm.

She rolled her eyes, reluctantly shaking his hand. "We almost had y'all."

Blake nodded. "I know. You're good at this. Just not as good as me." His strong, slightly calloused hand held firm to hers.

Her eyes narrowed. "We'll have to see next week."

"Oh, you haven't had enough yet? Gonna come back for more?"

She chuckled. "I'm not goin' anywhere. Does that scare you?"

His smile faded, his gaze falling to her lips. "Yes."

She hadn't realized how close they'd gotten. The feel of him near – combined with the smoldering look in his eyes – caused her heart to pick up its pace to a rapid flutter.

"Reese, catch." It was Tom's voice.

She looked over in time to see the football

speeding toward her face. Before she could think to act, Blake reached up and knocked the ball off its course. It flew clear over Betty's garden and landed somewhere behind the old shed.

Blake glared at Tom in a way that made Toms' eyes bulge in reply. "Sorry," he pled. "I didn't mean for it to hit her."

Blake shook his head. "Lucky for you, it didn't."

"It's fine," Reese assured. She hurried over to the shed and shuffled her way into the narrow gap between the weathered structure and the large pine tree that stood behind it. The fresh scent of pine made her think of Blake as she bent down to get the ball. She grunted as she reached, frustrated to find it lay just beyond her grasp.

"You got it?" Blake's voice made her jump, though the sound of it was low and gentle. He strode toward her from the other side, meeting her in the hidden place behind the shed.

"I can't quite reach. My arm's not long enough."

"Here, let me see if I can get it." Blake hunched down beside her and stuck his arm beneath the tree, squinting in concentration.

She tried not to get distracted by the feel of him so close. "Do you feel it there?"

"Yep. I just about got it." He stretched further before pulling away from the branches, a triumphant grin on his face. Had she seen him smile like that before? She was sure she hadn't. It was mesmerizing. He held the ball up for her to see, as if the sight of it could compete with a face like his.

"Thanks." Reese said, suddenly feeling unnerved. She reached for the ball but Blake moved his hand away from her.

"You want this?" A playful gleam brewed in his eyes as he straightened his legs, the great height of him towering over her as she hunched.

Reese came to a stand as well, fixed her eyes on the ball, and jumped to reach it, barely missing as he tossed the thing over his head. He caught it in his other hand with ease. His smile turned smug. Taunting. "You do have short arms, don't you?" he said.

"I guess I do, next to your gorilla arms." She jumped up again, missing as he tossed the ball behind his back this time. He lifted it straight over his head next, cupping it with his fingers extended for added height.

Reese eyed the ball as she stepped closer to him. And closer still, the heat of him warm against her skin. Blake didn't budge. Only rested a casual hand against the shed. As she contemplated what to do – how to get the ball from him – she shifted her gaze to his face.

He raised a brow. "Give up?"

"Depends," she said in a whisper. She hadn't meant for it to sound so sexy. So seductive. But it had. And to add to it, she'd stepped even closer, his strong muscular chest just a breath away.

Blake gulped. "On what?"

"On whether or not..." she let the words drift through the heated air before reaching for him. "...you're ticklish." Reese squeezed at either side of his waist, pleased when his arms buckled, the ball dropping within her reach. Quickly she snatched it from him and spun around, unable to hide giggles of her own.

She had barely secured herself against the shed when she felt him nudge up behind her, his strong chest flush with her back. "That was a dirty trick," he scolded. His warm breath drifted over her neck, triggering a euphoric thrill to rush through her entire body. "Drop the ball and I'll go easy on you."

Reese shrunk her neck into her shoulders, trying to free herself from the spellbinding sensation. "No way, Jose`," she said. But soon he had a hold of her wrists, his strong hands straightening her arms to either side. The ball dropped to her feet as Blake spun her around to face him, pressing her firmly against the shed.

The sound of their breathing was loud and labored as his eyes met hers. "You're really asking for it." Reese could swear she saw the mischief drain from his face in that moment. The playful expression being replaced by something more serious. Warm and alluring.

She was keenly aware of the hand he'd rested on the shed next to her. Could feel his warmth there too. They should get back to the group; she'd found what she'd been looking for. But something in Blake's demeanor said that he wanted something more.

She worked to slow the pace of her breath, to calm the sudden trembling she felt building in her chest. It felt good being there with him. Exhilarating. The private spot seeming to heighten the sparks that flickered each time he was near. And near he was. Coming closer even still, his shoes bumping hers as he moved in.

Reese dared to look up, a slight whimper escaping

her throat as she leaned her head back against the shed. She half expected to see amusement on his face – the show of that dimple in his cheek. But there was no trace of it.

The deep brown of his eyes stayed locked on her as he lifted his hand, slipped it over the curve of her waist.

Mmm. Closer still. The smell of his aftershave working wonders of its own. Every wordless action said he would kiss her. Right there and then.

Her eyes fell to his lips, and then closed altogether as he lowered his head. Softly, slowly, Blake ran his lips over hers, from one side to the next. She sensed hesitation there, and inwardly pled for him to continue.

He paused before offering her the slightest kiss. He kissed her again, too short and entirely sweet – a fleeting taste of bliss. His heated breath mingled with hers as he toyed with her there, pressing a delicate kiss to the corner of her mouth, and then to just her bottom lip, making her hungry for more. At last his mouth met hers in a stronger, longer kiss, his fingers squeezing her hip as the intensity grew. He tilted his head, urging her lips to part with the skilled movement of his own. Reese sighed, the phrase *heaven on her tongue* coming to mind. It was that very thing.

She lifted her arms, wrapped them behind his neck as he deepened the kiss, sighing at the sheer pleasure of it all. The moment made her feel like one of the characters from her books. Locked in a passionate kiss with a mystery of a man, the feel of his strong and certain hands on her body.

The thought had barely come when she felt him tense up in her arms. Without further warning, Blake broke from the kiss and pulled away. His breath was ragged and quick. "Sorry," he said, shaking his head. "I shouldn't have...we should get back. I'll go first." And with that – he left. Took off the way he came.

Reese brought a trembling hand to her lips as he strode out of view. *Sorry?* What for? It took her a moment to bend down and retrieve the ball, as scrambled as her brain was. Blake had given her one of the most heavenly moments in all her life, and then apologized for it.

She leaned back once more, reliving the encounter, desperate to memorize every spellbinding piece. His masterful mouth on hers. The smooth feel of his powerful lips. The contrast of the coarse, short scruff surrounding them. And the passion. She'd felt his kiss everywhere. At her waist where he'd gripped her, the back of her neck as he'd fisted her hair, and in a deep and lonely place in her heart. The place that longed for a man's touch. His kiss. His desire. With men from her past, Reese hadn't felt anything of the sort. Only pretended to feel the heat they seemed to be riding on throughout the kiss. Never had she imagined a man could evoke that kind of passion in her, or the sheer high that came along with it.

With a contented sigh, she closed her eyes, giving into the pleasure of the memory one last time before his voice replayed in her mind. *Sorry.* He'd followed it by saying he shouldn't have... Shouldn't have what? Kissed her at all? Taken it so far? What had he meant? A sick dart of pain welled in her chest. She wanted to vanish. To climb beneath the thick and hearty limbs of the pine until daylight was gone. Hide from every questioning glance or second thought. The great contrast in emotions made her head light.

"You coming?" Stockton peered around the edge of the shed, a slight grin on his face.

Reese nodded, disappointed that it wasn't Blake, but somehow glad about it too. "Yeah," she said, following him around the shed and across the yard. What would she possibly say to Blake now? How would she look him in the eye?

"Guess a person has to admit defeat once and a while, huh?" Stockton's comment made her wonder if he'd seen what had gone on between her and Blake. After all, everyone else had gone inside; she could see them lining up at the counter to dig in.

"The game, I mean," he clarified, though something in his kind eyes said he meant more by it.

"Oh," she said. "Yeah, we did our best. Hopefully we'll get 'em next time."

"Definitely." Stockton put his arm around her as they made it to the patio. "Let's go get some grub."

CHAPTER TWELVE

Blake could barely focus on a thing he did. The food he brought to his mouth – the same tempting meal he'd been craving since he'd walked through the door – tasted bland and flavorless. It was nothing compared to that kiss.

He groaned inwardly. What had he been thinking? He pledges to give this woman a safe haven from the dangers she faced, and then pounces on her the first chance he gets? In his defense it wasn't the first chance at all. He could have pounced several other times but had restrained himself. Not like he should receive a medal for it, seeing that he hadn't lasted much more than a week.

But oh, did it feel good. And right. Her kiss had brought him closer to heaven than he'd ever been. This woman did something to him, and the idea disturbed him. Was there something wrong with him that he'd enjoy her kiss more than any woman he'd dated before? Especially since he wasn't even dating Reese. Was it the whole kissing-a-stranger thing that made it exciting? No, he decided, Reese wasn't a stranger by any means. Plus there was that time he'd made out with a woman he'd only just met at Mike's party. She was gorgeous, but it hadn't done much for him. He wasn't about to say he was in love with Reese; obviously he wasn't. Still, he had to admit that she did something for him that perhaps no other woman had, which terrified him for two reasons: First, Reese wasn't there to stay. Heck, she'd be leaving in who-knew-how-long, never to see or talk to him again. Second, he was supposed to be caring for the girl, not ravaging her the moment he got her cornered with her flushed, pink cheeks and pretty little pout.

"Your new ranch hand is one hot tamale," Terrance said, breaking into his thoughts.

Blake looked up from his nearly untouched plate. "Reese?"

Terrance nodded, scooting his chair a little closer. Blake had come out on the deck for some privacy; looked like Allie's husband hadn't taken the hint.

"Yeah," Terrance continued, "I wish Earl would have brought her on at our place instead. I could give her a few things to do."

The comment fanned Blake's temper, but even more it put him on alert. He brought a finger to his lips to shush him. "Our ranch hands don't know why she's here. Yours don't either, do they?"

"No," he said. "But a gal like that sure makes a guy wish he was single."

Blake stiffened, shooting him a glare. "What are you talking about?" The words were coated in venom Blake hadn't known was there. But he couldn't help it; Terrance had everything a man could want. A beautiful wife – a faithful woman at that – and a couple of kids; the perfect family.

Terrance looked over his shoulder before answering. "I'm saying enjoy being single while you can.

Better yet, stay single and don't get married at all."

"Where's this coming from?" Blake asked. "I thought you guys were happy. Is something going on between you and Allie?"

The deck floor gained his interest as Terrance ran his shoe over it. Back and forth. "Allie doesn't think so." He shook his head. "I just feel suffocated. And it's only gotten worse since Alex died and I took over the ranch."

"I thought you volunteered for that," Blake snapped. "Weren't you out of work?"

Terrance shrugged, keeping his gaze at his feet. "I guess I'm just bored. And being a parent is a pain in the butt most the time. I don't know... I thought all of this was what I wanted, but now I'm not so sure."

"It's a little late for that," Blake spat. He'd never known Terrance to be so selfish. Where had this side come from? His daughters, Paige and Jillian, sat within view at the table, the oldest of the two smiling at Rowdy. Allie sat next to Reese, throwing her head back in laughter at something she'd said. A sharp rock seemed to form in his gut. He considered what it would be like to come home to a beautiful wife at the end of each day. One who belonged to him and no one else. How could this guy complain about such a life?

With a bit of effort, Blake turned back to face the man. He'd considered himself to be fairly close to Terrance, but wasn't sure if he dared ask the question that came to mind. After a blink or two, his curiosity won out. "You haven't...strayed have you?"

Terrance shook his head. Not an adamant shake like he was appalled by the question. Just a light, casual shake, as if he'd simply said no to a second helping of potato salad. The new information was disturbing. Made Blake want to somehow rescue his cousin, Allie, and their lovely girls. He wanted to lecture the guy in the least. Make him understand just what a treasure he really had.

"Listen, I know what you're thinking," Terrance said. He stared off in the distance, his face turning hard and cold. "But you have no idea what married life is like. All the responsibility in the world, and more limitations than you can imagine. Until you've been there you don't have a clue."

Blake came to his feet, no longer wanting the food on his plate. No longer able to listen to Terrance and his whining. Besides, at least one thing the man said was accurate – Blake had never been married, had no idea what it was like. "You're right," he said as he strode away, "I don't have a clue."

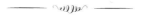

"I'll tell you one thing," Reese said, leaning into Allie as they sat on the couch. "I've never had such a disregard for calories in all my life. I swear they're gonna have to ship me out of here by cargo plane when the time comes."

Allie giggled, her pretty face turning thoughtful as she paused. "You look like you can stand the pounds. Plus you've got all that height going for you. Wish I had that."

Reese grimaced. "Makes finding a man hard."

Allie shrugged. "Not around here." She eyed Blake in all his tall, magnificent glory.

The two of them broke into laughter, but Reese's was more out of nerves than anything else. She felt like she wore Blake's kiss all over her face. Like anyone who looked at her could see what was going through her mind. The seductive kisses he'd given her behind the shed.

"So," she said, working to get herself back on track, "I got onto Betty's computer to see where the nearest gym was and my eyes about popped out of my head. It'd take half a day to get to and from the place. What do you do to stay so skinny?"

"I've got a treadmill," Allie said.

"You do?"

"Yeah. I didn't say I used it." She laughed. "But it's a real nice one. You're welcome to come run on it whenever you'd like."

Her shoulders lifted at the prospect. "Really? You wouldn't mind?"

"Not at all. In fact, I'll have Terrance hook up the DVD player in the office and we can watch chick flicks. You run. I'll eat popcorn," Allie said with a laugh.

Reese liked this girl. "Sounds wonderful."

"You about ready to go home?" By the sound of his voice, Reese could tell Blake stood a few feet away. But if she were going off the effect it had on her – the rich tenor of that low, masculine tone – she'd say he was speaking right against her skin. Or maybe it was the way he'd called it home – like it was *their* place. Reese was a dreamer if she'd ever known one, and she sure did like the image that brought to her mind. The idea of being married to the cattle-ranching, bull riding cowboy.

"Yeah," Reese finally said, coming to a stand. "I guess so." A part of her hated saying goodbye to Allie. But she was glad she'd get to see her throughout the week. It was like having a sister all over again. An older sister this time – one who seemed to have everything Reese hoped to gain one day. Already she looked up to the woman.

Allie came to a stand too and put her arms out, pulling Reese in for a warm embrace. More hugs followed. Blake's parents, and his aunt and uncle too. Each of them as kind and endearing as the next. But inwardly, Reese's mind was stirring on what might happen when they returned home – as Blake had called it. Would he kiss her again? Or was his apology an indication that he deemed it a terrible mistake? One he had no intention of repeating. It was a unique situation. Living in the same house with him, spending quality time in scattered doses. There was nothing to say they were interested in one another besides the occasional flirting. There were no dates. No real progression of first, second, or third time going out.

But that kiss. She sighed.

It was a manifestation without doubt. Blake was interested in her; he'd made it clear with every move of that passion-evoking mouth, and Reese wasn't willing to let things just slip away.

She continued to muse on that while they walked back to the house. Already, the stroll along the dirt road was a familiar thing, and she liked that. Walking beneath the twinkling stars – more stars than a city sky would ever show. She liked the crickets too – their rhythmic song adding to the enchantment of the night. But most of all she liked the way Blake took her hand and tucked it at the nook of his elbow. It was an old-fashioned gesture, but it was sweet and endearing all the same – the action said he wanted her safe from harm and close to him. She couldn't think of anything better.

At the porch, he creaked open the door. As promised, Blake had left the front room light on for her. "You sure didn't have a hard time getting the boys to agree, did ya? 'Bout the flag football, that is."

Reese stepped inside, watching as he locked up the door. "No," she admitted with a laugh. "I sure didn't."

Blake strode ahead of her, flipping the switch to light the hall. "You mind catching that light for me?" His request seemed to say something. That he had no intention of staying up and getting close. That he was ready to call it a night.

Reese glanced at the front room switch. "Sure." Once the room was dark, she walked briskly past him and proceeded down the hall. She spun around to see him still standing at the opposite end, his hand on the switch. She'd been content with the sparse conversation on the way home, had used the peaceful moment to reflect after all the noise and excitement. But now she could see that Blake had sunk back into that brooding state of his. He'd tried to hide it with the small talk about the game, but now she could see it clear as day.

"Is something bothering you?" she asked.

He looked down at his shoes, shifting his weight from one foot to the next. "Nope. Just got a long week ahead of me is all. I'm still hoping to pull on another ranch hand or two, but until then I might not be around too much."

Reese bit into her lip, irritated by the statement. "Not even for the nights I plan to cook?" she asked. "Got some good things on the menu this week." That was the truth. She and Betty had stocked up over the weekend. Reese had enough food for meals to last through the month.

Blake tucked his hands into his pockets, a hint of agitation on his face. "Just depends."

"Hmm. Well, sounds like I might be eating with the boys again this week," she said. "I plan to cook Monday, Wednesday, and Friday too. We'll eat at six-thirty."

"*Six-thirty?*" he spat incredulously.

"Yes. That's when the rest of the ranch hands get home. Can't very well have everyone waiting around until midnight for you."

He shook his head, his jaw looking tense and rigid. "Fine."

And there he stayed – at his safe distance down the hall. As if he was afraid to come any closer.

Reese forced a smile. "Well then, goodnight Blake," she said, and closed the door behind her.

CHAPTER THIRTEEN

Blake wiped at his forehead with the back of his hand, irritated when he saw grease smeared across the length of it. He'd look a filthy mess by the time he got home, not that Reese would be awake to see him anyhow. The darned swather had given him more grief than good this year; the blasted blades chewing up the hay tops like a herd of hungry cows, leaving rows of ruined crop in its wake. He muttered a curse under his breath, hating the visions that poured through his head. Tom, Stockton, and Rowdy enjoying a nice hot meal with Reese by their sides. Boy, did that boil his blood.

A burst of static sounded from the CB before Tom's voice came through. "Hey, Boss?"

Blake dropped the wrench in his hand, smeared the grease onto his tee shirt, and grabbed the small box. "Yeah?"

"I heard back from my cousin, Neil. Said he'd love to take the position if it's still open."

"You're kidding." It was the best news he'd heard all week. "Tell him yes. And to get out here as soon as he can." One extra hand wouldn't put an end to all their troubles, but it sure would help. "Neil's the one who has mechanical experience, right?"

"Right. And there's another guy who got laid off too. A friend of Neil's. You got enough work for him?"

Did he ever. "Sure do. They're coming from Colorado?"

"Yeah."

"Have them get out here right away. We can keep them on through fall."

"Will do," Tom said.

"Oh, and Tom? Just wanted to double check about the other guy. Your cousin knows him well? Just thinking of our situation, you know."

"Oh, yeah, I grew up with the kid. His name's Keith. He was born and raised in Colorado with us. No worries there."

Blake nodded in satisfaction. He hadn't heard it before, as interested as he was in the topic at hand, but as Tom last spoke Blake could hear the sound of Reese's lovely laugh in the distance. And Rowdy's too. Damn those boys. Couldn't they just take the food and go? Why'd they have to stay in her company all night long like a lonely pack of wolves? A small thought came to him then: perhaps Reese was doing this on purpose. Making him suffer for leaving her to eat alone so often. Naw, he knew better. She simply enjoyed the boys' company, was all.

An irritated growl climbed up his throat. Just last week Blake had been determined to come in on time. What had happened to his resolve?

He imagined what things might be like with two extra hands on staff. One who could fix the darned swather once and for all, and another who could help lighten the load where the hay was concerned. He let out a deep sigh as he pulled off his undershirt, wiping the grease off his arms and hands. The idea made him anxious is what it did. More alone time with Reese would be nice. Hell, it'd be better than nice. But it could do a lot of damage too. Digging into a bowl of frosting with no place to spread it. And what was frosting without cake? The substance of a lasting, meaningful relationship.

The light dangling above him seemed to dim along with his hopes. She was a heck of a woman, and a fine-looking one at that. But why start something he'd be unable to finish? With an elbow draped over one knee, Blake shook his head. Only a fool would do such a thing.

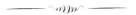

Reese slid the dish towel over the final pot before handing it to Rowdy. He smiled at her when he took it, a rather shy-looking grin, considering who it'd come from.

"I've been meaning to ask you..." he said in a low whisper, pausing to look over one massive shoulder. Tom and Stockton had already said goodnight, but the two still lingered in the laundry room, as if waiting to make sure Rowdy would join them soon.

Reese tightened the ponytail at the back of her head. "What's that?"

"I was wondering if you'd like to go on a date with

me this Friday night," he finally said.

A date? A deer in the headlights didn't begin to explain how she felt. It was more like a duck in the crosshairs. There was no place to run, no way to hide, and only her mouth to save her. Only she couldn't. Not if it meant turning him down. "Sure," she said. "That sounds nice."

The wide smile on Rowdy's face caused a knot of guilt to form in her stomach.

"I'll come on up here and pick you up around seven." He'd said it loud enough for Stockton and Tom to hear – their shock-and-awe reactions pouring from the back room. She could hear them grumbling next, and fought an uprising of dread. Would she feel obligated to say yes if the others asked too?

She sighed. Of all the men there at the ranch, Blake Emerson was the one Reese most wanted to go on a date with; too bad he'd be the only one too stubborn and proud to ask. It was irritating, really. All the other guys running around with their whistlin' and hooting, and causing up a storm while Blake stood by, cool as a cucumber, not a care in the world. Let the other guys be on the same football team. Have dinner with her throughout the week. And date her on the weekends too. She'd thought his kiss had meant something but now she was starting to wonder. Perhaps he'd been as insincere as the rest of them, only she was too blind to see it; this time she'd actually fallen for the guy.

It took a moment to realize it, but as the tips of her fingers began to ache, Reese noticed she'd been gripping the dishcloth far too tight. And who knew for how long? The men were long gone, and there she went over the same nonexistent spot on the countertop, scrubbing and scrubbing without purpose or aim.

Her shoulders fell. The dishcloth dropped. Had she been doing that in life? She'd received her bachelors' degree in child psychology. Nothing aimless about that. But had she been putting her time and effort into the wrong path? After all, what she wanted most was to be a mother. It's why she'd specialized in what she had. Sure, she figured she'd have it as a back up. Perhaps get on with a school district as needed. But Reese hadn't set her life up in a way that had led her to what she wanted most. Allie, for instance, had been dating Terrance since high school. All the years adding up to some untouchable connection the two held. A level of strength she may never have. All because she'd never found a guy she wanted to invest in. Not for long any way. But perhaps she'd been wrong. Perhaps Reese had been chasing after all the Blake Emersons out there, when what she really needed to do was settle for the Rowdy, Stockton, and Toms.

The voice in her head told Reese she was foolish. She'd been there shy of two weeks, and already she was pining after someone and coming to conclusions. Most likely all she needed was a good night's sleep. Something she hadn't had since she'd been there. The building sleep-debt was surely taking a toll on her in every possible way.

The sound of a twisting doorknob made Reese jump into action. Quickly, she tossed the dishrag over the faucet and sped down the hall, closing her door behind her. She panted there in darkness against the door, listening further. The sound of his boots across the floor. Slow and steady. The pause, where he was sure to be wondering where Reese was. She gulped when the muted creaking built along the hallway, leading to her room.

"Reese?" He hadn't said it loudly. Just offered the soft call of her name.

Reese froze. Unwilling to respond. He could simply heat up the plate she'd left in the fridge for him and eat all by himself. That was probably how he liked it anyhow.

Once she heard clattering in the kitchen, Reese snuck into the bathroom and got ready for bed. Sure she'd been waiting for Blake to come home the entire day. And yes, she was dying to spend a nice quiet hour or two talking with him about his day and hers. But the larger part of her needed Blake to want it more. If he wasn't willing to put time aside for her, then perhaps he wasn't worth the investment. Besides, all she needed then was a long and peaceful slumber. Perhaps tonight she'd finally get it.

CHAPTER FOURTEEN

"Would you like to dance?" The sound of his voice disturbed Reese, but his face sent her into sheer panic. She rolled onto her side, chasing the vision away. She was asleep – she knew it – and the dream was back. The conscious thought seeped deeper into her mind, raising her shoulders with confidence.

"No," she returned coldly. "I don't want to dance with you, Donald Turnsbro. And look..." She motioned to Sheriff Finn and Lloyd. "These men are onto you. And y'all are gonna take a trip down to the police station to discuss things." She watched in satisfaction as they put him in cuffs – the puny man with the round, baby face.

In a blink, the source of her panic shifted. They needed her on stage and she looked a wreck. Quickly she ran a hand over her gown. It was tattered, frayed, and filthy, but she had to go on. Her mother shoved the makeup bag in her hand as she made her way to the restrooms. The fabric folds of the curtain went on forever, nearly drowning her until she saw it. *Senoritas* carved in the wood. She ripped open the door, rushed to the mirror and began fixing the ruined state of her hair. It looked as if she'd been run over by a cowboy, his pickup, and his dog too.

"Can I get a little help in here?" The voice coming from the stall was familiar and soft.

"Uh. Just a second." Reese adjusted her crown,

fiddling with the bobby pins to keep it in place.

"*Please*," the little voice pled.

Reese spread a loaded powder brush over her face. Covering dirt scuffs and mascara smears in a frantic rush.

"Hurry. He's hurting me."

The brush slipped from her hand. Reese sped to the door. "Chelsea?" She pounded on the door to the stall. "Chelsea, don't let him touch you." Quickly she dropped to her knees, horrified when she saw two sets of feet. Chelsea's small shoes and white lace socks. Right next to Donald Turnsbro's towering boots. "Chelsea!" The sound of her own voice echoed in the small space, hurting her ears. Reese worked to climb beneath the stall, frantic to get to her sister, rescue her from the killer. She was halfway beneath the door when the gunshot sounded. The pain of it racked her body. The devastation. The loss and helplessness. Chelsea was gone and it was all her fault.

"Reese," a pair of strong hands startled her further. "Reese, are you alright?"

A deep shudder rippled over her skin before the truth set in. She'd been sleeping. It had only been a dream. Her mind caught on quicker than her body. The horrid chill still oozing down her back. Seeing Donald with his hands on Chelsea – she couldn't imagine anything worse.

"Are you okay?" The kind voice came again. Blake's. Thank heavens for Blake.

"Yeah," she managed, rolling onto her back. She clenched her eyes shut against the light from the bathroom, shielding her face with an arm. "Thanks for waking me up. That one was … it was awful."

The light dimmed, allowing her eyes to open once more. She saw Blake's tall, muscular figure as he pushed the door nearly closed, leaving only a sliver of light to show. "Still not sleepin' too well, huh?" His deep, raspy voice was thick with concern.

She shook her head. "No. I'm afraid not."

"I could stay for a minute and help you talk things out. Last thing you want to do is fall back to sleep and pick up where you left off. The night's early, after all."

"It is?" She propped herself onto her elbows, glanced at the alarm clock by her bed. "It's only *ten-thirty?*" The shock of it woke her even further. She rubbed her lips together, still able to taste the toothpaste on her breath. "Hmm. Feels like that dream lasted hours."

Blake shuffled closer, motioning to the bed. "Mind if I sit with you for a minute?"

"Not at all. Sit. I'd like that." She sat up and folded her legs beneath her, warmed as she felt Blake's weight sink onto the bed. It was then she noticed he was shirtless. "Were you in the shower?" She eyed him further. Small beads of water clung to his hair, the length of it slightly longer than usual – the moisture weighing it down to graze the strong angles of his jaw.

"Just finished up," he said. "Lucky for you I'd gotten myself decent 'fore I heard you." She eyed the sport shorts he wore. They almost blended with the deep shadows there. It was the white stripe down the side that set them apart.

She felt herself blush as her eyes ran over the rest of him. The light poured in just enough to play up the bronze contours of his gorgeous chest. And that scent – the smell of his aftershave toyed with her in a way that seemed like cheating. The room had never felt so alive. His strong, magnetic pull gripped hold of her, silently urging her to close the gap between them.

Reese gulped, realizing she was way out of her league. Here she'd been trying to make Blake long for her company. Thinking she'd punished him in some way by leaving him to eat alone for the night. She'd been wrong. Blake Emerson belonged on an entirely different playing field. One she should have never stumbled onto in the first place.

"So, do you want to talk about it?" Blake offered, his voice only adding to the spell.

About what? He was the perfect distraction. She pulled her gaze from him to think. Oh yeah – the dream. If she was being honest, Reese would rather discuss anything but, yet if it'd keep Blake in her room she'd talk about anything.

"It started out the same as the rest." She cleared her throat, hoping her voice would gain strength. "Donald Turnsbro asked me to dance. I was terrified at first, like always, but this time there was a twist. It was like, my conscious mind clicked on for a minute and took over. I told him no. That I didn't want to dance. And then the sheriff and Lloyd started putting him in cuffs." A humorless laugh escaped her lips. "The dream took this weird shift then, where suddenly I was worried about gettin' up on stage and handing over the crown.

For some dumb reason I looked like I'd been through a tornado the size of Texas." This time her laugh was real. The feel of it natural as Blake chuckled along.

"Okay," he said, amusement on his tone.

"So my dress is thrashed. My face and hair are a wreck. And all I can think about is fixing it all. Until..." She faded off, working to block the cruel images that rushed to the forefront of her mind.

Blake smoothed a warm hand over her shoulder and down her arm. The light caught the expression on his handsome face. The concern in his rich, brown eyes.

"Never once has my sister shown up in the dream," Reese said, dropping her gaze to the bedding. She traced a finger over the quilted pattern. "But she was there this time. She started crying for me from the bathroom stall. And at first I just kept going. I was fixing my hair and my stupid crown and powdering my face and she was in trouble the whole time. Beggin' for my help in this soft, tiny voice." Reese fought to control the tremble of her lip, the visions so real they hurt deep in her chest. "By the time I got over there, he already had her. A gunshot sounded... and then I woke up. Thanks to you," she added, glancing at him once more.

"That sounds awful," he said, concern evident in the furrow of his brow. "I don't like that you're still having those. I wish there was something..." He paused, tilted his head, and motioned to her pillow. "Looks like my method failed."

"What do you mean?" But then she remembered. The bed – she'd placed her pillow at the foot of it to sleep the opposite way – hoping it might stop the bad dreams as Blake suggested. Reese thumbed the corner of the sheet, inhaling another breath of musk-infused air. "Oh, yeah. It was worth a shot," she said.

There was that furrow again. "Let's see if we can take your mind off it for a bit."

The words should have sounded innocent enough, but all Reese heard was seduction. Sweet and alluring. Her gaze drifted to his mouth. Nothing would take her mind off the terrible dream more than being kissed by Blake again. Just thinking about it lulled her into a state of remembered bliss.

Blake licked his lips. Rested a hand on the bed, and peered at her through the dimly lit room. "What are some of your fondest memories with your sister?" he asked. "It seems like you mentioned going shopping with her, but what else did you enjoy doing together?"

The sensitivity weaved in his question warmed her to the core. She bathed in it a moment before answering. "You won't believe me if I tell you," she said with a laugh.

"Sure I will. Try me."

"Well, in the summertime my mama would let us run through the sprinklers in the baseball diamond close to our home. It was this gorgeous field of deep green grass. Only we didn't just run around in the sprinklers." She could see it in her mind as she continued. Chelsea in her blue striped bikini, Reese donning a matching one in red. "The pitcher's mound always got soaking wet. I'm talkin' puddles-of-mud wet. Chelsea and I, we would play in that mud for an hour straight. And not just making mud pies either. No, sir.

We'd smear that stuff all over our bodies like a couple of hogs in a pigpen. We'd wrestle in it. Throw it at one another. We even had a turn at spreading it over our lips like lipstick. Once the sprinklers went their last round, we knew it was time to rinse off."

She paused there to chuckle. "We missed it one time, and I knew we were busted. We were covered in mud from head to toe. All the way back to the house we worked on devising plans to hose off before my mama caught sight of us."

The low sound of Blake's chuckle encouraged Reese. Made her feel more connected to him as she relived the tale. "So we creep in through the gate, careful not to make a sound. And just as we round the lilac bush where the hose was, we hear a series of clicks. It was Mama, standing there with Daddy's big ol' camera, snapping pictures of us like the paparazzi." She laughed at the fond memory, warmed by the sound of Blake's laughter once again. "We were horrified. Or I should say *I* was horrified. Chelsea, she started struttin' in front of that camera like she was the star of her own personal runway, that girl. She was always such a character." The image was strong in her mind - her sister, primping her mud-plastered hair with a hand on one hip. It made her smile and bite back tears all at the same time. "I kind of hate that I've outgrown that."

"Who says you have?" Blake asked. "I'd play in the mud with you."

Reese chuckled. "I'll keep that in mind" A sigh escaped her lips then. "You know, it still hurts. Even after all this time. I mean, it's a different sort of pain. But

... I'll never stop wishing she were here. I'll never stop wondering what it would be like if she hadn't been in that car on that day."

Blake remained quiet as Reese thought further.

"This is healing, though. You know? Sharing fun stories. Keepin' her memory alive. It feels good." She shrugged. "Feels right."

Blake nodded. "I remember after my grandpa died, I hid myself out in the tree house for days." He chuckled, catching her gaze in the low light. "My mom brought my meals out. My old man hollered up at me from the deck. Trying everything he could to get me to come down. Eventually he hoisted himself up the rickety slats and climbed up there with me. Shoulda seen him up there. Big ol' Grant in that tiny space? Can you picture it?"

Reese nodded. "I almost can."

Blake shook a loose strand of hair from his face. "He didn't say a thing about staying up there as long as I did. Didn't tell me I had to come down or else. He just handed me a note and told me supper would be ready in an hour. That it was French dip, and would probably taste a whole lot better if eaten at the kitchen table.

"As soon as he left I tore open the note. It said that the pain I felt for Grandpa's loss – the fact that it went so deep in me – should be celebrated. Of course I thought he was crazy, but then I read on. And here's the part that's stuck with me; it read, 'The grief you feel is parallel to the love you've shared. Those who love deeply, hurt deeply too. But if they don't let fear get in the way, they chance to gain all the beauty this life has to offer." He nodded his head. "That's pretty word for word. Memorized the thing after reading it so much."

The phrase was as warm and comforting as a winter's quilt. Yet enlightening just the same. Could that be part of the reason Reese had never fallen in love? Fear?

"He went on to warn me," Blake said. "Told me not to close myself off in the future, which many people tend to do after a loss of some sort. Said that my love for Grandpa helped make his life complete. And that it was my job to go out there and live my own life the best I could. In a way that'd make him proud."

"That's beautiful," Reese said. "You know, so many people spoke with me after Chelsea died. And I know what they said was helpful, but I just can't remember any in particular that did the trick, I guess." She lifted her gaze to meet his. "Your father was wise to write it down like he did. On paper, words are silent, but they're lasting. And there's something special about that."

Blake gave her a nod in agreement.

"Do you still have the letter?" she asked.

He nodded once more.

"That's neat."

"I don't know a whole lot about women," he said, grimacing when she lifted a brow. "But I do know that you seem to have these motherly instincts from an early age. The way Allie worried over us so much. Watched after us. You'd think she was our mother with the way she'd fret. I just have to think that – what you felt for your little sister must have been even stronger than the bond I have with Shane and Gavin – and that says a lot."

Stinging tears built up in her eyes as she nodded,

fighting the sudden storm of emotion building inside. When Blake extended an arm toward her, Reese gave into it for a moment, bowing her head as he wrapped her in his solid embrace.

She sniffed. "After she was born," Reese said, the soft sound of her voice echoing against Blake's chest. "I used to carry her around like she was my own, personal baby doll. I nearly drove my mama crazy with insisting I change her and clothe her and feed her." She pulled away as his arms loosened, just enough to look at him. "I was always in a hurry to teach her the things I'd learned to do. Ride a tricycle. Play hopscotch. Jump rope. I begged and begged my mama to let her get her ears pierced early, and finally she gave in." She stopped there as emotion choked back the words. "I just feel so terrible that she's not here anymore. That she didn't get to do all the things I did. She isn't just a step or two behind anymore."

She held her breath as Blake tucked her hair behind one ear, the slightly calloused tips of his fingers lingering at her jaw. "I'm sure in a way she still is."

The significance of that statement resonated in her heart like the echo of a flawless chime. She bit at her lip while wiping the tears from her cheeks. "I think you're right."

"Here," Blake said, pointing to her pillow. "How about I lay next to you – promise I won't get fresh – and we can talk until you fall asleep."

That sounded good to her. More than good – perfect. She scooted over to the edge of the bed, turned onto her side so she faced the wall, and rested her head on the edge of the pillow. A warm dose of anticipation flittered over her skin as she felt him lay onto the bed behind her, his weight encouraging her body to slide backward, closer to him. She scooted further away instead, hugging the edge as he began to speak.

"There was a time when my grandpa brought me along for my very first hunting trip," Blake said. From the sound of his voice, she imagined he lay flat on his back, his words drifting toward the ceiling at a slow and easy pace. "My dad and grandpa said Gavin and Shane weren't old enough just yet, but my cousins – Allie's twin brothers – came along. Big mistake."

And as Blake told of the mischief and grief he and his cousins had caused during the trip, Reese smiled, laughed, and gave into the persistent pull she felt behind her, an inch at a time. Soon her back was flush against his side. A comfortable fit as she shared stories in turn.

Since arriving on Emerson Ranch, Reese had noticed a list of admirable qualities in Blake. Strength. Honor. Determination. He was a leader. But as they went back and forth, sharing bits and pieces of their past, that list seemed to double. He was loving. Charming. Good-humored. And at one point in life – light-hearted. A quality that had somehow slipped over the years.

"So to his dyin' day, Grandpa Emerson refused to let me handle his gun."

Reese chuckled as she turned onto her back. "Well who can blame him, after the whole bullet-through-the-boot incident?" She wiped the moisture from her eyes as their laughter died down. They were shoulder to shoulder now, the warmth of his bare skin penetrating the sheer fabric of her night shirt. Without so much as a pause, she shifted to her side to face him, propping herself with one elbow. Her vision had adjusted to the scanty light long ago, allowing her to take in each magnificent feature of his face. A face that meant more to her than it did an hour ago. They'd shared something beyond simple stories. They'd shared their hearts. Dear and tender places – parts she imagined he'd guarded as carefully as she had throughout the years.

The word fusion came to mind. When fluids mixed, they fused together, quickly becoming one entirely new body. But there were exceptions. Oil, for one, worked to stay separate no matter the mate. For her, men had always been more like oil – or perhaps it was her. Either way, through dating and talking and getting to know them, the separation had always remained.

Yet in the time she shared with Blake on that night, she'd felt something truly unique, and it thrilled her. Reese's heart had opened up to him. Wide and vulnerable. And just as a spark of fear flared in her chest in response, Blake's words played in her mind. If she wanted to gain all the beauty this life had to offer, she couldn't let fear get in the way.

"Think I got your pillow a little damp," Blake said, lifting his head to run a hand through his hair. The moisture was nearly gone from it, and Reese had the urge to run her own hand through the rich, chocolaty waves. He was just inches away, yet she wanted to get even closer. To wrap her arms around him then and there. Blake had proven he was a gentleman. That he could lay by her side, keep his hands to himself, and his mind set on the topic at hand. But Reese was ready for more. She wanted his cowboy's kiss once again. She only hoped she was brave enough to act on it.

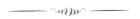

Blake's gaze dropped to Reese's hand as she reached for him, scooting even closer than she'd been a moment ago. Her fingers, smooth and silky, rested on his bare shoulder before sliding down the length of his arm. The energy in the room took a sudden shift. From warm and cozy, to red-fire hot. His other arm rested beneath the pillow, propping him as he lay on his back. He was half-tempted to move it, wrap it around her slender figure in return. But he waited.

"I'm really glad you came in here tonight," she said, that sexy southern tone adding to the heat.

"I'm glad too," he said in a whisper. He closed his eyes to appreciate the feel of her fingertips as they slowly drifted from his elbow to his waist. Soon her palm slid up the contours of his bare chest. Skin on skin.

He muffled a groan as his pulse raced. He'd enjoyed his time with Reese in her room. Had kept his focus on her and his hands to himself. But he hadn't seen this coming. A jagged breath pushed its way through his lungs.

She'd reeled him in real good this time. Flag football had been different. The entire game had felt like a tease. A series of flirtatious smiles and loaded glances. Heat – pure and simple – had driven him on. Urged him to taste her mouth that day. And though he felt the need stronger than he ever had – Blake knew it came from an entirely different place. They'd built something in the moments they'd shared. And he dared think – if only for a moment – that perhaps Reese was what he'd been waiting for all these years. And here she was, soft and warm by his side. Pulling herself up against him. Her hands moving against his bare chest.

Blake had to wonder if he'd fallen asleep while he lay there. The moment felt like more of a dream. To assure himself it was real, he keyed into the feel of her breath on his arm as she nuzzled into him, skimming the tip of her nose across his bicep. She ran her lips over the area next before pressing a kiss to his skin. Every part of him responded to the gentle touch. The teasing gesture. And he could no longer contain it.

The bed creaked beneath him as he moved onto his side. Reese shifted to lay on her back as he did – an invitation he couldn't refuse. After propping himself with an elbow, Blake cradled her face in his hand. The sheets were soft and smooth beneath him, but it was nothing compared to the heated silk of her skin. He breathed in her lovely scent as his gaze drifted to that pretty pout.

Through the dim light Reese met his gaze, slightly trembling it seemed as Blake glided a thumb over her bottom lip, desperate for a taste. Her breath was hot and moist against his skin as she sighed, shallow and halted. Her eyes flittered closed. She was so beautiful. From the suntanned appearance of her flawless skin, to the flushed appeal of her cheeks, visible even in the shadows.

At last he lowered his head, grazed his cheek over hers, and teased her with the coarse stubble along his jaw. Back and then forth, her sweet scent making him weak. Gently, he came in for the softest kiss, surprised when she lifted her head from the pillow, extending the touch of their lips. Something about the action lit a fuse. And he couldn't hold back any further. No more soft, playful touches or innocent teases. He wanted her mouth on his. Reese had asked for more, and he would oblige.

A groan sounded deep in his throat as he pressed a demanding kiss to her full and tempting mouth. He was pleased when she met his passion, encouraged by it too. He let her set the pace, a steady rhythm of heated kisses, teasing tastes, and pleading whimpers for more.

Reese was a slice of heaven on earth if there ever was one, and Blake secretly knew he'd do anything in the world to get back to this place. This moment. No anxious need to push faster and further, only the desire to relish the feel of her slick and heated lips. To share in a passion greater than any he'd known. The raw and simple intimacy drew him deeper. Pulled him under. Reese belonged to him, and nothing had ever pleased him more.

As the hour passed, Blake realized it would never be enough. The night was late, and he needed to let her rest. At last he pulled away, smoothed a hand over her hair before kissing her one last time. In wordless actions, he encouraged her to turn and snuggle her back against his chest. There, he cradled her. Planned to hold her until she slept.

There was confidence in his action. He knew they had come to this place in a natural and honest way, and that the warm embers burning between them would still be there come morning. Already, he was looking forward to what it would bring.

CHAPTER FIFTEEN

Reese bit at her bottom lip while gazing out the window. The sun had sunk just low enough to send its citrus-colored light over the land – adding to the rustic beauty of the fields out back. At any moment Blake would be home. The ranch hands were fending for themselves tonight, and he had promised to come in on time. In fact, he'd told her not to bother making dinner at all. He wanted to take her out tonight. She had no idea where the closest restaurant was, and she didn't care either. Only knew she couldn't wait to spend more time with him.

She sighed as she closed her eyes, reliving some of the moments they shared the night before – blissful bits and pieces at a time. Blake was a rugged man – as strong and masculine as they came. A true and honest cowboy. Reese had never known that a cowboy's kiss could be so gentle and patient. So loyal and strong. The passion laced in those moments would have made her faint straight away had she not been so actively yearning for more. More of him, of his mouth, of his strong yet gentle hands at her throat. She smiled, recalling the way his finely trimmed facial hair felt against her cheek. The coarse feel of it around his warm and certain lips. Reese was ruined from that point on and she knew it. No other man's kiss would measure up.

A bit of shyness crept in as she heard the handle of the front door jiggle and turn. She grabbed a fresh washcloth out of the drawer, ran it under the faucet, and began wiping the spotless counter. She stayed focused on the action as the sure and steady sound of his boots tread across the floor. He stopped in the entryway to the kitchen. She could see him in her peripheral, leaning against the doorframe while folding his arms across his broad chest. Her cheeks warmed as she felt him watching her.

"Howdy," she said, throwing him a smile over her shoulder. "How was your day?"

Blake cleared his throat. "Fine. Not as fine as my view is now, but..."

Reese draped the washcloth over the faucet, then pumped a squirt of lotion onto her hands. She rubbed it into her skin while stepping closer to him, wishing she had something witty to say. "Felt strange not cooking anything today," was all she came up with.

"Oh, yeah?"

She nodded. "Got all the laundry done though."

"That's great," he said with a smile. "You're going to like the place I'm taking you. At least, I hope you are. Hey, you mind if I jump in the shower real quick? I can be out in five."

"Not at all," she said. As soon as she heard the bedroom door close, Reese sighed. She felt nervous suddenly. A bit awkward about the formal setting. She hoped the nerves would die down soon.

Blake was true to his word. Not more than five minutes later he came striding down the hall, the smell of his intoxicating aftershave drifting through the air. The scent told Reese he'd managed to shave his neck in the shower, which always accented the contrast of his solid, scruff-covered jaw. She spun around to see a clean pair of Levis hanging on his hips, and a deep blue snap-up shirt complimenting his olive skin. He'd placed a different cowboy hat on his head, hiding only some of his still-damp hair. She smiled as she caught herself staring at him. "You look nice," she said when their eyes met.

A grin tugged at one corner of his lips. "Just trying to keep up with you. I looked so rugged 'fore I feared folks might think I was holding you at gunpoint to keep you in my company." Blake flipped off the hall and kitchen light, pausing at the switch in the front room. "We'll leave this one on." He held his elbow out for her once they reached the front door.

A dose of warm, tingly heat seeped into her body as she wrapped her hand around his bicep. It was nice – spending time with him in an entirely different way. Tonight was something he'd asked for. In a few direct ways, Blake had shown that he was interested in Reese. The occasional flirting. The kisses he'd given her by the shed. And then last night. But going out together – on a real date – something about it felt big. He'd quit his work early, ready or not, and set some time aside for her and her alone. She liked that.

After helping her into the truck, Blake climbed in and roared the thing to life. "Can't tell you how glad I am about getting some extra help," he said. "I mean, if I can get these boys to carry some of the load we've been hauling, it should give me a whole lot more free time like this."

Reese tried to hide the smile she felt blooming. Didn't want to show him how much his simple comment had affected her. "That sounds nice," she agreed.

"Did I tell you about that little devil calf that's threatening to destroy me?" He switched gears as he sped onto the main road, the sunset casting a tangerine glow over his skin.

She gasped, laughter bubbling in her throat. "Did you just call an innocent baby calf a devil?"

"He ain't so much of a baby anymore, and there's nothing innocent about the little bugger. I tell ya, I knew he was hell on hoofs from the day he was born."

She chuckled some more. "So what's he doin' to cause you grief now?"

"Little guy's getting past our fence and sneaking into the neighbor's clover patch. Trouble is he doesn't know when to quit. I seem to always find him soon enough, but one of these days I'm going to head out there to see his belly bloated like a thanksgiving blimp."

"From overeating?"

"It's called pasture bloat. And it's terrible cuz the animals will eat themselves right to death."

"You're kidding," Reese said. "There's a whole lot to cattle raising the average person just wouldn't know, I guess."

Blake shrugged. "Just like anything else. I wouldn't know a whole lot about pageants. Or college either.

Didn't you say you got your bachelor's degree? That's quite an accomplishment."

She nodded. "Yeah. I studied child psychology because I love kids. I never really planned to take it as far as I did even. I just found it so fascinating. Plus that's where my mama was convinced I was going to find a man."

Blake glanced over at her and winked. "Good thing ya didn't."

He had no idea what that wink did to her. Not to mention the words. He was flirtatious tonight – much more than usual – and she liked it. "So what about you? You never found the woman of your dreams?"

"I thought I had a few times," he said. "Was wrong."

"Hmm." Reese couldn't help but get caught up on the fact that Blake had actually found women he'd thought were Mrs. Right. Would it frighten him to know she had never really had that sort of connection? That she'd never been in love?

As they drove further on, the country tunes playing low in the background, Reese glanced at Blake in time to see that playful spark brewing in his rich brown eyes. "You're pretty far away," he said.

She tilted her head. "What's that supposed to mean?"

"I mean, you're practically in a separate zip code over there." He rested an arm along the back of the seat, his hand barely grazing her shoulder. "Ya see, there's more than one reason we cowboys like our pickups. The space in back, for our tools, our dogs, and our dirt. And that space right there." He nodded to the black leather surface between them. "That there's for our ladies."

Reese chuckled in response. "How romantic," she said, sarcasm thick on her tone.

"Yep." He patted the space. "Don't get shy on me now, my little rose. We're fixing to see some city folks right quick and I want everyone to know I'm riding with my date, not my sister. If I have men hitting on you I don't want to go starting a brawl."

She laughed again, realizing he was serious about her moving by his side. "Well, alright then." With a quick click, she unfastened her seatbelt and slid on over. Besides, she kind of liked the idea of the women seeing Blake with her too. As she pulled the lap belt over her, Reese breathed in that woodsy scent of him.

"There," he said. "This isn't so bad, is it?"

Reese shook her head, enjoying the way his arm rested around her now. It wasn't bad at all.

"Here, if ya don't mind..." The sentence died as Blake lifted his arm from off the back seat. He surprised Reese by gripping her hand and locking his fingers through hers. She didn't mind that either. In fact, the warm, masculine feel of his solid hand cradling hers – it felt wonderful. She'd had men hold her hand on dates before. While escorting her into a movie or out to the car. But she'd never had anyone reach for her hand while they sat side by side. She recalled the way she'd seen his father, Grant, kiss Betty in the kitchen. More than once. In the few times they'd gone over there, the older, rather attractive man had wandered Betty's way only to wrap his arms around her and plant a kiss to her cheek. Or her neck even, which her own mother would have found to be terribly tacky.

"My parents aren't very affectionate in public," Reese blurted. She wasn't sure why she'd felt the need to share such a thing.

Blake laughed. "Wish I could say the same. Heck, ever since I was little my old man would tip my mom back and smooch her long and hard right in front of everyone." He chuckled some more. "All us boys, we'd always moan and get all disgusted by it. But secretly, I was glad to know they were so in love. Eventually I started looking forward to doin' that with my own wife."

Reese wasn't sure why, but she was enchanted with the idea. Of having a couple of boys of her own. Ones who would moan and gripe each time their daddy came into the kitchen to give her affection. She wanted the ranch life too. It felt ridiculous to admit to herself, but it was true all the same. She wanted to live the fairytale.

The move to Emerson Ranch had been a frightening one. But as the days went on, her experience was starting to look more and more like something out of a romance novel. And even though it was premature and silly and unlikely to say the least, Reese wanted her happy ending to be with Blake Emerson. She sighed, letting the comfortable quiet fill the space as they came to the town.

"Now, this is a place we've been coming to since I was a young one," Blake said as he pulled into the parking lot of the small joint. A blinking sign in the window told Reese the place served Mongolian BBQ. She'd never even heard of such a thing.

After killing the engine, Blake helped Reese out his side of the truck and walked her up the steps, offering his hand over his elbow this time. She gladly took hold of it, imagining what it might feel like to belong to him.

"Hey, Gan," Blake called as they stepped inside.

A short, older man with kind eyes and leathered skin waved a hand over his head. "Blake. I see you finally brought some lady company. No more bringing in all of your workers, huh?"

"Not tonight. Gan, this is Reese. Reese, this is Gan, owner of the best joint in town."

"Oh, you're just trying to get free drinks from me, aren't you?" The older man reached a hand across the counter. When Reese extended hers, he took hold of it with both hands and brought it to his lips. "You are very beautiful," he said. "I think you should go on dates with *my* son. Not this horse-riding wearer of boots and hats."

Reese giggled.

"Let the woman go, Gan," a female voice rang out. "I swear I let him out of my sight five minutes..." The older woman, short as well, came up from behind, throwing an arm around Blake. "How are you, child?"

Child? Reese hid a smile. Blake was nearly twice her size.

"Doing great, Heesun," Blake said affectionately. "Got a quiet table for two someplace?"

"Quiet? Ah, yes. I do. Come." The little woman turned on one heel and shot like a dart through the small dining area. Behind a partition lay a spacious room with several large tables. "I give you our private room since nobody reserved it today. Pick your place."

Blake stepped ahead of Reese, eyeing the tables. "How about that little booth in the back?"

"Fine," the woman said. "I'll get it ready. You go get food."

Reese liked the woman's no nonsense way. "She's been doing this a while, huh?" she said as Blake led her to the serving bar.

"You could say that." He slid open a refrigerated display case and retrieved two bowls. "Here," he said, handing one to her. "This is your meat. Now if you want to fit anything else in your bowl, you're going to have to do this." He proceeded to set the bowl onto the narrow counter top and mash the raw, frozen meat strips with his palm. Reese's eyes nearly bulged out of her head. She glanced at the small family ahead of them. One kid piled a helping of noodles into his bowl, while another mashed the toppings on his own. The father, just two steps ahead did the same.

"Okay." Reese couldn't help but giggle as she pressed at the frozen strips, feeling them soften and mush beneath her hands. "Is there sanitizer down there?" she asked.

"No. But there's a bathroom if you feel like you've got to wash up afterward."

Feel like it? "Well, yeah – I don't want to get salmonella, so…"

Blake simply smiled at her like the idea was preposterous. "Now for the good part. For each ingredient you add to your bowl, you have to divulge something about yourself. Something I don't already know. 'Course I gotta do the same." He reached for the first item before them, pinched a bunch of cabbage with the tongs, and released it into his bowl. "I don't like cats," he said.

Reese gasped. "You don't? That's horrible."

He motioned for her to go next. "Okay..." She decided to go for the cabbage too. "I'm a singer. I've performed on stages ever since I was a little girl, but I prefer to sing in church the most."

He stood there, staring at her in stunned silence. "Would you sing at service here? So I could hear you?"

Reese shrugged. "Sure."

Blake shook his head, looking baffled. "You're beating me at this." He reached in and spooned on a couple of tomato slices. "I cannot sing."

Reese skipped the tomatoes and dished up some pineapple. Lots of it. "I've gained seven pounds since I've come here. Half-a-pound for each day."

He paused to look her up and down approvingly. A dose of heat skittered over her flesh with his gaze. "Looks good on you." He heaped on a pile of shredded potatoes and spoke as he mashed it all down. "I used to have a crush on my cousin, Allie. Was upset when I found out I couldn't marry my own cousin. Forget about the fact that she was several years older than me, I still thought I could land her."

Reese laughed. "I'm not surprised. She's a beauty." She grabbed the potatoes next too, smiling as she squished them beneath her hand. "Last night I didn't have any more bad dreams," she admitted. Her face warmed as he smiled at her.

He added noodles to his bowl, but set his eyes back

to her before speaking. "I had a pretty good dream myself."

Her body responded to that in ways she couldn't grasp. She felt like she needed to fan herself suddenly. As if the heat of his words showed in her face. She cleared her throat and set her eyes on the options at the bar. Noodles looked like a good idea. "I've never been in love," she said. Her lips tightened after she'd said it.

Blake didn't look at her this time. Only reached toward the bar and got some sprouts. He took a moment to answer, as if pondering what he might say. Or what she'd just revealed, she wasn't sure. "I sometimes feel like Gavin leaving was my fault."

She could see emotion in his eyes as he'd said it, but he still didn't look at her. Only reached for a napkin at the end of the bar. He'd shared something more deep this time. Was it because she had?

Reese piled on her last ingredient, making a mental note to pry about his brother later. She kept her gaze off him until she spoke her final fact – confession, was more like it. "Rowdy asked me to go out with him this Friday," she said in a small, tightened voice. "I said yes."

His face went blank. He reached back toward the bar, grabbed a single sprout with the tongs and added it to the mounding top. "I really hate Rowdy."

CHAPTER SIXTEEN

Blake leaned back against the seat, eyeing Reese as she sipped from her straw. The place had been cleared out for a while, only a few late-comers sat in the main dining area, finishing up their food. Blake and Reese had been done for a while. Had merely been enjoying the relaxing conversation in the comfortable space. His Texan rose had revealed quite a bit about herself that night, and Blake had devoured every sweet, southern word of it. Still, he wanted to know more. Part of him had been tempted to bring up what she'd shared while at the bar – the fact that she'd never been in love. For whatever the reason, she'd seemed ashamed to admit it. Though he wasn't sure why. Unless ... unless she feared she'd never fall in love at all. How close had she gotten to men in the past, anyway?

"You about ready to go?" he asked her, opting to save it for another time.

Reese sighed contentedly. "Yeah. I had no idea what this mishmash of stuff was going to taste like with all those sauces and spices we added toward the end. But that was ..." she paused, giving him a flirtatious grin, "*almost* heaven."

His pulse raced in response. "Almost," he said with a wink. He gripped hold of her hand and escorted her out of the restaurant, saying goodbye to Gan and Heesun along the way. Though inwardly all he could think about was the night before. The moments he'd spent with her in his arms. The tempting taste of her pretty mouth. He had a habit of falling too hard too fast when it came to women, and wasn't too pleased with himself for how he'd acted while in her bed. But what choice did he have? Reese had made her desires known – scooting close to him, running her hand over his chest. He might have more willpower than some, but Blake was still a man. And boy, did that woman ever make him weak.

"I was wondering if you'd be open to talking a bit more about your brother, Gavin. The fact that you sometimes feel like it's your fault that he left."

Blake knew he should be focused on answering the question, but a voice in his head went in another direction. If she'd asked about Gavin, perhaps he could ask about what she'd revealed too. "Well Gavin – he never got along with my old man real well. They butted heads about all sorts of things. Gavin's the type to always push. His brain can get going a hundred miles an hour. What new techniques were folks using out there? How could we be saving time? Making more money?" He shrugged as he accelerated through the intersection. "I was interested in that stuff too. But I always had a better grip on my dad's limits. I knew he didn't want to hear about it if he didn't come up with it himself. The first few times I brought up suggestions, they were shot down without so much as a thought. But I was more content to just do things his way and leave it at that. Gavin wasn't."

Reese tilted her head. "So what does their relationship have to do with you?"

"I just think I could have stuck up for him, is all. My father's pretty set in his ways, and I didn't want to go rocking any boats. Especially 'cuz I thought Gavin would just learn to deal with it the way I did." An image of his brother came to mind. "Guess he's just not designed that way."

"Do you think he'll ever come back?"

It was a question Blake asked himself nearly everyday since he left. "If he's anything like me he will. Most men who were born on the land, they just ... it's in their blood. It's what they want to be. How they want to live. Guess it just depends on how different we really are."

Reese nodded. "I'm gonna pray for him," she announced. "I bet your mama prays for him to come home every night of her life. Your daddy too." She took hold of Blake's hand as he dropped it from the wheel. "Yeah," she repeated with a nod. "I'm going to pray that he'll return."

He was warmed by the gesture. Blake considered himself to be a God-fearin' man, and he'd offered a fair amount of prayers in his lifetime. But for whatever reason, he didn't dare admit that he'd prayed for that very thing too. "That'd be nice," he said, squeezing her hand. She leaned into him then, snuggling her cheek against his shoulder and sighed. The warmth of her kindness spread further now, a new dose of heat adding to the flame. He couldn't help but wonder how many times she'd shared moments like these with other men. And why was it she hadn't fallen in love with any of them? Not even once. Of course, it wasn't as if he'd fallen for hundreds of gals himself.

Though the question lingered somewhere near the tip of his tongue, Blake never asked it. Perhaps he was better off not knowing. Maybe this time was different – for both of them.

——— ༄)))ﾟ ———

The television glowed bright in the night, the silent fuzz lighting the room as they spoke. Reese pulled herself off Blake's chest with a reluctant groan. "You're going to hate me in the morning," she said.

He furrowed his brows. "What for?"

"For making you stay up two nights in a row now."

He shrugged. "Maybe I'll sleep in tomorrow."

"You'd really sleep in and leave the ranch hands on their own for a while?" She could hardly picture it.

Blake chuckled. "Depends on how tired I am."

"Well I don't want to keep you up any longer," she said. "Besides, I can't go interrupting your perfectly happy dreams about drowning cats or riding bulls or whatever it is you dream of."

She giggled as he shook his head in response. "I'm pretty sure I know what I'll be dreaming about tonight." His eyes narrowed as he looked at her suggestively, causing a dose of heat to spill over her body. He chuckled low in his throat as he reached for the remote and shut off the TV, leaving the two in sudden blackness.

"Did I ever mention that I'm afraid of the dark?" Reese asked, reaching out for him. Her hands found his chest, her fingers running over the snaps on his shirt.

"You are?" He sounded amused.

"A little," she lied. Truth was she was terrified of it.

"Then how about I guide you down the hallway?"

"Okay." Reese stared blindly before her as she came to a stand, glad she had Blake to hold on to. She remained quiet as he spun her around, placing her back against his solid chest. His strong arms wrapped around her waist next. The warmth of his breath on her neck caused goose bumps to spread over her skin like wildfire – hot and dangerous.

"I'll keep you safe," he crooned in her ear. His lips grazed her skin, and Reese felt as if she might burst with anticipation. She wanted to know how it would feel for him to kiss her there, at such a tender and intimate place.

He shuffled one foot forward after the next, urging her to do the same. "Are your eyes starting to adjust yet?" he asked.

"I thought they were until we got to the hallway. It's really dark here."

He'd come to a stop, letting her know they were close to their bedrooms. "If it's that dark," he said against her skin, "then nobody can see me take advantage of you in the late hour."

The fire returned. Rushed through her chest as her body melted. "You wouldn't do that," she said in a whisper.

"Oh yes," he warned, "I would." His lips glided over her neck, just beneath her earlobe in a heated, pleasing tease. The coarse feel of his finely trimmed facial hair thrilled her in an entirely different way. Not only did his facial scruff feel good against her skin, it spoke of his true masculinity, and she liked that.

She closed her eyes, sighing as his teeth grazed her flesh ever so lightly. She had folded her arms over top of his while they walked, but now, as he worked his spell over her, Reese moved one hand to the back of his head, glad he'd removed his hat during the show. She fisted his hair as he pressed a hot, passionate kiss to her throat. The action seemed to affect Blake as he – without notice – spun her around and brought his hands to her face. At once he moved in, pressing his heated mouth to hers. He set a sensual cadence with slow and steady moves. Persuasive. Patient. Masterful.

Reese wasn't sure where things would lead. What she was meant to do with the feelings he'd conjured in her. She only knew that nobody had ever made her feel so perfect.

A slight moan sounded from Blake's throat as the rhythm of his kisses began to slow. He pulled away slightly, rested his forehead against hers. "If I don't say goodnight now... you'll be the one hating me in the morning." There was something lurking in the strained sound of his voice – a silent plea for her not to test or tempt him. His thumb slid over her collarbone as he waited for her to respond.

At last she nodded. Blake seemed to have more experience where these things were concerned; perhaps she should take his word for it. "Goodnight then, Blake." She gulped, trying to get control of her quickened breath. "And thanks for the date. I uh..." she felt herself blush in the darkness. "I had a wonderful time."

He pulled her close and gave her one last kiss. "Me too, my little rose. Me too."

CHAPTER SEVENTEEN

The stars shone bright overhead as Rowdy brought the truck to a stop. Reese stayed in place as he rounded the small, white pickup. It'd been a nice evening of hot pizza, cold drinks, and a giant screen playing wrestling matches overhead. Reese was glad Rowdy hadn't gone to any great lengths to impress her; he'd just been himself, which was refreshing.

After opening her door, Rowdy took her hand to help her down the way Blake often did, only it hardly seemed necessary; Blake's pickup was twice the size.

"Wonder if Blake stayed up," Rowdy said, his voice tense. Only a sliver of light glowed from the cracks in the blinds in the front room.

"Yeah," she said, "I wonder too." Throughout the evening, Reese had done all she could to keep things platonic. She'd forced herself to cut back on the flirting; not an easy feat since it was such a part of her nature. But she was most thrilled about succeeding to pay for half the bill. No need to lead him on when there was no real potential there. As it was, Reese was into Blake. She sighed, barely catching the look that had settled over Rowdy's face. *Oh, no.* She was familiar with that look.

Had seen it on one too many porch steps.

"Thanks again for the fun evening," she said. "That place had great pizza. And it's been a long time since I've watched wrestling on TV."

Rowdy didn't reply. Only nodded silently as he moved closer. "I'm glad you came with me," he said.

Reese looked down at her shoes. "Well, I'll see ya–"

Her words were interrupted when Rowdy captured her chin in his hand, lifting it to where their eyes met. His gaze dropped to her lips as he moved in for a kiss. At once Reese turned to the side, offering her cheek instead.

Rowdy pulled back and tilted his head, a near-shocked expression on his face.

Reese gave him a coy smile and tapped her cheek.

"Oh," he mumbled. "Goodnight then." His large shoulders dropped a notch while he contemplated. At last he moved in, kissing her half-heartedly on the cheek.

"Goodnight, Rowdy. See you tomorrow." The door was right within her grasp. She took hold of the handle, pried the thing open, and gave him one last smile as he strode away toward the back entrance.

She was glad the small lamp inside had been left on, decided to bask in the warmth of it as she rested her back against the door.

A loud clank sounded from the kitchen, making her jump. Reese pressed a hand to her heart as a vision of Donald sped to her mind. An image of a bloodied Blake came next, accompanied by a sharp and frigid fear. "Blake?" she called, rushing further into the room.

"Yep. In here." His deep voice sounded oddly muted, but even still it was the sound of angels in that moment. She leaned to peek into the kitchen as she moved toward it. Blake's upper body was tucked into the cabinet beneath the sink. A list of tools littered the surrounding area.

She stepped closer, feeling shaken and disturbed. And it wasn't the awkward moment at the door that'd done it. It felt like her mind had only just been poisoned – the sheer idea that Donald Turnsbro could find them there made her ill. Reese had felt so safe on Emerson Ranch from the start. Had been haunted only by distorted replays of the event back in Texas. Not one of the nightmares had him entering her life there on the ranch.

But what if? What if Donald found her there somehow? Actually showed up to finish the job? And why hadn't she been fearing it all along? The man beneath the sink – the growing love she felt for him – that's what had her so afraid. The idea of losing Blake. Losing him to some crazy man who was out for her blood. She glanced down at the sea of tools at her feet, working to calm her heart and clear the ugly images from her head. *It's fine, Reese,* she told herself. *Donald isn't here. It's fine.*

With that thought serving to calm her, she stepped over a large wrench, found a clear spot on the floor, and lowered herself beside the open toolbox. "So... is the sink clogged?" Her voice sounded strained; she hoped Blake hadn't noticed.

"No," he said with a grunt.

Once she set eyes on him, a bit of the tension drained from her limbs. The sight of him alone making her feel warm and safe.

Shadows played across the contours of his muscular arms as he worked. "I just thought I'd get you a garbage disposal," he said. "We've never done enough cooking in here to miss it, but I reckon it gets kind of old having to move peelings and what not into the garbage."

Reese couldn't help but be warmed by the gesture, and pleasantly distracted by it too. "Why, that's really sweet of you, Blake." She looked over the messy floor, spotting items she hadn't noticed before. An unopened instruction manual, an empty disposal box, and a few nuts and bolts. "Can I help you out at all? Maybe read you what the manual says?" Her father never did anything without an instruction manual.

"Naw," Blake said. "I know what I'm doing." His bicep bulged as he cranked the wrench around the pipe over his head. "You could stand by and keep me company though. Maybe tell me how your date went."

Reese worked to hide the smile that came over her face at his request. She loved that he wanted her to stay in there with him, and even more that he admitted to being interested in what happened between her and Rowdy. "Well," she said, grabbing a nearby screwdriver. She twisted the thing in her hand while considering what to say. "He took me to a bar. Got me drunk. Then took advantage of me in the parking lot."

A tool clanked. Blake scooted out from under the sink enough to prop himself on one elbow. The kitchen light graced the stern look of disapproval on his handsome face. "Listen," he said. "You might not think so, but I can take that kid faster than he can blink."

Reese tightened her lips, musing that Blake looked exactly like someone who could take Rowdy down. Especially in that moment. All anger and promise.

"Joking around about stuff like that ain't gonna lend me an ounce of humor. But it might just get the boy beat to a pulp. So tell me what really happened, and if you repeat what you've already said, I'll go do what needs to be done."

Was he kidding? Geez. Reese might have sounded off when she came into the room, but she couldn't have sounded entirely sloshed. After a moment Reese spoke up – anxious to erase the tormented look from Blake's eyes. "I was kidding, of course. We had pizza. Watched wrestling. Came back."

He studied her before nodding in satisfaction. With a bit of shuffling around, he was back under the sink, cranking another bolt into place. "Was he a gentleman at the doorstep?"

Reese paused before answering, nearly feeling Blake's deadly threat lingering in the air. "Sure was. Walked me to the door. Gave me a kiss on the cheek."

"Did he try kissing your lips first?" Blake asked, his voice strained from the task at hand.

"No," she lied.

"The guy's smarter than I gave him credit for," Blake said.

A smile tugged at her lips.

"Well, I guess I won't worry so much if you go out with him again then."

Worry? "You were worried about me?" She liked the idea way too much.

"Maybe," he said.

Reese ran a knuckle over the side of Blake's denim covered leg. "I'm not going to go on any more dates with Rowdy," she said.

Blake continued to work, grunting as he cranked the wrench along the opposite side. "Oh yeah?" His voice sounded nonchalant, barely interested.

"Yeah. I kinda like someone else right now."

"Hmm. Who's the lucky guy?"

"Oh, just someone who was kind enough to take me into his home. He's been pretty good to me. Managed to stop a mean-streak of nightmares from ruining my sleep. Doesn't mind if I put on a few pounds. And he kisses better than any man I've known."

Blake set the tool down. Scooted himself out, and ran a hand through his tousled hair. "It's Tom, isn't it?"

Reese leaned forward and rested a hand on his shoulder, drawn in by his natural allure. And comforted by the closeness they shared. She closed her eyes in time for his lips to meet hers in a soft, playful tease. After the short kiss, Reese pulled away with a sigh. "I better let you get back to your work–"

Before she could speak another word she was tipped back in Blake's arms, the bend of his knee supporting her. "Trust me," he said. "The sink can wait."

CHAPTER EIGHTEEN

The sun streamed bright through the kitchen window, warming Blake's back as he watched Reese move about the place. She'd insisted on making him breakfast that morning, along with every other morning since their official first date at the Mongolian BBQ. Three weeks had past since that night. Three weeks filled with heated glances, stolen kisses, and long, late-night conversations about things that mattered and stuff that never would. She was easy company. And he'd be damned if he wasn't falling in love with the woman.

Reese had been at the ranch over a month now, and they hadn't heard so much as a word from her home town. Blake dreaded the day the call would come saying they'd found their man, had him locked up in custody, and the date for trial was set. Sure it was selfish, but Donald Turnsbro couldn't possibly find Reese in Montana. Here, she was safe. And here, she was with Blake. If he had it his way she'd never leave, but that was just him falling too fast in love again, and that never had gotten him anywhere good.

"You sure you wouldn't like any help?" Blake asked, anxious for a distraction from his musings.

Reese tucked a few blonde strands behind one ear. "You could grab the syrup." She flipped the pancakes as Blake did just that. When he came up behind her to slide it onto the counter, Reese's lovely scent toyed with him the way it always did. She hadn't changed out of her pajamas yet. A pink pair of silky shorts with a matching tank top. The color brought out the warmth in her cheeks. The light in her eyes. And the glow of her flawless skin. He nuzzled his face into her neck, rubbed the scruff of his facial hair over her shoulder. "You heading over to Allie's again today?" he asked.

Her shoulders raised around her neck as she giggled. "Yes," she said through a squeal.

The ideas racing through his head in that moment led him down a path he couldn't take. Not yet anyway, so he released her and strode back to his barstool.

"Did I tell you her treadmill is just like the one at the gym I used to go to?"

He shook his head. "Is it?"

"Yeah. It's a real nice one. And have I mentioned how much I love Allie?" she asked.

He nodded, a smile pulling at his lips. "A few times."

"I'm tellin' you, that woman is my soul sister."

Blake was glad to hear it, was happy Reese and his cousin were hitting it off so well.

She glanced up from the skillet. "So tell me about your ex-girlfriends. You mentioned that you'd been in love before. I'm just curious." A hint of embarrassment showed on her face as she dropped her gaze back to the pancakes.

Blake cringed. There were two deadly topics where women were concerned: weight and exes. Not a man alive – no smart one anyway – dared breach them.

Trouble was, staying silent was worse than saying the wrong thing. And with a woman's weight or a man's ex-girlfriends it was always the wrong thing.

Blake blew out a deep breath, thinking he may just as well go dig himself a hole out back and climb on into it. He rapped a knuckle on the counter. "There was Tami," he said. "I fell for her quick. And hard too. Boy, was I in love. Or so I thought, anyway. But after close to a year of dating, I realized – mostly due to the fact that she never wanted children – that we weren't right for each other. Wasn't that she *couldn't* have them, mind you – only that she never wanted them and I do."

He scratched at the back of his head. "That one hurt, but not as bad as my breakup with Shantelle. That's the relationship I'm most upset with myself over. Mainly because I spent almost two years with the woman. I think I just liked the idea of it all. Being a man who took care of his woman. I didn't take time to consider whether or not I had the *right* woman. She was never satisfied, you know? Had this spoiled side to her 'cuz of her upbringing." He shrugged. "'Course she had her good sides too. They both did or I'd have never fallen for them in the first place. Anyhow, along the way I realized it would take a certain kind of man to keep Shantelle happy, and it had become clear that I was not that man, nor did I want to be."

He turned to look over his shoulder at the scene outside. The barn in the distance. The horses grazing. "I dated other women too, of course. The beauty pageant gal, a dental hygienist, nothing real serious. But then I just got busy with running this place." One final thought came to mind, but it was nothing he'd say aloud. Yet it meant something all the same. In just one month, Reese had somehow managed to make Blake feel more than he'd ever experienced in those other relationships.

When Reese remained quiet, Blake turned back to look at her. Her expression was thoughtful. Her brows pinched in the center while she bit at her lip. It made him wonder how deep he'd dug the hole.

"Do you think it's weird that I've never fallen in love before?" she asked. "I mean, I've had guys say they loved me. But I never could say it back." There was a sincere quality in her question. An innocence in the concerned expression on her face. Reese couldn't have possibly known it would hurt him, but it had. She'd said – in not so many words – that she *still* hadn't fallen in love.

He wanted to say no, that it was a good thing. But the words wouldn't come. He managed to shrug. "Just takes finding the right guy, I guess." Was it foolish to hope he was the right guy? After all, they'd been dating, spending time, hitting it off. Just what would it take for this woman to fall in love?

"Hmm." Reese piled a few pancakes onto his plate, slid the butter and syrup his way. After grabbing the pan of eggs off the stove, she placed them on the counter and joined him at the bar. She glanced over at him, opened her mouth to speak, but then shook her head, tightening her lips instead.

"What?" he asked.

"Nothing." Her cheeks had turned pink. He could nearly feel the heat from her blush.

"C'mon, rosebud, what were you going to say?"

Reese had dropped her gaze to the counter, but at his prompt she glanced back up, meeting his eyes. She searched his face for a moment, her expression igniting some sort of flame within him. One that burned to the point it ached. Would she say she'd found the right guy in him – like he hoped?

"Nothing. Actually, I want to plan something for us on Saturday. A date." Her voice had changed, assumed a higher, sort of nervous pitch.

"Oh yeah?"

She smiled. "Yeah."

It was plain to see that Reese was holding something back, and it disturbed him. Then again, maybe he was too. Blake was holding back the depth of his own feelings where she was concerned. Guarding them for a time. "Okay," he answered. "I mean, now that we've got the extra help I can take the whole day off. How about I plan something for Friday night, and Saturday will be all yours."

She drizzled the syrup over her buttered pancakes. "Sounds good to me."

 Reese reached for her hand towel as the treadmill came to a stop. The chick-flick they'd watched had her wheels turning faster than the gears of the equipment beneath her feet. "Blake told me a while back that you and Terrance were high school sweethearts," she said, dabbing her face and neck.

Allie motioned for Reese to follow her into the kitchen. "That's right," she said. "We started dating clear back then."

Reese took a seat at the barstool while Allie tugged open the fridge. "Had you ever fallen for anyone else – besides Terrance, I mean?"

Allie sighed as she slid a large pitcher of water over the counter. A sad expression draped over her pretty face. "Yes. There was somebody else I really cared for. And it was hard because I worried for Terrance a lot. I always knew that the other guy I liked – it was actually Terrance's best friend – I always knew he'd be fine. He seemed to have his head on straight. His priorities right." Allie paused to look over her shoulder. Of the few weeks Reese had been going over there, Terrance had only made an appearance a couple of times.

Looking satisfied, Allie leaned in closer. "I really cared for both men. I did. But I remember praying so hard for Terrance. That he would settle down. Be satisfied somehow. Maybe find a woman who would love and care for him through all his restless ways." She shrugged, her eyes fixed on a distant spot across the room. "Guess God answered my prayers."

A light, prickling sensation moved up Reese's arms. She could nearly feel the truth in her new friend's words. "So it hasn't been easy?" she asked.

Allie shook her head. "I'm not sure marriage ever is. There's got to be some give and take in any relationship. And I'm sure it's natural for one of the two to do a little more giving than the other." She gave her a warm smile then. "I'm content. I told the Lord I'd be happy if I could have a few of his choice spirits to raise and look what he gave me. A couple of the sweetest little angels a mother could ask for. And you wouldn't believe how much they adore their dad." Something about the tender tone of her voice caused Reese to pause in responding. Had her contemplating what she'd said instead. Allie had said – in not so many words – that she and Terrance didn't exactly have the perfect marriage. It made Reese wonder if such a thing could even exist.

"How are things with you and Blake?" Allie asked. "Still going well?" The smile that owned the sweet woman's face nearly lit the room ablaze. Genuine, kind and full of promise.

And though Allie had only just opened up to her about some of her hardships, Reese somehow knew it was safe to show the joy she felt in her own budding romance. Allie would appreciate the good news. "You know," Reese said, "I wouldn't say I've ever been in love before. But what I feel for Blake..." She shrugged, unable to form the words to finish her thought.

"Feels a lot like it?" Allie said, her brows raised in a hopeful arch.

Reese nodded, feeling vulnerable once she'd agreed. Like the news had been secretly spread to the entire world in that very moment.

"Oh, Reese, that's wonderful!" Allie squealed as she jogged around the counter, extending both arms toward her.

Reese shrunk back a bit. She didn't want to be rude

and resist her new friend's affections, but she wasn't so sure there was something to celebrate. What if things didn't work out for her and Blake? "Sorry," Reese said, embarrassed by her half-felt hug. "I don't want to get you all sweaty and gross." She dabbed at herself with the hand towel to give merit to what she'd said.

"Oh, I don't care about a little sweat. What I care about is that two truly amazing people are finding the love and happiness they deserve." It was obvious Allie's spirits weren't dampened. In fact, the topic seemed to pull the somber expression from her face – the one she'd worn while speaking of Terrance. "So you're going to be in charge of your date Saturday; right? Have you decided what you're going to do?"

Reese smiled. "Yep. And I might need your help finding just the right place, if that's alright."

"Okay," she agreed. "What do you need?"

A vision of what she had planned flittered through her mind. "Mud."

CHAPTER NINETEEN

"So how are things going with your new ranch help, son?" Grant's question was natural enough, but Blake couldn't help but feel uneasy.

He squinted against the afternoon sun. "You mean Reese?"

"Well, I was talking about the two you just brought on. Tom's friends."

A rush of heat climbed up the front of Blake's neck. He was grateful for the breeze that picked up. Hoped it would help cool the color spreading over his face. He tilted away from his father and set his eyes on the calf he had pinned against the post. "They're great," he said. "Neil's real good with the swather, and Keith's a hard worker too. They've got the entire hayfield covered between the two of them."

"That's good," his father mumbled. "But uh, since you mentioned her a minute ago, how's Reese coming along?"

Blake hesitated to answer. He took his work seriously, and didn't want his father to think he'd let himself get distracted.

"She doesn't seem to do a lot of griping or fussing," Grant continued. "'Course it's just my perspective, but that girl seems the type to make flowers grow 'round her rain or shine."

"You're right. She ..." Blake paused, wondering if he should open up about how close the two had become. A burst of fear tightened his throat – fear that his father wouldn't approve. That he'd think he was shirking his duties on the ranch to spend time with her. "She's just like you said."

His father took a look at the thermometer. "No fever," he said, stepping away from the calf.

Blake released the little guy and surveyed him some more. "Think it could be the onset of pneumonia?" he asked. "I mean, I know it's not exactly the season for it, but his eyes are all weepy. His nose is starting to run."

Grant shrugged. "We'll have to keep an eye on him. This ain't the one getting into the clover patch, is it?"

"No," Blake said. "But I'm about ready to kill that one myself. I tell ya I can barely keep track of that bugger. If there's a weak link in the fence someplace he's gonna find it and flee."

His father strode over to the corral's gate and released the lever, watching as the calf ran free. "Sometimes just one little devil can disrupt the whole herd," he said. "He'll outgrow it soon enough." Grant wiped down the thermometer before replacing it in the kit. "Seems as if Reese has taken a real liking to ya."

Grant always was one for shootin' straight, and Blake couldn't help but shift awkwardly under the man's all-too-knowing gaze.

"Aw, c'mon, son. Ain't no shame in fallin' for a woman like that. Fact, she'd make one fine addition to the Emerson family tree if you ask me."

"Geez, Pop," Blake groaned, feeling like he was twelve years old again.

His dad chuckled under his breath. "No need to get wound up over it. I can see the way you look at her. I'd have to take you into Doc Johnson if a woman like that didn't affect ya none."

It was true enough, but that didn't change the awkward nature of their conversation. Still, as they strode over the land, eyeing the cattle wandering about, Blake couldn't help but muse on what his father had said. The man had a lot of wisdom when it came to women, and perhaps it wouldn't hurt to open up about a few things before Shane came back with the truck.

"Was Mom the first woman you ever fell for?" he asked, kicking a rock beneath his boot.

"Oh, heavens no. I was a man – or boy I should say – who liked being in love. From the time I was young I was chasing after one gal or another."

Blake nodded, his shoulders rising a bit. "So how'd you know Mom was the right one? Or that the other ones weren't?"

His father bent down to observe a set of tracks before lifting his head. "I started paying more attention. Like I said, I'd fall for a woman so fast your head would spin. And they didn't have to be so great to get me to do it either. But over time I learned that I'd allowed myself to fall for some real stinkers, and that scared me. I wanted what Grandma and Grandpa had, and I knew that some of them women were more likely to give me years of grief than anything else." He furrowed his brow while tapping the tips of his fingers on his jeans. "And that's just it, ya see? They'd have hated being married to me too cuz we weren't a good match."

A familiar spark lit up in Grant's eyes as he glanced over. "And then I met your mom. She was a ray of sunshine if there ever was one. I'd never met anyone with a brighter outlook. And she brought out the best in me too. She made me want to be the best man I could be, simply by loving me for who and how I already was. And that's how I knew that she was my match. And I vowed to do what I could to stay worthy of her for as long as I lived."

The thought warmed Blake from the inside out. Because he'd found a real gem in Reese Taylor, hadn't he? She had more reason to gripe and nit-pick than the rest of them. Living with him day to day as she did. Getting an up close and personal look at all his flaws and imperfections. But she had a way about her that made Blake take notice of them himself – like the way she'd spent time with the ranch hands during his late hours. She was smart, that one. Reese Taylor – more than any woman he'd known – made him want to be a better man. Simply by loving him the way he was. The phrase was so prevalent in his mind Blake hardly noticed the conclusion he'd drawn. But he knew in his heart it was true. Reese did love him – whether she knew it or not – confessed it or didn't – he was certain she did. And Blake knew beyond a shadow of a doubt that he loved her too.

CHAPTER TWENTY

Blake shifted uncomfortably in the passenger seat, squinting against the late morning sun. He'd agreed to let Reese be in charge of their date, but hadn't guessed that her driving his truck was part of the deal. "You do know where you're going, right?" he couldn't help but ask. It was obvious she'd driven onto his Uncle Earl's property, was headed toward the orchard they owned.

The grin on Reese's face widened. "Sure do." Boy, was she cheery this morning. If their breakfast had been a round of poker, her face said she held the winning hand, and he couldn't help but wonder what the woman had in store. It made him nervous, truth be told. He was used to holding the cards – not to mention the steering wheel.

She directed the truck along the dusty dirt road until she came to the edge of the orchard. A variety of colorful apples grew thick on the green, leafy branches, the familiar sight making him guess once again at what she had in store. Reese shoved her foot down on the parking brake and shut off the engine.

"We walk the rest of the way," she said. In seconds Reese was out of the truck where she retrieved the mystery bag she'd thrown in back. He didn't like the way she'd hopped out without waiting to take his hand. Or the way she seemed to be playing the man's part in the whole thing.

Blake cleared his throat, prying the bag from her grip and hoisting it over his arm. He offered his hand to her next, pleased when she slid her small, silky fingers through his. She led him straight through the main row of fragrant fruit trees, a chipper little skip in her step.

"You really like keeping me in suspense, don't you?" he accused.

She glanced over at him, a wry smile on her heart-shaped face. "Maybe."

He nodded. "No, you love it. I can tell. Makes you feel powerful."

That earned a laugh from her. "It's been fun keeping you guessing like this. And yes, it makes me feel very powerful. Like some sort of ruler. Or ancient dictator. You're sorta at my mercy today."

"Well, princess, in case you haven't noticed, I am forever at your mercy. You just say the word and I'll relinquish everything I have to you."

Her cheeks flushed red. He hoped his hadn't done the same. He'd meant for the words to be part of the easy banter, but what he'd shared couldn't have been more true. Reese Taylor owned every part of him, and the truth of it had only grown more evident since his talk with Grant.

Once they'd made it beyond the orchard, the new view hinted to what Reese might have in store. Several yards ahead lay the pond on Earl's property, hidden by a ring of massive oak trees. A pond he and his brothers used to swim in with his cousins. He relaxed a bit, glad to have figured it out. The bag no doubt held towels and swim suits. They'd have to change their clothes there, he realized, which would prove to be interesting to say the least.

The thought was enough of a distraction that he hadn't noticed she was leading him to the wrong end of the trees. He hated to speak up and let her know he was onto her, but she had to realize he'd catch on at some point. "The opening to the pond is on the opposite side," he said. "We can't really get in any other way."

She chuckled. "Show's what you know. And if you think we're going for a swim you're wrong. For the most part, anyway."

Blake shook his head. The woman could barely wipe the grin off her face. What in heaven's name did she have in mind? And just what had Allie told her about this place? Surely there was nothing here he hadn't discovered in his youth.

Reese sped up once they neared a small break in the trees. Blake's brows furrowed as he noticed a bright blanket spread over a cluster of matted grass in the shade. A wicker basket sat in the center with a small cooler by its side. "What's in there?" he asked.

"Food, of course. For later. But first..." Reese crossed her arms before her, gripped hold of the sundress she wore, and tugged it off over her head. A red and white swimsuit partly covered her slender, yet curvy figure. "Yours is in the bag," she said, pulling her hair into a ponytail at the top of her head. "I'm going to get a head start."

"With what? I thought you said we weren't swimming." Blake stripped off his shirt while he waited for an answer.

"Did you not look at the water here?" she asked. "This little nook is too shallow to swim in. 'Fact, it's nothing but mud."

Mud. He recalled the story she'd told about her and her sister playing in the mud. That didn't sound bad either. He reached for his belt buckle, pausing when Reese's gaze caught his. He raised a brow. "You're welcome to do this part for me," he said, lifting his hands in the air.

Reese gasped as she turned her eyes away from him. "*Blake,*" she scolded. "Don't get me all bothered like that."

He dropped his drawers and reached for the suit she'd packed him. "My comment got you bothered?"

"Of course it did." Her face was nearly flush against a nearby trunk.

Blake smiled, enjoying the woman's innocence. "In a good way?" he asked in a low, sinister tone.

Her small shoulders shrugged. Blake chuckled as he tied up the drawstring on his swimsuit. "Well, miss virgin eyes, I'm decent."

Reese spun to face him, her gaze wandering over his body from head to foot. "I never said I had virgin eyes," she said, tiptoeing her way toward the edge. And sure enough there was mud. A small pool of it, separated from the rest of the water by a strip of land.

Blake stashed her comment away for another time and followed her into the sludge. "Can't believe I never knew this was here," he said.

"Allie said it doesn't stay muddy like this for long.

In fact, she said she'd bring a bucket and add some water from the pond if needed."

Blake figured she'd done just that. "So she's the one who set up the picnic for us?"

She nodded. "Yep." Her feet had been submerged in the goopy mess, but at her final remark, Reese stepped further into the mud, plopped down onto her knees, and then lowered herself onto her belly. "Thought it'd be kinda fun to act like a couple of kids today. See if playin' in the mud's as fun as it used to be."

The dark goo crept up the sides of her thighs and waist, hid her stomach completely, and climbed up her arms as she rested on her elbows. She tucked her hands neatly under her chin, eyes locked on him. And there was that smile, causing heat to flare up in his belly. Blake smiled in return, amused by the sight before him.

Reese began piling the stuff before her, mounding it to a peak, then paused to look up at him. "Well, what are you waitin' for?"

The dark mud clung to contours of Blake's back as Reese ran a finger down the length. She'd finger-painted back in school as a child, but nothing compared to the canvas of Blake's well defined back. The massive muscles along his shoulders and the narrowing lines that led to his waist only added to the glory. "There," she said. "Can you tell what I drew?"

Blake chuckled. "Nope."

"Seriously? That should have been easy. I'll give you a hint and then do it again." She skimmed the surface of the muddy pond, gathering a bit of liquid to smear over his back. It hadn't cleaned it completely, but at least it wiped the slate. "Okay, your hint is… our first kiss."

He remained very still as she proceeded to trace her mud-covered finger over his back in the shape of an almond. "I drew it vertically the first time," she said. "Now I'm going horizontal." She made a line across the center, put a few stitches through that, and was pleased with the appearance of the football she'd drawn. If Blake could see it for himself he'd be impressed. As it was, he had to picture it through her movements on his back.

"Uh… it's not lips, is it?"

Reese groaned. "No, it's a football."

"A football?" Blake sounded surprised. "Oh, yeah," he said. "That makes sense. My turn."

Crusted mud coated the front of her body. She waited for Blake to come out of the mud before taking his place. For the most part, his face had remained mud free. Only a few random smears marked streaks along his forehead and jaw. She liked it. Had visions of standing in a warm shower with him, wiping the mud off him with a heated washcloth.

"Okay," Blake said once she was on her stomach. "You said this is the last one, right?"

"Right," she agreed. She had no way to keep track of time, but by the growling of her stomach she guessed that more than an hour had passed. She closed her eyes, tuning into the sensual feel of Blake's hand, running the watery part of the mud over her back to clear it off. His large, slightly calloused hands moved slowly over her form, longingly. Lovingly.

"I like playing in the mud with you," he said. The deep tenor of his voice made her melt.

"I like playing in here with you too." She was glad to hear that he'd enjoyed it, and had somehow known that he would. Blake was as easy to please as he was to love, and she thanked her lucky stars she'd had the chance to do both.

"You know that piece of property my father gave me?"

She tilted her head at the shift in conversation. "Yeah."

"When I build on it – when I build our home, that is, I'm going to create a mud pond in the back, just like this one."

Our home? Those two words sunk deep into the center of Reese's heart. And her mind. As if mud – thick and unmoving – surrounded them, forcing them to remain at the forefront of every fiber. She pulled in a jagged breath, repeating his words in her head again and again. *Our home.* What a thing to say. And so casually too. Had she heard him correctly? Other thoughts managed to break past the barrier, flooding her mind with words spoken from the past. Men making promises. Speaking of love much too soon. Saying things that were far from genuine, lacking even an ounce of sincerity. Not once had those words wooed her. Made her feel anything but doubt and disbelief. Yet this was different. Blake's simple comment had felt more like a promise. One that had managed to thrill and terrify her all at once.

She worked to relax her shoulders as he trickled more water onto her back, seeming to put extra consideration into what he'd draw this time. They'd started off with building mud castles, sea creatures, and even mud clothes. Their child-like activity shifting into the drawing game they played now. They'd kept it simple. Blake sketching dogs and trucks on her back. While she'd drawn hearts, flowers, and butterflies on his.

A small breeze blew as Blake removed his hands, allowing her back to dry off before he started. "Okay, you ready?"

She nodded. "Yep." The blunt tip of his mud-coated finger pressed against the left side of her back. One straight, vertical line. She kept the image of that line in her head as he moved slightly to the right, making an identical line. *Letters?* she wondered.

A bit off to the right of that came a circle. Or an O. Her heart sped up as she felt the next shape traced over her back – V. And then the E. I love. He'd spelled I love. She closed her eyes, let out a jagged breath as he confirmed what she'd been guessing.

Y. O. U.

Reese stayed silent, unmoving, eyes shut tight.

"Well," he prompted. "What did I say?"

She let her eyes flitter open. Her gaze fell to where her elbows sat, submerged in the mud. It wasn't as if he'd really declared his love for her, she realized. They were merely playing a game. But then she felt him coming closer, leaning low to where his chin grazed her shoulder. His lips circled her ear, the incredibly soft surface teasing her senses.

"I love you," he whispered tenderly. "I know it hasn't been long, Reese, but I do."

This time the words were warm and inviting. Pure and truthful. Twice she'd had men utter such a phrase to her. And twice she failed to find a hint of sincerity in their tone. Yet even as she faced away from Blake, his words pasted across her back, his whispered breath still tickling her flesh, she could feel the truth of it. Reese turned her head, ran her cheek along the side of his face, devouring the beautiful knowledge. Blake loved her. And she loved him too.

With the stretch of her neck, she got close enough to press a kiss to his roughly shaven jaw, hints of his aftershave luring her deeper under the spell. She dug her elbows from the mud before shifting onto her side, and then her back, anxious to get close. Closer to him. To every part of him.

Blake responded by laying down as well, and pressing his mouth to hers in a heated, demanding kiss. She hadn't known him to skip the gentle teases and playful steps. But something in him had changed. She met his passion with an urgency of her own, thrilling in the blessed moment of discovering love at last. She had, and she knew it.

The rhythm of their kiss slowed as Blake moved, scooping her under his arms. He came to a stand before walking them to the island of land, and motioned to the pond with a raised brow. Reese nodded, realizing she now had mud along the back of her hair. Gently, Blake set her to her feet, and then jumped into the pond without another sound. Reese did the same, relishing the feel of the cool water against her skin. She pulled the elastic band from her hair, slipped it around her wrist, and tousled the strands beneath the surface. When she came back up, the water reaching her neck as she stood, Blake swam over to her.

Without so much as a word, he reached out, cupped some water in his hands, and trickled it over a spot on her shoulder. Softly, he rubbed at a clump of remaining mud, his caressing touch far too alluring. Soon the fine grains were gone and there was nothing but him – the feel of his touch on her skin. She closed her eyes as he brought his mouth to the sensitive spot, kissing it with firm and persuasive lips. Reese sighed as she shrunk into him, looping her fingers through his hair while his kisses traveled up the side of her throat, the ever-present feel of his scruff thrilling her along the way.

As he burned a path to her lips with his heated mouth, Reese replayed his words one last time. He loved her.

His skin was cool against her palm as she cradled his face, yet his mouth offered nothing but heat. A fire and ice contrast as his kiss became hers at last. Blake tilted his head, parting her lips with his own, groaning as his large hands slid over her bare back. The water worked as a cloak, giving Reese the confidence to indulge in his touch without concern for who might see.

It was their moment, and she would give into it.

A pleading whimper escaped her lips as he deepened the kiss. The grip of his hand at her hip was familiar in all the right ways. But never had he touched her bare skin there. The calloused touch of his fingertips, the feel of his masculine hands on her waist planted a restless urge within her. A feeling that was entirely new. Anxiously she hiked one leg around him, and then the next. Her arms seeking more of him too, wrapping firmly around his broad shoulders and back. Blake pulled away just an inch, ran his tongue over the length of her lower lip before demanding her kiss once more. She wasn't sure exactly where things would lead, only knew she didn't want it to end.

Blake released another groan that echoed in the sliver of space between them. She felt the tension in his grip, but didn't pay any mind. Only tuned into the feel of his mouth, the taste of his kiss as he slowed the movements to a near taunting pace. She clung to him, silently begging for more.

"Reese," he mumbled. She kissed him again, working to regain the rhythm they once had.

"Reese," he said once more between kisses. "I'm going to need your help here."

She pulled back, eyes wide with question. "With what?"

His deep brown eyes searched hers. She could hardly believe the masculine beauty of him in the moment. The tousled-to-perfection hair. His perfectly trimmed facial hair. And the alluring way he moistened his lips before speaking. "From what I've gathered, this is pretty new to you."

She nodded.

"And I don't want to … you know, take advantage of that. I mean, I want to keep going, but I know it wouldn't be right."

"You think we should stop?" she asked.

Blake's lips tightened as he nodded. "For now."

Reese became keenly aware of her legs. The way they were wrapped solidly around Blake's muscular build. She loosened her grip on him and let them drift to the base of the pond. "Okay." The single word sounded small and weak. It wasn't as if she didn't know where things could lead, but she hadn't been thinking so far ahead. Only going with what felt right.

Blake ran a hand over his face, a tortured sort of look creasing his brow. With awkward movements Reese made her way to the edge of the pond, hoisting herself onto the dry land. Wordlessly, he followed suit. It was easy enough to dodge the mud on the way back, the narrow strip of land leading to the blanket Allie had set up for them.

Blake grabbed the towels first, handing one to her before drying off himself. How was he still moving? And thinking? Reese had left her brain somewhere between that kiss and Blake's suggestion that they stop. She hadn't meant to get so carried away, but it was obvious to her then that she had. She could hardly even remember what they were doing there. How they'd gotten there in the first place.

"I have to say," Blake tucked both hands behind his head as he lay back in the sun, closing his eyes before continuing. "I never thought playin' in the mud could be so… interesting." His tone was cool and easy, but a pained expression lingered in tight lines along his forehead.

"Yeah," Reese managed. She didn't feel even near normal yet, but at least she could fake it. After lowering herself onto the crumpled towel, she began pulling out the food she'd taken to Allie's earlier. Cold cuts and cheese. Mayo and mustard. Pickles and bread. She grabbed an icy can of soda and rolled it over to Blake, smiling when it landed against the side of his body.

"Brr," he mumbled with a grin. He pried open one eye to look at her before sitting up and opening the can. "Thanks."

With the release of a deep breath, Reese thrust her mind back on track. She had planned a nice lunch and an even better dessert, and she needed to focus and enjoy it. Later, when the lights were low, Reese would think back on the moments they shared. She'd think about what he'd said when he stopped things between them, and ponder what exactly he meant by it all. But for now, she'd enjoy her day with Blake, and leave the rest for another time.

CHAPTER TWENTY-ONE

Blake brought Tucker to a slow trot as he neared the men on the field, happy with what he saw. The cut hay was drying up nicely. With any luck, they'd be able to bale it in the next couple of days. He eyed the sky, glad to see there wasn't a cloud in sight.

"Looking good out here," he said as Keith and Neil approached. "Looks like the weather's going to cooperate."

"Yep," Keith said with a nod. "My father always said the heavens watch out for farmers and such. Guess it's true."

Blake nodded. Boy had he lucked out in finding the new help. One who knew equipment, and one who knew his crops. They sure had made a difference. Allowed him to take it a little easier this summer. Spend more time with Reese. Just the sheer thought of her had him spinning the horse around. "Well, I sure appreciate all your hard work." Just before he got the horse to pick up speed, one last thing came to mind. "Hey, you haven't seen that bugger of a calf out this way, have you?"

The men shook their heads. "No," one said. "He hasn't been around much this week."

Blake nodded in satisfaction. "Alright then.

Thanks." It seemed his four-legged friend had finally grown out of his taste for munching clovers and causing trouble. It was a good thing too, seeing that Blake didn't spend nearly as much time on the land as he used to. He wasn't neglectful by any means, but for once in his life, he'd learned how to balance things out. Let his hours on the land find their end so he could enjoy the evenings cuddled up beside Reese.

He urged Tucker to pick up speed, his mind racing back to their moments spent together at the pond. He'd never had such a difficult time slowing things down with a woman before. But he'd never felt so right about it either. Reese Taylor was the one he wanted – in every possible way – and he wasn't about to mess that up by moving too fast for her.

"Hey, Blake?" His father's voice boomed from the CB at his belt.

He brought it to his lips to reply. "Yeah?"

"We've got half-a-dozen bloated calves out here. I need you to get hold of Doc. Allen as quick as you can. Looks like we're about to lose 'em."

"Bloated how?" Blake asked, gripping hold of the reins with one hand. "Neil and Keith said they haven't seen them at this end of the pasture all week."

A burst of static proceeded his father's words. "It wasn't the Jenkins' clover they got into. Bring the vet to the wheat field on Eleventh West."

"Eleventh West?" Blake was stunned. "How'd they get clear out there?"

"I was hoping you could answer that question," his father said. "Now go get the vet and we'll talk about this later. We can't afford to lose these cows, Blake."

"Trust me," Blake said, thinking of the hired help they'd brought on this year. "I know."

———— ~·))﹚﹚·~ ————

"I'm telling you," Reese said to Allie, "it couldn't have been more perfect."

Allie grunted as she pulled into the next sit up. But rather than lay back into another, she stayed there, eyeing her with a creased brow.

"What?" Reese looked down at the way she was pressing on Allie's shoes. "Am I puttin' too much weight on your feet?"

Chocolate brown strands slipped from Allie's ponytail as she shook her head. "It's not that. Just… go back to the part where he wrote that on your back. He leaned down, whispered it in your ear, and you…"

Reese had replayed the scene in her head a thousand times. "I nuzzled into him a little, then turned around to kiss him. Then he picked me up and–"

"No, I know," she interrupted, her face solemn. "And don't take offense, I'm just wondering why you didn't say it back."

What? If Reese had been on the ride of her life, Allie's comment had just ripped her right off the tracks. "I basically did tell him – not in words, I guess. He has to know. Of *course* I love him." Reese shot to her feet and began to pace. "In what world would I not have fallen in love with him by now? He's been everything I could want in a man. Everything." She spun around to see Allie smile.

"I know. But Blake might not. Don't worry," she added, coming to a stand herself. "You can tell him tonight. Are you cooking for the group or just him?"

Reese worked to relax, assuring herself what Allie said was true. Still, she couldn't help but feel some sort of urgency about the whole thing. "I'm going to tell him for sure. Ugh. I really wish I would have now. I can't believe I didn't."

"It's fine." Allie headed into the kitchen, motioning for her to follow. "Obviously he didn't seem to mind. You guys followed it up with some nice smooching and all."

She nodded. "Beyond nice. It was exactly heaven on my tongue, like he'd said it would be." She sighed. "And it's all I've been able to think about the entire weekend."

Allie chuckled as she reached into the fridge. "I bet," she said, handing Reese a bottle of water. The creak of a door sounded from around the corner, causing Allie to tilt her head. "Terrance?" she hollered. When no answer came, she strode through the dining area and stuck her head into the mudroom.

In the short pause, Reese's mind shifted back to an unpleasant thought she'd had a while back – that sick worry over Donald Turnsbro finding her there. Her heart drummed a frantic beat while she watched Allie stride over to the back window. She pictured him there on Allie's property, terrified that she could possibly put the lovely family in danger.

"Huh," Allie said. "It was just Terrance. He must have had to grab something. Probably his work boots."

That put Reese's mind at rest, but only for a moment. She ran through their recent conversation, wondering what Terrance might have overheard. "You don't think he'll say anything to Blake, do you?"

"No." Allie shook her head. "Besides, it wouldn't matter if he did. Come tonight, Blake will already know you're in love with him too – in case he had any doubt."

Reese nodded as a rush of nerves spun in her stomach like an angry swarm of bees. A combination of upsets. The first caused by the fear she had about leading a killer to Emerson Ranch – putting the families she'd come to love at risk. The next was brought on by something equally pressing in an entirely different way. Blake.

"Yep," Reese replied at last, hoping she'd have what it took to follow through. "After tonight, there won't be any doubt."

CHAPTER TWENTY-TWO

Blake ran his fingers through his hair, kicking at the strands of straw at his feet. The sun had settled low in the valley, leaving an odd, muted light over the dreary evening. Half-a-dozen calves had escaped. On his watch, no less. Doc Allen had managed to save two, but four calves were lost – the blasted demon calf among them. That little bugger had given him more grief than good, but inwardly Blake had grown fond of him. And the image of his dead, bloated body would haunt him for years to come.

"Wheat," he hissed. "Of all things..." He reared back his foot once more and kicked the side of the barn, cursing under his breath. He should have known better. He'd wanted so badly to prove to the ranch hands, his father, and himself that he hadn't slipped. That he could run the ranch as well as he ever had while cutting back his hours. But it had backfired with a vengeance.

The hum of an engine sounded from beyond the barn, causing Blake to roll his eyes. How many times did he have to tell them he wanted to be left alone? Without bothering to identify the approaching pickup, he rounded the corner and shuffled inside the weathered old barn, plunking down on a bale of hay. Streams of setting sunlight pushed their way through the cracks in the structure, lighting specks of dust filtering through the air.

"Hey, Blake?"

Blake lifted his chin, recognizing the sound of Terrance's voice. "Yeah?"

Terrance stopped in the doorway. "I heard about what happened."

Great. Grant had already started telling the whole town about what an incompetent mess of a son he had. He dropped his gaze to the floor, preferring the view of dirt and straw beneath his feet. Anything but looking another man in the eye at such a time.

Terrance scuffled closer. Took a seat on a nearby stool. "Listen," he said. "I know how it feels. Get so wrapped up in pleasing a woman that everything else takes second place."

The comment pricked his defenses, but inwardly Blake knew he was right.

"I debated on whether or not I should tell you about this," Terrance continued, "but sometimes I overhear the girls talking. Reese confiding in Allie. 'Course Allie tells me stuff too."

The hesitation in Terrance's voice infused Blake with a strained sort of dread. His muscles tensed. His head began to pound. "Mmm, hmm," he urged.

Terrance cleared a circle on the barn floor with the toe of his shoe. "First off, she really misses home. And I guess it's something she doesn't bother telling you, so she doesn't hurt your feelings. But Reese was really hoping to be home in time for her brother's football games. I think she was actually going to see about getting transferred to a place closer to home. See if she could still have occasional contact with her family and all."

Blake glared at the bare spot Terrance had cleared, feeling as if a similar space was being hollowed out inside the center of his chest. Reese wanted to leave? Move closer to home? It didn't make sense. Sure, she was into her brother's football games. Was practically his number one fan, from how she put it. But... "How long ago did she say this?" he asked. "Her and I have been getting a lot closer lately. I mean, she might have felt that way in the beginning–"

"Well, that was the other thing I wanted to talk to you about."

Blake cringed. Just how much did this guy know? He eyed the stupid spot in front of Terrance once more. With each swirl of his foot, the circle grew bigger and bigger.

"I overheard them talking just today. Reese didn't know I was there but, well, basically she said you told her that you love her."

Blake dropped his gaze back to his boots. "Yep."

It took a while for Terrance to continue. "And she didn't say it back?"

He'd said it like a question. Blake looked up now, eyeing his friend in the low light. "What do you mean?"

"I mean you were the only one declaring your love that day, Blake. You're being played."

Blake shot to his feet. "Played *how*? She kissed me.

She didn't have to say it back. I could tell she felt the same way." He broke into a pace, treading dirt and straw over the clear spot on the floor. It felt as if the barn was caving in on him, one massive wall after the next. The hefty weight crushing the air from his lungs. It was right with Reese; he was sure of it.

"All women play men, Blake. They lead you on, make them think they love you, and wait until you're whooped to drop the bomb."

Blake strode to the further quarters of the barn, a dark and dusty corner that muted out almost every ounce of light. "Not her," he said. "Reese isn't like that."

"Classic denial, my friend." The sound of his voice grew closer. "You know what? If you like living in this sad little dream world then go right ahead. I don't like being the one to shatter it. Reese can do that well enough on her own. Like she did with the other men who fell for her."

Blake spun around, recalling the other guys she'd spoken of. The ones who'd professed their love and she hadn't been able to do the same. "How do you know about them?"

Terrance leaned a hand against the barn wall. "I told you. I heard her talking all about it. She's worried that she'll *never* fall in love."

The words were poison. A deadly mix of it gushing into his chest with a searing burn.

"Like I said, I debated on whether I should say anything. But when I found out about the calves, heard how badly you were slipping, I figured you might want to know that you're investing in a lost cause."

Blake nodded in understanding. "Thanks," he finally mumbled.

Terrance gave him a pat on the arm. "Sorry, bro." The man dropped his chin and shuffled slowly toward the barn door. He paused there and spun around. "I'm here, ya know. If you want to talk or go for a drink. We can go find you a hot little number to take your mind off things if you'd like."

Blake gritted his teeth. "I'll let you know."

CHAPTER TWENTY-THREE

Steam seeped through the hot pads as Reese pulled the potatoes from the oven. She squeezed each gently, testing them in turn, pleased to find they were baked to perfection. After setting them on the counter, she looked over all the toppings one last time, smiling as she eyed the dishes that held them. Back home, her mother had always kept nice china. There wasn't so much as a pie plate or tea cup that didn't match. Here it was just the opposite. A pale yellow bowl held the sour cream. A shallow dish with olive green leaves displayed the chopped ham. And the shredded cheese was heaped into a small crystal bowl. The word charming came to mind, making her smile. She was charmed by everything about the ranch. The scenery, the family, and the cowboy she'd fallen madly in love with.

"Oh," she blurted, recalling one last thing. She spun to grab the butter, smiling at the way it looked next to the other dishes. A deep sigh fell from her lips. Allie had really thrown her for a loop that afternoon – shining a bit of light on things the way she had. Reese hadn't seen it on her own, but Allie was right. Blake deserved to know, in case there was any doubt, that she had fallen deeply and entirely in love with him in return.

It hadn't taken long to come up with a plan. It was

inspired by their first date, actually. She decided that the game they'd started at the Mongolian BBQ could continue there; for each topping they put on their potato, they'd reveal something more about themselves. It might have been unoriginal, but Reese couldn't worry on that. She only needed to tell him that she loved him. That she was sorry for not telling him sooner. The words had been balancing on the tip of her tongue nearly half the day. Since she left Allie's anyway. And the urgency to say it only seemed to build with each tick of the old kitchen clock.

She eyed the scene at the barn through the sliding glass window, realizing – in the muted light – that Blake's truck was no longer there. Suddenly her nervous jitters turned into full-blown panic. He'd be there any minute.

She recalled the way Grant had paged her on the CB, letting her know Blake would be a bit later that evening. And while he hadn't given her specifics, Reese gathered they'd had a particularly hectic day. She hoped she could help him unwind and relax for the evening. That he'd open up to her about his difficulties. The ranch hands had returned over an hour ago, the bustle of their activity below dying down to a quiet hum.

The roar of an engine sounded out front, followed by the slam of his truck door. Sooner than she expected, she heard his boots on the steps. The front door burst open, and Reese pulled in a deep breath.

"Hi…" It was the only word she could get out. The stern expression on his handsome face silenced her. "What's wrong?" she asked.

Blake lifted his hat from his head and flung it across the room. "You want to know what's wrong?" His eyes were hard and angry, the look foreign to her. "While I was busy falling all over you and confessing my love the ranch was falling apart. *That's* what's wrong."

She flinched at his aggressive tone. "Falling apart how?"

"We lost four calves out there today, Reese. *Four!* And I may have Grant and Shane and five other ranch hands helping me out, but in the end *I'm* head foreman and there's no one to blame but myself." He threw her a loaded glare.

"Blake, that's awful. I'm so sorry." Reese started walking toward him, ready to offer some comfort, but stopped cold once her temper caught up to speed. What was he blaming *her* for? He'd stated only a second ago that it was his fault, yet he looked at her as if she was the source of all his grief.

"I know what's going on with you, Reese," he said, taking a backward step. "I'm sure you thought you had me tricked like one of your lovesick losers back home. The ones who'd gush about their love for you while you just stood on by."

A dose of sick heat pooled into her throat. Burning like a mean shot of acid, seeping further as she took in his words. "Blake, it's not like that."

"Sure it is," he said. "We're just in our same old patterns, aren't we? You wishing you could fall in love, knowing there's not a chance of it. And me falling for a woman who's not even worth my time."

Reese gasped. "You're wrong, Blake," she spat,

marching around the coffee table. She grabbed hold of his arm, attempting to get eye contact but Blake yanked away.

Reese persisted. "Look at me!"

With his back to her, Blake lowered his chin, shaking his head slowly. Reese narrowed her gaze as she waited, folding her arms over her chest.

At last he turned to look at her over one shoulder. His brown eyes held no love. No compassion. It was as if he'd changed into someone else. "Why?" he demanded. "So you can finally tell me the truth? Because what you really want is to get back to your life in Texas. Isn't it? Why don't I call Earl and have him place you somewhere closer to home. Then you can see your brother's games and try out for more pageants and lead on more men than you can shake a stick at."

Without another thought Reese reached up and slapped him soundly across the face. "Maybe I will," she spat.

The floor was a blur as she sped over it, her legs like numb, moving machines. She'd made it partway down the hall when she heard Blake pipe up once more.

"You were supposed to be a guy," he yelled. "You know that?"

Reese froze in her tracks, somehow forcing her feet to stop. What had he meant by that?

"When I left to pick you up at the airport that day, I thought you were going to be a man. Somebody who could actually help me out around here, not distract me to the point that I let the whole dang thing go."

The new information hurt, added fuel to the raging

fire within her. After yanking open the drawers, she grabbed fistfuls of clothes in a frantic rush and shoved them into her bag, anxious to get away from Blake. Away from the ranch.

Betty had told Reese she could keep her car overnight. Said it'd save her the trouble of walking down to get it in the morning for her trip to Allie's. The thought made her sad. She would miss Allie. And Betty too. She wouldn't have the chance to say goodbye to either of them. Reese planned to go straight to Earl's – the retired marshal who'd arranged the whole thing. Perhaps if he knew how desperate she was to get away he'd do all he could to make the move as quick as possible.

While shoving her bathroom items into her bag, Reese stewed on every terrible word. If she had her own car there, she'd leave the ranch on her own. Forget about the stupid papers she'd signed, and be done with the whole thing. Her circumstances had taken a dramatic twist and there was no keeping her there. Not after how horribly wrong things had gone.

She wiped at the tears that streamed down her face, catching a glimpse of Blake's aftershave in the mirror. Without a second thought she reached for the bottle and shoved it in her bag. She might be angry with him. Heck, a part of her down-right hated him. But deep down she'd only begun to fall in love, and she knew it would take time to get over him.

The walk down the hall was a tortuous one. She refused to look into the kitchen. The sight of her thought-out dinner preparation would be too much to handle. She wasn't sure where Blake had gone off to, but she didn't catch sight of him as she barreled through the living room, the bulk of her luggage slowing her down. After grabbing the key off the end table, Reese took one last look at the place, saying a silent goodbye in her heart.

"Wait," she heard Blake say.

Her defenses kicked in, ready for battle. Too bad if he wanted to take things back now; he'd gone too far, and Reese wouldn't stay there another day. Or perhaps he wanted to argue further. Get in a few more jabs while he could.

The sound of his boots on the tile told Reese he'd been in the kitchen. Once he rounded the door frame, his gaze caught hers. His broad chest rose and fell at a quickened pace as he strode toward her, stopping only once he stood just inches away. Reese squared her shoulders and narrowed her eyes.

Wordlessly, Blake reached out a hand and gently pried her luggage from her fingers. He proceeded to remove the bag from her shoulder and tuck her handbag under his arm. Soon she was left with nothing but her purse. He turned to open the door for her next, his gaze shifting aim to the view outside.

Reese gripped onto her purse straps and stepped onto the creaky porch. The sky overhead offered none of its usual beauty. No twinkling stars to light her path. Not even a sliver of sunset to warm her way. Just a flat and muted view of the land. She slowed her pace as Blake loaded the truck with her things, surprised when he moved to open her door for her as well.

Reese slid onto the seat in silence, and stayed close to the edge as he closed the door. Once Blake had climbed into the truck and roared the engine, he turned to her. "I can take you to my folk's. Or Allie's if you'd like. Just until Earl can get you another place closer to home." The tight and trained sound of his voice said he was biting back his anger even still.

Who cared? She was angry too. Furious was more like it. "I planned on going to Earl's," she spat, keeping her gaze on the floor of the cab. "I think things will move along faster that way." What she'd said was true; Earl was the one who'd arranged things. May as well go straight to the source. But there was more to her reasoning than that. Reese wanted to avoid seeing Betty, Grant, and Allie too. She'd never felt so humiliated, and couldn't fathom looking even one of them in the eye at the low moment.

Blake didn't argue. Only steered the truck toward Earl's house in silence.

Reese fought with herself all the way there. It seemed her mind was determined to ruin her. She couldn't help but relive every tender moment the two had shared since she arrived: The dare at the diner, their first kiss by the shed, and the tenderness in their late night talks. All the while the ache in her heart stretched and swelled. The anger did too. How had things gone so terribly wrong?

At Earl's place, a dim light glowed within the modest-sized home. "I don't want you to come to the door with me," Reese said as they came to a stop.

He had looked over at her – she could see that

much in her peripheral. After a moment she glanced back.

"I'll take your items to the porch," he said. "And then I'll leave if you want me to."

Reese pushed open her door. "I can carry my own things." She made it to the back of the truck in time to see Blake retrieving her luggage just the same. She rolled her eyes and stomped past him in an irritated huff.

Once at the doorstep, she folded her arms while Blake rested her bags on the porch. When he was finished, he glanced at her through his lashes, offering one, single nod. If replaying their past hadn't ruined her completely, seeing the hurt in his sad, brown eyes did. She watched him climb into his truck for the last time, wanting to drop to the old wooden porch and bawl. Or to cry out to him, try to remedy things one last time. Make him see that she wasn't the monster he thought she was. Instead Reese wiped the quiet tears from her cheeks, gathered her luggage, and knocked on the door.

A dog barked from within the home as the porch light glowed to life. The curtain in the window pulled back next, revealing Allie's mother, Lilly. Her blue eyes bulged when she saw her, and the drapes fell back into place.

"What in heaven's name?" the woman bellowed as she opened the door, an anxious collie prancing at her heels. Concern pinched at her slightly wrinkled face. "Come on inside, dear. Come on in."

Reese turned sideways to allow space for her luggage to fit through as well. She felt silly suddenly for bringing it with her when she hadn't even spoken with them about coming.

"Earl," Lilly hollered. "You better get in here."

In moments flat Earl came racing around the corner. A spark of joy lit his face for a flash, and then it was gone, replaced by the distressed expression his wife wore. "Well what do we have here?" The man shuffled toward her, lifted one of the bags off her shoulder and set it to the floor.

Reese straightened up and cleared her throat. "I want to leave," she said. When it looked like Earl might protest, she persisted. "I know I signed some papers sayin' I'd go along with all this, but I can't stay. And so help me, if y'all can't find me another place to go I'll call someone from home myself and have them come get me."

Her lip quivered as the kind man searched her face. The gentle look in his furrowed brow softened her approach. Wilted her posture. And caused a fresh stream of silent tears to fall down her cheeks.

At last the man nodded, cupping a solid arm gently behind her back. "Alright, sweetheart. If that's what you want. Come this way. I'll have you out of here first thing in the morning."

CHAPTER TWENTY-FOUR

For some reason, the four a.m. phone call seemed fitting. It wasn't as if Blake had been sleeping. Not by a long shot. He'd been pacing along his bedroom floor enough to wear a hole clean through the floorboards. The phone rang once more before he could get to it. The old one in his room didn't have caller ID, but he was sure he knew who was calling just the same.

"Yeah," he muttered, bringing the thing to his ear.

"Blake?" It was Allie. She was his second guess. Betty had been his first, seeing that he figured that's who Lilly would call once she laid eyes on Reese in all her distress.

"Yep," he said, gearing himself up for war.

"What did you do to Reese?" she shrieked.

Blake shook his head. "Nothing. I just let go of something that wasn't mine to begin with."

"Who says she wasn't yours? Blake, you ruined that poor girl."

"Ruined *what*? Her ongoing record? Her let's-see-how-many-guys-I-can-get-to-fall-in-love-with-me game?"

"What are you talking about?" Allie asked.

"I've been enlightened," Blake spat. "Thanks to your husband."

A knock came from the front door. Blake tilted his head in confusion.

"Come let me in," Allie said. "I'm at your house."

"What? That's you?" Blake marched down the hall as a fresh dose of anger shot through him. "What are you doing here?" He opened the front door in time for her to answer.

"Trying to save you from losing the best thing you'll ever have." All sweats and messy hair, his cousin pulled the phone from her ear, pushed past him, and barreled into the house. "One hour," she said. "That's as long as you get. At five a.m. Earl is going to pack Reese into that car and take her to the airport. From there, she'll go to a place he's sworn to keep private, and you'll never see her again."

The image was a blade in his head. Every angle sharp and cutting. "She doesn't even love me, Allie. I fell in love with that woman. Like an idiot I told her and she ..." he shook his head. His hands tightened into fists.

"Blake, I don't know what Terrance told you, but take it from me – the person Reese has confided in since your first kiss by the shed."

The sentence stopped him cold. Ripped the words from his mouth.

"I have no idea if you've ruined things for good, but that woman loves you. And if you don't try to get her back I swear it will haunt you forever." She stepped into his line of view, her blue eyes set on him, and gulped.

"Trust me."

A knot of nerves bunched at the center of his back, pulled at his shoulders and neck. "Why wouldn't she tell me? I told her I loved her, Allie, and I was so blind that I didn't realize she never said it back."

"She regrets that. She told me herself just yesterday. She figured you knew. Of course Reese loves you, Blake. And if you hadn't done whatever you did when you got home last night, you would've heard the truth of it yourself. She planned on telling you." Allie took hold of his arm. "You are everything to her right now. She would've married you if you'd asked, but instead you turn her away?" She released his arm, letting her hand drift back to her side. "You've got to fix this."

Blake shook his head, unable to believe it. "No. She misses her home. Wants to go back with her brother so she can watch his games."

"Of course she misses them, but she'd give it all up for you." Emotion seemed to slow her words. A pool of tears welled up in her eyes. "Reese is in love with you, Blake Emerson. And if you're too stubborn to swallow your pride and do what it takes to get her back, then you certainly don't deserve her."

Allie's words hovered in the air as she stormed out of the house, throwing one last glare over her shoulder. Blake sighed, the late hour complicating the natural pattern of his thoughts. It was all chaos and regret. Regret and confusion. Regret and ... The knot at the back of his neck sunk, settled deep into an aching spot in his stomach. *What have I done?*

The seconds on the clock ticked on, prodding at his wounded brain with each echoing click. She loved him. Reese really did love him. He hadn't been imagining it. Except now he'd messed everything up. Blake sunk onto the couch and dropped his head in his hands, groaning as the pain radiated further – stretching, reaching, strangling. Two sentences replayed in his head: *You are everything to her. She would have married you...*

Shortly after he'd professed his love for her, Blake imagined doing just that. Why had he so easily believed what Terrance said? The chaos clambered about in his mind. His rampant thoughts scattering like dry grass in a wicked breeze. But among them, one remained in place: Reese could one day be his wife.

He had to wonder if what Allie said was true. And if he decided to act on her words, would Reese have it in her heart to forgive him? There was only one way to find out.

CHAPTER TWENTY-FIVE

The early morning sky looked similar to the view last night. No sunlight or stars to speak of. Just a mass of pale grey hovering overhead. "You'll like this new place you're going to, hon," Earl said. "It's real pretty there too. Lots of greenery and shrubs. Flowers and trees. Real nice."

Reese nodded, hardly able to focus on what the man said. She only knew he was attempting to lighten her mood, and for that, she was grateful. The man couldn't have known it was a lost cause. She'd lost something that had taken a lifetime to find, and though Reese knew she'd been blessed with a resilient spirit, she feared she might never fully recover. Still, she forced out a reply. "Thank you." It had come out in a whisper, so she cleared her throat and tried again. "I appreciate you going out of your way this morning. Takin' me to the airport so bright and early. And takin' me in last night."

"Glad to do it, hon." He draped a wrist over the steering wheel. "Just uh, hate to see you leaving so soon."

She managed less-than-half a smile. "I'm sorry I was so pushy last night. I just... couldn't do it." There was truth in the statement, enough to fill her with momentum once again. It felt better than the pain she'd suffered through the long hours of the night, so she embraced it and went on. "There's absolutely no way I could have stayed here another day. I'd rather go face-to-face with Donald Turnsbro myself than see Blake again," she said, hardly caring if Earl knew of their not-so-secret romance or their recent spat or anything in between. In fact, she may as well set the record straight while she had the chance. Earl was sure to hear more than a mouthful from Blake, and who knew how his perspective had become so warped?

"You may as well know that I fell in love with Blake. I don't care that I knew him shy of two months, or that it takes some couples years to fall in love. What I felt for him I've never felt for any other man, and he wouldn't even give me the air to so much as breathe those words to him last night."

"Hmm..." Earl shook his head. "I've never known the boy to be such a fool. I wonder what got in–" One short buzz sounded from the cup holder, and Earl paused to eye the cell phone resting there. "Let me pull over so I can get that message," the man said, flicking his blinker on.

A nervous dose of energy shot through her as he pulled the truck off the side of the road. Reese didn't want to go missing her flight and get stuck staying an extra night. She was ready to move on no matter where she was headed or who she'd be with.

"Huh." Earl's eyes rose in surprise. Reese sighed as he tapped the buttons on his phone with his rather large-looking fingers.

"There we go," he said, giving her a wink. He checked his rearview mirror before setting his phone back in place. The blinker clicked on, and at last he pulled back onto the road, not bothering to finish his sentence.

She might not have been paying much attention, but Reese was certain Earl had been going much faster before the text came. "Anything wrong?" she asked, wondering if the flight had been delayed.

"Naw," Earl said. "We're still a headed to the airport. Just don't want to get picked up by any patrolmen. They flock around these parts." His face had changed, she was sure of it. The deep and sullen lines that had shaped it only moments ago had smoothed. There was a hint of a smile there even. She considered the text he'd received, wondering what it had said. Whatever it was it had lightened his mood significantly. The shift in his energy put new distance between them. Made her feel as if she could no longer open up.

"I'll tell you one thing," Earl said, sparking the conversation once again. "I nearly messed things up real good with Lilly."

Reese glanced out the window, seeing vague outlines of cattle grazing in the distance, their dark color a slight contrast to the shades of grey.

"See," Earl continued, "I'd sort of promised myself to another gal. But then that gal left for school and while she was away I found myself falling head over heels for the lovely Ms. Lilly Burns. We dated for a bit before I decided perhaps I'd been making a mistake. That I was supposed to be waiting for this other woman. Mostly due to guilt, mind you, since the gal's old man found out about Lilly and approached me. Anyhow, I tried breaking things off with Lilly. And I did it all the wrong way cuz I sort of blamed her for the whole thing." He sighed. "Don't know where I'd be if she hadn't forgiven me."

Forgive? Why was he talking about forgiving in a moment like this? There'd been no apology from Blake. No effort to erase the damage he'd done. Blake wanted her out of his life. Would be glad when she was gone. And Reese was left feeling more broken than she'd been on the day she arrived.

Earl eyed the rearview once again, his pace seeming to slow more and more by the second. Out of curiosity, Reese eyed the passenger-side mirror. A truck sped along the road behind them, standing out against the grey like the cattle. It was black.

Her heart sped. Did she dare dream it could be Blake?

Soon the metallic sheen of the grill came into view. Earl flicked on his blinker once more and pulled over to the side of the road. The large truck veered off too, the familiar black body of it causing Reese to gasp. It *was* him. But why?

"I received a special request from my nephew," Earl said, turning to look at her. A spark of mischief danced in his brown eyes. His knowing smile affirmed what her heart hoped it knew. Maybe Blake had learned the truth. Especially if Allie had anything to do with it. Surely she'd have told him how Reese really felt. Explained to him just how wrong he'd been.

She tilted her head to look through the mirror once more, noticed Blake striding toward her side of the truck.

"Well, go on, then," Earl said. "The boy ain't got nothin' to say to me."

Reese nodded, fighting to strangle the mounting hope rising within her. And failing. All she could do was hope. Hope that he'd seen how wrong he'd been. Hope that he planned to apologize and ask her to stay. Hope he'd give her a reason to forgive him.

Her fingers fiddled with the lock before she managed to creak open the door. As she looked down at the ground, placed her feet on the running board, Blake's strong hand came into view. But she wasn't ready to take it just yet. Not when she didn't know where he stood. What he wanted. Or what he'd come for.

She pulled her hand in and hopped down on her own, closing the door behind her. With the flick of his head, Blake motioned for her to follow him back to his truck. Reese kept her eyes on the bumpy gravel and tall grass, feeling as if she might fall or faint or die. It was too much to take. She stopped there, not wanting to get into the truck with him. Anxious to hear what he'd say.

"What are you doing here?" She folded her arms as her chin rose, barely meeting his eye in the muted light.

The vision hit her like a mean slap to the face. His

brown eyes fixed on hers, the intensity there making her ache, a longing that burned deep in her chest.

"Reese, I am more sorry than words can say. I screwed up. I mean, I flipped out pretty good after I lost the calves. Then Terrance came in telling me that he'd heard you saying that you didn't love me. That you wanted to go home and were thinking about getting transferred even to someplace closer." He shook his head and stepped forward. "I just, I mean I started convincing myself that I'd made another mistake. That you fell in line with the list of gals I'd only thought I loved before." He shrugged. "I was never so sure that I deserved someone like you in the first place. Guess that made what Terrance said a little easier to believe."

Reese worked to sift through what he'd told her, realizing why he'd been so upset. Why would Terrance tell Blake she didn't love him? And that she planned to leave?

Blake ran a hand over her bare arm. "Allie told me everything. Terrance hadn't heard right and I had it all wrong. I ruined the best thing that had ever come into my life by turning you away. Please. Forgive me, Reese."

Moisture welled up in her eyes. Reese hadn't exactly known how Blake could redeem himself, but after hearing what he'd been told, it made sense. She nodded, unwilling to let a mere misunderstanding get in their way . "Of course, Blake," she said.

Blake rushed in to kiss her – sure and firm on the mouth. The tips of his fingers were slightly rough against her cheek as he wiped her tears away. "I love you, Reese Taylor," he whispered reverently.

Reese sighed, grateful she'd finally been given the chance to return the sentiment. "I love you too. I'm sorry I didn't say it back at the pond."

But Blake had rushed in again, began kissing her once more, proving that it no longer mattered. He pulled back to gaze at her and smiled. Her eyes were adjusting to the scanty light. That, and a hint of sunlight seemed to be peeking over the nearby hilltop.

"I don't want to lose you, Reese. Ever. Will you come back home?" The unassuming look in his eyes warmed her heart.

She nodded. "I'd love to."

———— ꞏ⠶⟩⟩ꞏ⠶ ————

Blake rubbed his palms over his levis, nervously watching the recorded game. For the millionth time, he felt the small box in his pocket, assuring himself it was there. Ready. Reese sat on the edge of the couch, eyes wide as she watched her brother run down the field. Her mouth dropped open slightly. Her hand clenched into a fist before her. Further and further he ran. Touchdown!

Reese was at her feet in an instant, cheering like only a woman could. And though Blake was caught up in what he knew was coming after the game – the part he'd watched over and over to make sure it was right – he forced himself to stand as well. "Man, that kid can play," he said.

"Darn right," she cheered, throwing her arms

around him. "This is the best gift you could have ever given me, Blake. The very, very best." She'd said the same thing when he'd arranged for her to speak with her family a few weeks ago. Earl said himself their situation was unique. They didn't suspect that Donald Turnbro had any big connections. The guy had no ties to gangs or anything of the sort. In this case, they could be more lenient.

Blake smiled. "I'm glad you like it." It hadn't been easy to do what he'd done. And if he hadn't had Earl on his side with all the strings he could pull and conversations he'd managed to arrange, things might not have worked out so well. As it was, there was an even greater surprise coming at the game's end. Reese stayed on her feet as they went for the field kick. Wasn't a crucial point by any means; her brother's touchdown had already won them the game.

Reese shot another fist in the air when they made that as well, her smile bigger than Texas. "I swear I'm the happiest woman alive right now," she said, sighing as the team celebrated.

Suddenly the scene faded to black, and Blake nudged the small box once more. Her parents came on the screen. "Hey there, Reese," her father boomed.

"Hi, baby," her mother said, her eyes slightly red with emotion. "We miss you so, so much," her mother continued with a sniff.

Reese sniffed too, was lowering herself onto the couch in silent awe, eating every spoken word.

"We want you to know how much we miss you, darlin'," her father said next. "Your mama and I are praying this gets over with soon so you can come back and visit."

Blake wondered if the word *visit* would tip Reese off for what he had in store. She didn't seem to catch onto it, only nodded her head as she listened to her old man's tenderly spoken words. "It sure was nice talking with you last month. And it did us a lot of good to hear how happy you are there. We're glad you wound up with such good folks."

Reese glanced at Blake through tears, shot him a smile before pasting her eyes back on the screen. "I'm sure you'd like to hear a little something from CJ," her mother said. "So here he is."

Blake's heart pounded into double time as her brother flashed onto screen. The football field behind him, his team – for now – hidden from view. He started off with what had to be an inside joke, making Reese laugh and wipe more tears all at once. He told her how much he missed her next, but that it had only forced him to keep extra women on hand. And then came the part Blake had been waiting for.

"Me and the guys put a little something together for you," CJ said as he backed away from the camera. He motioned for the rest of the team to join him on the field, and the cheerleaders too. They scattered across the field before lining into position. The cheerleaders created a pyramid, gaining a bit of height. The football team filled in below them, some dropping to their knees, each holding a rectangular board.

Reese's smile had remained wide with entertainment and joy. Blake watched closely as her expression changed. He glanced at the TV. The first few signs flipped over. One after the next, revealing the first two words: *Will... You...*

A gasp pulled from Reese's throat as she threw a hand over her mouth.

The rest of the message was revealed, one giant letter at a time. *Marry... Me?*

CJ, holding the question mark, ran toward the camera as the folks in the bleachers cheered wildly. The coach had told everyone that the proposal had been requested by an out-of-town alumni. No name had been given in case Donald somehow caught wind of things.

"The proposal's from Blake, in case you didn't know," he said into the camera, his voice nearly drowned out by the sound of the crowd. "So, sis, what are you going to say?" The kid's smile was wide with approval. After he flashed a quick thumb's up, the screen went blank, and a sudden silence fell over the room.

Reese slowly turned to him, a million emotions playing in her eyes.

Blake dropped to one knee. Secured the trusty box at last. "Reese, back when you first came, I was wondering what on earth I was supposed to do with a beautiful woman here on the ranch. I never knew the answer to that would be... fall deeper in love than I'd ever been before." He cleared his throat. With a flick of his fingers, the box clicked open, revealing the ring – a thin gold band holding a square-shaped diamond. "You saw me struggling back at my folks' place, unable to recall the happiest day of my life," Blake continued. "All because I hadn't lived it yet. Reese Marie Taylor – make this the first happiest day of my life and tell me that you'll be my wife."

Reese nodded silently at first, her teary eyes locked on his. "Yes," she finally blurted.

The word was an explosion in Blake's chest – like a burst of warm, liquid confetti. He shot to his feet, reveling in the simple word, and wrapped his arms around Reese. With her feet off the ground, he spun in place, repeating the blessed words in his head once more –Reese Taylor would be his at last.

He hadn't welcomed the next thought that came to mind. In fact, Blake pushed it away the moment it came. Yet the idea returned with a vengeance. He wasn't the only man who wanted Reese for himself. Somebody else out there wanted her in an entirely different way – wanted her dead. And though he'd always felt Reese was safe there at the ranch, a rush of inner doubts shot to the surface as if making up for lost time.

With his unsettling fear gaining life with each breath, Blake wrapped his arms more tightly around Reese, assuring himself that no matter the circumstance – he could keep her safe.

CHAPTER TWENTY-SIX

The golden reflection of sunlight poured through the massive church windows, illuminating the old chapel like a dream. Reese stepped back behind the wall after taking a glimpse. There were more folks there than she'd imagined. The wooden pews filled several rows back.

"You ready, darlin'?" Her father held his arm out for her, a soft grin on his face.

She smiled in return, thinking of how very blessed she was to have her family there. It'd been fairly short notice, but at least they'd already known the proposal was on its way. Known before her even. "I sure am, Daddy," she said. A rush of emotion shot through her as she tucked her hand into the nook of his elbow. Soon he'd hand her over to another man. Soon her dad would say goodbye.

They rounded the corner. The music played. The crowd rose to their feet. And then Blake spun in place, eyeing Reese from the end of the aisle. He smiled, and the butterflies in her tummy stirred. Tall, dark, and more handsome than laws should allow, Blake showed everyone there just how good a tuxedo could look on a man. Every inch filled to perfection. Next to Blake stood his brother, Shane, a smile on his face as well.

As she strode down the aisle at the slow pace, Reese caught sight of several familiar faces. More than she expected to recognize. The ranch hands stood toward the back. While passing them she received wide grins, a thumbs up, and the weak sound of a cat call. *Rowdy,* she decided. Betty and Grant were toward the front, wiping at tears. Lilly and Earl did the same.

The next two faces Reese saw brought on a fresh wave of emotion. She worked to fight back the tears, but could hardly contain them. CJ's grin always made her heart swell, the shape of it so much like Chelsea's. She thumbed the charm bracelet her mother had brought – something borrowed from her little sister. In the holy place, Reese felt Chelsea's dear spirit, could picture her standing at the front next to Allie, wearing a soft pink dress to match. Her mom looked more beautiful than ever, even with the small blotches of mascara dotting parts of her eyelids. She wiped at her eyes with a Kleenex, then tapped a hand over her heart. Reese was glad they'd been able to spend a few days there at the ranch before the wedding. It would make saying goodbye a little less painful.

It wasn't until they got closer that she noticed another man standing next to Blake. Tall and handsome, he looked like a mix between Shane and Blake, save the sandy blond hair and tattoos peeking from his rolled sleeve. The stranger looked her up and down, a subdued smile on his face. Reese looked at Blake in question. "Gavin?" she whispered.

Blake nodded, emotion held in his eyes. It was an answer to a prayer. Even if his wayward brother wasn't there to stay, he had come. She uttered a silent thanks as the crowd lowered back into their seats. Her dad turned and faced her, lifting her veil to kiss her solidly on the forehead. "My girl," he whispered against her skin.

Reese set a hand over his, fighting more tears of emotion. A flood of memories rushed in: him spinning her in circles on the plush grass, or carrying her high on his mighty shoulders so she could reach the peaches in the backyard. He winked at her before replacing her veil, and then rested her hand in Blake's. The significance of the action warmed every inch of her body.

Blake gave her hand a comforting squeeze. Reese glanced up in time to catch a smile that reached the dimple in his cheek. Her heart sputtered out of beat.

The preacher conducted the ceremony, and soon Blake was reciting his vows. And then it was Reese's turn. She'd expected to be so nervous that the words would come out in a rush, but it wasn't that way at all. Looking into Blake's deep brown eyes gave life to every word she spoke, every promise she made, and she couldn't wait for their new life as husband and wife to begin.

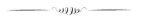

"I cannot imagine that wedding being any more perfect than it was," Reese said, snuggling up to Blake as he drove.

Blake couldn't argue with that. "I agree, Mrs. Emerson."

"I mean, my family was there. And Gavin came. Did

you know he was going to come?"

"I had no idea." He recalled the shock he'd felt when Gavin walked through the chapel doors. "Betty told me that someone wanted to see me, and there he was standing at the entrance. More muscled than I remembered, with that same devilish grin on his face." Blake shook his head and chuckled. "Boy, was it nice to see him."

"It was nice to meet him too," Reese said. She ran a single finger over the inside of Blake's arm, tracing a line along the curve of his bicep. The sensation caused his belly to burn with anticipation.

"I'm so happy that my family got to come. And that they'll be able to send me all of CJ's games and we can talk a little more often now." She sighed. "I don't know. Part of me feels like there's not a whole lot to worry over where Donald Turnsbro is concerned. That he's just a coward who'll never come out of … whatever hiding he's in."

Blake nodded, wanting to agree. Only he couldn't muster the words. He couldn't help but wonder if they'd jeopardized her safety in some way. Taping the proposal. Flying her family out for the wedding – something he'd never deny her, considering the circumstance as it was. But still, had they somehow compromised the secrecy of her location?

The sun had long gone down, leaving the great glow of the full moon to light the night. That, along with a massive array of heavenly stars. They got a later start than they'd meant to, but Reese didn't want to leave for their honeymoon getaway until her family left for the airport.

"There it is," Blake said as they passed his property. "We'll want to start building right away, get into our own place as soon as we can."

"Sounds good to me," Reese said.

They remained in comfortable silence for part of the drive, drifting in and out of conversation as topics arose. Soon they arrived at the old bed and breakfast, a place Reese handpicked from a site online. He recognized the Victorian home from the photos she'd shown him, and smiled as he thought back on his surprise that she'd prefer that place to a hotel. No maids coming in to clean the room. No room service arriving at the door. The owners didn't exactly run the place anymore, so they'd have the quaint little home to themselves. Just the two of them. Mmmm. His belly warmed again.

Once he pulled the truck up to the drive, the home's automatic porch light flicked on. Blake typed the code into the lock box and retrieved the key. After unlocking the place, he strode back to the truck to carry Reese over the threshold, the tempting scent of her making him weak. "Stay put," he said, placing her gently on her feet. "I'll be right back with our things."

His mind raced as he carted their luggage to the room. His pulse raced too, as he entertained thoughts of what would come. In no time he had the groceries on the counter and a fire roaring in the cozy front room where Reese stood.

While removing his sport coat, Blake watched her from behind. Her wedding dress – a mix of satin and lace – hugged every curve she had. Her blonde strands were tucked neatly at the back of her head, only a few wavy locks hung loose around her face. She'd wrapped her arms around herself, hands cradling her elbows as she stared at the fire.

"You cold?" he asked, striding over to check the thermometer. He paused as he heard her answer, the words sounding shallow and unsure.

"Not really."

Blake turned back to look at her, eyeing the timid slope of her posture. The way she averted his gaze. She was nervous, he realized. Blake had done a lot of thinking about the evening he'd spend with Reese, and each time it did all sorts of things to his insides, but nerves had never been a part of the equation. Longing. Anticipation. Need, yes. But not fear. He'd need to keep that in mind. Go at a slow and comfortable pace for her – *his wife*. The word thrilled him, had him quickening his pace as he strode to her. He shut off the lights along the way, stepped out of his shoes once he neared, and loosened the tie from his tux.

While inhaling her sweet and seductive scent, Blake wrapped his arms solidly around Reese from behind. She felt rigid to his touch, almost. The nerves tightening every limb. "Hello, my little rosebud," he crooned.

She released one small, nervous laugh. "Hi."

The surface of her skin felt like silk as he traced his fingertips over her arms in a slow and caressing motion. That is, until a ripple of goose bumps rose there.

She nuzzled her back into his chest. "That feels

nice," she said.

"Does it?" He continued the motion along the sensitive, impossibly smoother inner part of her arms, up and then back, paying close attention to the tiny tendons along her wrists. Her palms were next. She surprised him by lifting the tips of her own fingers to graze over the inside of his hands as well, her touch like a feather. Desire shot through him, the anticipation building as he savored her touch.

With slow and certain movements, he brought his hands to the zipper at the back of her dress, a new wave of chills showing on her skin in the warm glow of the fire. The tiny latch slid seamlessly at his will. Blake thrilled in the way the heavy material slid off her figure, leaving her in a silky slip that barely went to her knees. Once she stepped out of the dress, Reese draped it over a nearby lounge chair.

Blake set back to work, tracing small circles at the upper nape of her neck with his fingers. At last he lowered his mouth to her skin, trailing kisses along her bare shoulder. "You smell so good," he murmured against her skin.

She made the small sound of a laugh.

He slid his tongue over her next, nudging her thin strap until it slid down around her arm. She tasted good too.

This time Reese let out a slight whimper. The tension drained from her body, the feel of her turning warm and soft, like putty. Slowly she spun around and began further loosening his tie. Once done, she removed it altogether. He wondered if she could feel the tremendous beating of his heart as she moved to his buttons, unfastening one after the next. Blake's eyes closed as she tugged the bottom of his shirt from his pants, unfastening the final button before sliding it down his arms where it drifted to the floor.

Blake's hands sought her hips as he leaned in and pressed his mouth to hers, driven by a hunger greater than any he'd known. The push and pull of her kiss was gravity. All-powerful, persuasive, and impossible to resist.

He moaned with pleasure as Reese's hands moved longingly up his bare chest. She threaded her slender fingers through his hair next, gripping with a near desperation as the rhythm of their kiss increased. There was no telling who'd set the pace. It was all yearning and need. Longing and love. A tenderness that made him ache as the kisses slowed into lingering, cherishing tastes of one another.

Reese slid one hand slowly back down his chest, causing his muscles to tighten beneath her touch in a ripple. She took a step back then, reaching for the stack of clean linens on the sofa. It took him a moment to realize she was creating a bed for them right then and there. The great sheet unfurled with a quick snap, and drifted in a soft and flowing wave until it rested over the plush carpet below. All satin and skin, beauty and allure, Reese lowered herself onto the sheet, her slightly narrowed eyes fixed on him. His heart nearly stopped beating completely when she moved from a sitting position to lay on her back.

Blake dropped to his knees, reveling in the sound

of her sigh as he lowered himself over her. His hand slid up the back of her leg as she wrapped it around him; a groan rumbled in his throat. The feel of her warm body beneath his was better than he'd imagined, even through the slip she wore.

Her kiss was gentle but yearning, and filled with a tender innocence that made him feel weak and empowered all at once. Through it all, a constant awareness remained at the back of his mind: this night was all about Reese. It was her night, and he planned to make sure it was everything she ever dreamed of.

The soft feel of a subtle breeze played gently across Reese's face, rousing her to awareness. She smiled. Knowing just where she was, who she was with – and loving it. She stretched her leg behind her, feeling for him with her foot.

The sheets were smooth, cool, and seemingly endless. "Blake?" she said, turning onto her other side. The moon shone through a crack in the blinds, leaving a streak of silver where he should lay. "Blake?" she hollered again.

"Out here." His voice was distant. Coming from somewhere within their honeymoon getaway spot. Perhaps by the fire? After shrugging into her white, silky robe, Reese strode down the hallway. Colorful reflections from the crackling fire danced along the wall as she went. It was hard to know which would warm her more – the magnificent flames glowing from the fireplace, or the glorious man standing in front of it. As she neared his flawless build, covered only by a loose pair of boxers, the answer was clear.

She came up behind him, pressing herself flush against his back, and rested her cheek on the muscular contours there. When her hands wrapped around his chest, the heated thumps of his heart met her palms, reminding her of the time they shared earlier. That, along with the addictive smell of his aftershave, had her longing for more already.

"Whatcha doin' out here?" she asked before planting a kiss to a prominent curve along his shoulder blade.

His back swelled as he sucked in a deep breath. It wasn't until he exhaled that she detected a level of stress in him. "Just uh... couldn't sleep." The strain was evident there too, in the sound of his deep voice.

"Don't tell me *you're* having bad dreams now."

"Naw." He shook his head.

Reese waited for him to elaborate. When he didn't, she urged on. "So what's the matter?"

There was a moment of delay, and then a defeated sounding sigh. "I fell asleep for a while, but out of nowhere I just woke up in a state of panic. My brain just started in on me and no matter what I tried doing I couldn't shut it off."

"Mmm, hmm," she prodded, pressing the tips of her fingers into the strong muscles at his chest. "Panic over what?"

Another sigh passed through his lips. "About the

fact that you've got some … guy after you. I woke up thinking stuff like, *did we really fly your family out here? And, why had I used half the high school team to propose to Reese when she's supposed to be in hiding?*" He shrugged. "Stuff like that."

It sounded like guilt. "You told me yourself no one knew the proposal was for me – except my family and the coach." When he remained silent she spoke up again. "We don't talk about Donald Turnsbro very often, but I meant what I said yesterday. I don't think he'll ever find me out here. We don't even know if he's trying to find me or just working to stay under the radar, you know? "

He gave her an absent nod in reply.

"We have to move on sometime," she said. "And I know it might seem soon, but it's been empowering – just going on with our lives despite it all. I don't want that man to affect me anymore." She didn't want him affecting Blake either.

"Well, I already checked the place out. Grabbed my gun, took a stroll around the property. Made sure we were really alone."

She chuckled. "You walked outside dressed – or undressed – like this?"

"Just like this," he mumbled.

Reese could feel the tension along his rigid limbs. Hear it in the tightened tenor of his voice. She wanted to melt it away for him. To make him forget the troubles that had taken him from their bed. She wanted to take him back there with her.

"So now that you've assured yourself we're alone…"

She loosened her grasp on him and walked to his side, fighting the streak of shyness that threatened to creep in. It was obvious that words weren't going to work Blake out of his disturbed state of mind. But perhaps something else could. As she rounded his side, Reese trailed her fingers over his bicep, pressed a kiss to his shoulder, and then moved to stand directly before him. She dropped her chin, the warmth of the fire at her back, the heat of his breath grazing her forehead. "You uh... ready to come back to bed?" She looked at him through her lashes, surprised at how entirely inept she felt in that moment. It was just that – harmlessly flirting with a guy was one thing. Teasing words and playful glances. Never had she tried to straight-out seduce a man before. Of course, Blake was her husband now. The thought caused a thrill to sprout in her chest.

Blake's gaze shifted from the fire to her, the flames accenting the warm color of his skin. A hint of a smile tugged at one corner of his lips. He cleared his throat. "Sure. I'll be there in a minute."

Her shoulders dropped an inch – her confidence too. Yet before she moved to step around him, head down the quiet hallway alone, Reese decided she wouldn't give up so easily. With a fresh wave of determination urging her on, she brought her hands to either side of his neck. She pressed herself onto her tiptoes next, brought her mouth to his jaw, and traced over the short stubble with her parted lips. Once at his earlobe, she gave him a playful nibble, knowing the sensation of him doing that very thing had driven her crazy.

Suddenly Blake brought a hand to her hip, the solid feel of his grip warm through the cool silk of her robe. She smiled, and then moved to the other side, repeating the action while her hands traced down the front of his chest. She became more playful with that earlobe, teasing it with her tongue before sinking her teeth into it, ever so lightly.

This time he groaned, gripping her waist with both hands now. At once his mouth met hers in a hungry kiss. She indulged in it, savoring the smooth touch of his tongue. The seductive skill of his strong lips. And the bristle of scruff surrounding them.

She barely recognized the sound of her own whimper, the one she couldn't squelch when he deepened the kiss. And when he moved to sample the tender hollow of her throat, she moaned with pleasure.

In sheer seconds he had her lifted off the ground, but he didn't take her to the bed. Instead he lowered her onto the couch and tugged at the tie of her robe.

Being married was a beautiful thing, she decided. A spark of courage and a little effort, and Blake was all hers. And heaven knew that Reese – for as long as she lived – was all his.

CHAPTER TWENTY-SEVEN

Blake smiled at Reese as he scooted beside her in the truck. It'd been only a week since they'd come home from their honeymoon, but it'd been one of the best weeks of his life. Forget about the fact that they were still at the house, and that they would be until their home was built, married life was all Blake had dreamed it might be. Waking up beside Reese made each day a blessing, one he'd cherish his whole life long.

"I forgot to ask how you slept last night," Reese said as they pulled onto the main road. She took hold of his hand, ran circles over it with her fingers. "Have any more bad dreams?"

Blake didn't like to worry Reese, but he hated the idea of lying to her even more. "A couple," he admitted. He flipped her hand over, brought it up to his lips to kiss the back of it. "Too bad we can't just stay up all night," he said. "I wouldn't mind that a bit." He wasn't kidding. By their second night at the bed and breakfast Blake had been fighting off nightmares that had him fearing for Reese's safety more than ever. Since then, he'd battled the dreams by night, and worked to keep a level head by day. There had to be a good balance between being cautious while maintaining the normalcy of everyday life; Blake was still struggling to find it.

Soon the conversation turned to the day's plans. Reese wanted to pick out some new jeans at the department store, while Blake planned to stock up on some much-needed supplies for the fast-approaching shift in season. Already the chill of autumn was upon them; soon it'd be time for the annual cattle sale – the event that earned them the one check they'd get all year. A sum that would last them until the following autumn.

"How long do you think you'll be?" Reese asked, bringing him back to the conversation at hand.

He shrugged. "Shouldn't be too long. This would've been a lot easier had you just borrowed Bettys' cell phone, you know?"

Reese only shrugged, not offering her usual list of reasons she didn't like doing so. Each was centered around the fact that she didn't want to impose.

"I'm going to get you your own phone today," he decided, his shoulders lifting at the thought. "Yep. While we're right here in town. In fact, for now I want you to take mine –"

Reese jerked back like his hand was on fire. "No," she shrieked. "You have no idea how many calls you get about this or that. Even on the weekends. I don't want to be stuck with that thing."

Blake eyed her while considering. Keith and Neil were ready to take off for the season. But first they planned to spend the day on the field; they'd likely have a few questions about one thing or another.

"How about we meet at the Mongolian BBQ," Reese said. "I can walk there easily enough from the department center."

Though he forced himself to nod in return, Blake felt a level of discomfort in the suggestion. What she'd said was true – the place was less than half a block away. So why was it he wanted to suddenly abandon all the errands he'd put on his list and join her instead?

Reese tilted her head to look at him. "Blake?"

"Sure," he said in return. He didn't want her living her whole life in fear, after all. "I'll meet you there. What time's good for you?"

She bit at her lip. "Depends on just how much weight I've gained," Reese said. "It's hard accepting the cold hard act of moving up a pant size. Let's say 1:00, that'll give me a bit of wallowing time. And if I've gone up two sizes I'll need time to come up with a game plan."

Blake sent her a look of warning with narrowed eyes. "Now don't you go messin' with those curves, babe." And he meant it. Reese was absolutely perfect the way she was. He slowed as he approached the shopping plaza. "Is this the place you wanted to start?"

"Yes. Perfect." After offering a measly kiss to his cheek, Reese scooted toward the passenger door and flung it open.

"I would have let you out, Reese," he scolded.

She closed the door and rested her hand along the open window frame. "No need." Reese gave him a playful wave before strutting toward the glass doors in her frilly skirt and red boots. She paused to blow him another kiss, causing Blake to shake his head in wonder. How did he ever get so lucky? He checked his rearview while inching away, satisfied when he saw her step inside.

Blake's destination was just over ten minutes away. He used the time to relive the morning he'd shared with Reese. The warm and slender curves of her body. Her smooth and heated kiss. He could hardly wait to climb back into bed for the evening. The mere thought had him driving faster, anxious to get back to her.

There wasn't a whole lot of traffic surrounding the hardware store. Blake was glad; he'd be able to finish up early and join Reese while she shopped. Who cared if shopping wasn't his thing? He didn't like being separated from her. Not with the uneasy feelings he'd been having where her safety was concerned.

A quiet rumble sounded as the automatic doors wrenched open. Florescent lights shone bright on the high stock shelves, its green-tinted light playing off the grey concrete floors as he walked. Blake secured a flatbed cart and strode toward the aisles, wasting no time in finding his supplies.

Soon the cart was loaded with enough items to fill the flatbed, making the industrial carrier hard to turn at the corner's end. He piled another sack of fertilizer onto it and sighed. A little sleep went a long way. And the lack of it seemed to be taking a toll on him. The recurring nightmares tiring his body as well as his mind. As he hunkered low, securing yet another sack in his grip, Blake heard the buzzing of his phone.

Reese had been right; the calls were starting already. He glanced at the caller ID for only a blink before bringing the thing up to his ear. Hmm. A number he didn't recognize, with an unfamiliar area code too. "This is Blake," he said, straightening to a stand.

"Mr. Emerson, this is Sheriff Finn calling from Pearland, Texas. I need to speak with you about a new development in the case."

The familiar sights and smells of the bright department store made Reese feel right at home. Of course, this place was much smaller than what she was used to, but it was pleasing all the same. Reese liked knowing she'd have some of the luxuries she'd enjoyed in Texas not too far from her new residence on Emerson Ranch.

Unknowingly, she'd come nearly an hour before the place was to open. But thanks to an older gentleman – the manager of the place – she'd been allowed to come inside early to look around. She'd have to wait to purchase anything until the other employees were on hand, he'd told her, which was just fine by Reese.

She'd already spent nearly half-an-hour melting over items in the baby department. Baby booties and bonnets, blankies and bottles. Her dream of becoming a mother was finally within reach, and she could hardly wait to welcome a warm little bundle into her and Blake's lives. It took her a while to tear herself away, but once she did, Reese moved onto cosmetics, testing out some of the fragrances along the way. Back at home, she'd spent hours in similar departments, searching for just the right shade of lipstick and nail polish to go with each gown. Of course jewelry and handbags were a consideration all their own. Things had sure taken a shift; now, as she looked at the diamond bracelets and gold chains before her, all Reese could think about was the tiny little suit she'd seen in the baby boy section.

Just as a handbag caught her eye, one made of red leather to match her boots, Reese heard a soft voice speak from behind.

"Can I help you, ma'am?"

Reese jumped, realizing she hadn't seen any other employees yet – just the kind man who'd let her in. The woman who'd asked stood behind the counter, busying herself with a stack of perfumes, shifting the boxes to make a pyramid on the glass display case.

"No, thank you," Reese said. She stepped a bit closer, inspecting her for a moment. Short, thin, and timid, the gal kept her eyes pasted awkwardly on the job before her.

"Well, on second thought – could you direct me to the jeans department?" Reese asked. The place may not be open just yet, but she'd most likely need the extra time to find a pair of jeans that fit her just right. Perhaps she could explore a few of the other shops before meeting Blake for lunch.

The question seemed to take the employee off-guard. At once she lifted her chin, her locking directly on Reese. Beads of sweat dotted the woman's upper lip. Hints of further perspiration showed in the slick sheen along her hairline. She dropped her eyes to the cabinet before her. A small map lay there. The woman waved a finger over the single page before settling on a spot with a long, painted fingernail. "Women's wear. Just head to the south end of the store." The tone she'd used was so quiet Reese had to lean forward to catch it all. Why did this woman seem so… frightened?

"Why, thank you," Reese said, hoping to ease the odd tension hanging in the air. "You just saved me from wandering 'round the place 'til the wee hours of day, I'll tell ya that." Yet as Reese strode toward the south end of the store, she couldn't help but muse on the reserved employee. The strange, nearly whispered sound of her voice. The way she'd held her gaze with such intensity. Reese tightened her grip on her purse straps.

With only half-an- hour to go before opening time, she would have expected to see more employees by now. The place was so quiet. Eerily so. And though the baby and cosmetics sections were bright with glowing lights above them, a number of departments remained dark and vacant. She squinted, realizing only the outer edge of the women's section was lit up. She walked on, guessing she could use the neighboring light to find the switch herself.

Each step she took seemed to echo throughout the entire store before bouncing back to her. While she moved past the power tools one tentative step at a time, a flash of movement caught her eye. Reese stopped walking and threw a hand over her heart, the rhythm picking up pace as she worked to catch her breath.

Slowly, she ran her gaze over the long aisle of riding lawn mowers. The lights in that department were out as well. Power saws and pliers loomed in the shadows, but nothing else was there. Perhaps she'd just seen the cast of her shadow, stretching across the lonely floor.

Suddenly a set of lights flickered on in the back corner. A distant hum sounded as the giant squares of neon glowed to life along the ceiling – lighting the very department she was headed to. Reese knew this should please her, but it puzzled her instead; she looked over the endless racks of shirts and tops, dresses and skirts. Unable to see the person who'd flipped on the lights.

After a moment of delay, Reese lifted her shoulders, pulled in a deep breath, and proceeded past the power tools as quickly as she could. She was on edge now; there was no denying it. Moist heat gathered on her palms. Her heart pounded in excess. She was starting to wonder if it'd been a mistake to enter the place early. She hadn't come to Montana on vacation after all, she'd come here to get away from a crazy man who wanted her dead.

With the shake of her head, Reese strode on, jumping as she heard someone knocking, the sound coming from the very doors she'd come through. Good. More employees had arrived. Soon other customers would too. She had thought it'd be a rare treat to browse without any fellow shoppers, but now she couldn't wait for the place to fill up.

She relaxed as she envisioned the bustle of store

clerks, each filtering through the place to their own departments. The image offered instant comfort; allowing her to focus on what she'd come for – the jeans. And there were some cute ones too. With the first pair she grabbed, Reese accidently snatched the size she usually wore. "Oh yeah," she said, recalling the reason she was buying the things in the first place. She pulled a size larger off the rack, and the size above that just in case. If she'd gone up two sizes over the summer she'd force herself to go lighter on the food.

With that depressing thought, Reese picked a dark studded set of jeans, a lighter, slightly faded pair, and some shorts that looked as if she'd cut and washed them herself. One of her favorite looks. She proceeded toward the dressing rooms, set her purse down on the small stool there, and latched up the door. Off went her boots. And then her skirt. She opted for the shorts first, thrilled when the size one up from hers fit just right. A little snug perhaps but she didn't mind.

She reached for her boots once more, anxious to see how the pair would look with them, when suddenly the lights went out with an audible snap. A gasp pulled from her throat as she lifted her chin. Every sliver of light was gone. Replaced by an endless mass of black.

Darkness, thick and menacing, surrounded her from every angle. Reese pulled in a deep breath, working to calm herself as she patted around for her purse. She wasn't sure why, but she felt that having it on her lap would offer a sense of comfort. The items in there were familiar, the feel of it was too. She'd hold onto it until the lights came back on. Which, of course they'd do at any minute.

She gulped, wondering just when her eyes would adjust. Her attempt to see her own hand in front of her face was an utter fail. She glanced where the mirror was and saw no reflection there either. No hint of light, flickering bulb, or exit sign. The thought gave her an idea – *an exit sign.* Who cared if it would lead her outside where she'd be locked out until the place opened to the public, Reese wanted out. Planned to find her way out of there if the lights didn't come back on soon. She gave herself a number – one hundred. If she counted to a hundred and the lights didn't come back on, she'd explore the place on her own – go looking for an exit.

While gripping the straps of her purse, Reese released a deep breath and began to count.

CHAPTER TWENTY-EIGHT

Blake might not have been so alarmed by the call if it weren't for the grave tone of Sheriff Finn's voice.

"How are you, sir?" Blake asked, hoping he'd managed to sound calmer than he felt. His eyes fixed at a spot on the package before him as he waited for the dreaded response.

"Is Reese there with you?"

Blake shook his head. "No, she's at a nearby department store. Is everything alright?"

"Wish I could say it was. Truth is, we've discovered the body of Molly Turnsbro, Donald Turnsbro's sister."

Blake's jaw dropped. "*What?*" The sound of his voice echoed down the aisle. "She's dead? Was it Donald who did it?"

"We're afraid that's a strong possibility."

Dead. This guy had killed his own sister now? Heavy knots seemed to build in Blake's stomach, the wrenching heat of them weighing him down. Had

Reese's location been compromised? Was Donald headed there now to finish the job? "How worried should I be right now?" he asked, barely able to get out the words. "Do you think she's in danger?"

"It's hard to say. But there's something more you need to know. Molly's body was found in a storage unit. The owner said that Donald was delinquent on his payments, so he replaced the padlock months ago. No one's been in there since."

Blake tilted his head. "How many months?"

"Close to five now."

"That's impossible. Reese told me you met with his sister after the shooting."

Sheriff Finn cleared his throat. "We met with who we believed to be Molly Turnsbro. We now believe we had been speaking with Donald that day. That he was in disguise. And that he's been living as a woman since Molly's death."

"How is that possible?" Blake asked, not really expecting an answer.

"Our documents show that Molly got a stewardess job at the Austin-Bergstrom airport back in April. We suspect they hired Donald posed as her."

It was an odd puzzle to piece, but Blake worked to click things together just the same. "And you guys think that Donald's going in each day disguised as his sister."

"Yes."

"So where is he now?"

There was a short pause. One that made Blake's pulse race to a painful degree. "Taking some personal leave, according to her boss. Molly's last flight was on

June twenty-fifth. To Billings, Montana."

A curse fell from Blake's lips. The floor squeaked beneath his feet as he barreled toward the door, his loaded cart all but forgotten. "You mean he's been here the entire time?"

"Apparently he claimed to have family there. Said he had some personal affairs to take care of before returning to work. We get the impression he meant to finish his business long before now."

His business being to kill Reese. It wasn't something he could say aloud; the gripping echo in his head was painful enough. The automatic doors slid open, revealing a parking lot that looked a whole lot different now. Everything he saw was an obstacle. Something to keep him from being with Reese. From protecting her. "How the hell did he know where Reese was?" Blake boomed.

"Fellow employees is all we can guess. The schedule says Molly wasn't on the actual flight. But a friend of hers might have been." The sheriff had been teetering back and forth – addressing Donald as *him* one minute then *her* the next. The airport staff had been convinced Donald was a woman. Must be one heck of a disguise.

"Does Reese carry a cell phone?" the sheriff asked.

"She uses my mother's phone sometimes, but she didn't bring it today." He cursed under his breath once more. "Sheriff, can you contact Sheriff Call and have the nearest officer head to Center Hill Plaza? Reese is there now. I'll head there as quick as I can, but I'm certain an officer could beat me to it. We really need to make sure she's safe."

"I agree. I'll do that now. But son, don't you go speeding and chasing and causing a scene. The man's been there for months without so much as an incident. Chances are Reese is just fine. We'll arrange for you to take her someplace out of the state until we can locate Mr. Turnsbro. We have an advantage now. We know his disguise, the name he's been using, and we have a locational vicinity to work with as well. Trust me, we'll find this guy in no time."

After ending the call, Blake slammed his truck door and roared up the engine. He sped out of the parking lot and tore down the street toward the plaza as words from the officer sped through his mind. Only the facts seeped in. Donald Turnsbro had killed his own sister – even before the shooting. He'd been posing as a woman ever since. And lastly, he'd been in Montana nearly as long as Reese had.

The truth of it made him ill. This guy was nuts. Had been there for months. And was biding his time somewhere nearby. Working to get details from the locals. Disguised as a woman, no less. His foot sunk lower, pressed harder as the truth of it drove him to near madness. As soon as he got his hands on Reese, they would leave the state, just like the sheriff said. Now he just needed to get to her.

CHAPTER TWENTY-NINE

Reese's parents had always worked to calm her fears about the dark. *It's harmless,* they'd say as they flicked on the light to prove it. *See? Nothing has changed.* And with that, they'd snap the light off once more, pull her door to a near close, and leave her with the monsters who lurked there. Of course, Reese didn't believe in monsters anymore. No – that wasn't exactly true. She'd come to a knowledge that was more haunting than all the rest: monsters *did* exist – were all around. It just took more than mere light to see who they really were.

A slow and aching shiver trickled slowly down the center of her back, catching on each ridge of her spine. Donald Turnsbro was a monster. And though she had tried to deny it while dancing with the man – his dark energy had spoken to her in wordless breaths. Screamed for her to run. And she hadn't.

Three hundred. She'd counted to three hundred now. All the while inwardly pleading for the lights to kick on. For the backup lights at least. Places like this had generators, didn't they? Power failures happened and they needed to be prepared. But something told

Reese this wasn't a power failure. She shook her head, her mother's exasperated voice playing out in her mind: *Stop it, Reese. Stand up and find your way out already.* She nodded. The lights might not come back on for a long while, and there was no reason to linger in the darkness. *Like a sitting duck*, an inner voice said. Reese worked to silence it, trying to think of just when her morning had taken such an unpleasant twist. Because, if she was being honest with herself, it happened before the lights went out. Finding the place closed hadn't bothered her; even if the kind gentleman hadn't let her in, she'd have just strolled throughout the plaza until she found an open shop.

The smooth surface of the door met her palm as she patted blindly before her, fumbling for the latch. It took her a second, but soon the cool, metal knob was in her grasp, reminding her of the stubborn latch back in Pearland – and the sight she'd seen from the cracks. The very thought pulled her mind back to her morning. If the store hours hadn't bothered her, then what had? Not the baby clothes by any means. That was all joy and hope. Dreams and pleasure. Oh, how she longed to have a child of her own. She'd gone to the cosmetics next. Been directed to the jeans department, and heard a scuffle along the power tools. Only she'd already been off by that point.

Slowly, Reese pulled back the door, disappointed to see nothing but blackness. The sound of her breath was magnified in her head as she took a step into what felt like nothing. She gripped the leather straps of her bag, hiked them over one shoulder, and reached for the opposite wall. She pictured the panes of glass at the entrance. Once she cleared this section, there would be outdoor light to illuminate her path toward the exit. She wondered if the doors would be open by now, but knew they wouldn't. Not for another twenty minutes or so. It might have felt like an eternity since the lights had shut off, but Reese figured it'd been maybe five or six minutes at best.

With small and cautious steps, she followed the wall, her palms too sweaty to slide smoothly over the surface. They skidded instead, the way Donald's hand had skidded over her wrist, all sweat and moist heat. Desperation and wiry strength.

The wall seemed to go on forever. Making her wonder if she'd gone the wrong way. Of course she hadn't, but the mere thought had her taking longer, more stretching strides. She just needed to get around the bend, the hallway that seemed to trap the darkness in place. Her other senses kicked in. Making her aware of the small beads of knotted carpet beneath her socks. With each step she felt for the change in texture, the cool smooth tile that would tell her she'd made it to the foyer.

A small clatter sounded from a nearby department, and Reese didn't know whether to be relieved or scared. Neither, she told herself. There was no danger here, just a temporary power outage. Nothing that should send a grown woman into a state of panic. The thought offered some level of comfort, so she told herself again – there was nothing to be afraid of. She'd simply find an exit, get out of the building, and head back in to get her boots and skirt when the place opened. And pay for the shorts she wore too, she reminded herself.

At last, the planes of smooth tile slid beneath her foot. Encouraged, Reese moved faster, patting further, thrilled to see a spot of pale morning light around the bend. She sighed in relief as shapes and shadows came into view. With a deep inhale, she summoned a bit of bravery and stepped away from the trusty wall. Parting with it was more difficult than she imagined, but it was the only way to get closer to the light. She put both arms straight out before her, not quite able to see enough to keep her from bumping into things. The area nearby was still very dark. It was the departments further down that caught most of the outdoor glow.

A cool, metal bar met her stretching fingers – a clothing rack. Reese felt at it, assessing how large it was. She reached out with her foot next – lifting it to make sure there wasn't anything that might trip her – when the flat part of her shin met a sharp lower bar with a brutal jab, making her coil in return. She sucked in air through her clenched teeth and pressed a hand against the aching spot. That was sure to leave a bruise, she thought. But the moisture against her leg told Reese it'd do more than that. She was bleeding. Great. She'd look a wreck by the time the lights kicked on. Like she'd just survived some natural disaster – the day the lights went out in the department store.

A small chuckle bubbled in her throat. More nerves than humor but it still felt nice; worked to calm her to a degree. Suddenly a beam of bright light shone from across the department. A flashlight, Reese realized.

Whoever held it was coming her way. "Oh, thank the heavens and sing their praise," Reese said, lifting a hand to mute the brightness. "I've been scared silly over here all by myself."

No response came, yet the light continued to near at a slow and steady pace. Its brilliant center – a massive orb of white – was accented by a wide, stretching halo that reached both the ceiling and floor, the strength of it more blinding than the dark.

"Hello?" she tried again, squinting against the brightness.

Still no answer came. The approaching stranger was all silence and progression.

No words.

Just steps.

Their pace building with each forward shuffle, the light staying ever focused on Reese. Enveloping her in the strange and unfriendly glow.

Reese felt her heart kick – a jumpstart to a new and panicked pace. Quickly, she spun around, grateful to find she could now see that half of the women's department, thanks to the light at her back. Without so much as a second thought, she ran straight ahead. Away from whoever held the light, into the illumination it lent.

She scurried past racks of workout clothes. Tight shiny pants and colored tanks. Each loaded rack jumped out at her as if she were maneuvering through some sort of obstacle course. Ducking, dodging, spinning even, to stop the knobby edge of a rack from catching her shoulder. She lost her purse along the way but didn't care.

A sign. A sign. She needed an exit sign. She needed... Suddenly the light went out once more. The one at her back, carried by her quiet pursuer.

A heavy breath fell from her lips as she allowed the looming question to play out in her mind: Was it possible that Donald Turnsbro had found her? She grasped for another explanation – anything – but what else was there? Who else would chase her as this person was?

At last the green glow of four lovely letters caught her eye: E X I T, just a few feet away. With her hands out before her, Reese moved quickly toward it no longer caring that she couldn't see. The edges of cloth-covered hangers jabbed her cheek as she passed. She slammed into a counter next, but slid her way quickly around it, wishing she were quiet enough to hear the sound of approaching footsteps. No matter, soon she'd be safe outside.

Once she stood beneath the sign, Reese patted at the door, confused when no metal push bar lay across the center. She felt at it some more, desperate to get out in the open, when a round knob met her fumbling fingers. With a frantic twist, she pushed the heavy door open, and spun around to lock it before making another move. Locked it, because she was not outside as she'd guessed she'd be.

Above the knob, Reese detected a deadbolt lock and flicked that too before sliding back into a corner to survey the place. A stockroom of sorts. High, vaulted ceilings, rows of massive shelves holding equipment, and tiny box-sized windows that barely lit the place.

Blue shadows stretched over the area. Reese looked for the darkest spots, considered hiding in them, but recalled the light her pursuer held. That is, if she was really being pursued. She panted while taking long and certain strides away from the door, and then stopped short to listen. Nothing. She took a few steps more, pausing when she heard something. It hadn't come from the door though. Instead, the muffled grunt sounded from one of the wide, industrial aisles.

"Is anyone in here?" she whispered, wondering if she'd lost her mind altogether. Yet the grunt came again. The cool shadows lit her way, shifting and creeping as she moved past one empty aisle. Folded sheets in packages. She could see masses of them on the next shelf as she moved, one of the only spots of bright, unhindered light streaming into the place. Another bit of sun peered in, revealing a strange figure in the center of the next aisle. She was scared to move toward it at first, yet as her eyes ran over the sight, Reese realized there was a man there. Small and old. The one who'd let her into the place.

"Hello?" she asked, her heart dropping as she noticed the reason for the grunting. His mouth had been covered by a thick strip of duct tape. And though he sat on an office chair of sorts, his arms had been pinned and tied behind his back. "Oh, my goodness," Reese said with a gasp. She sped toward him, began working to tear the tape off the man's face, and froze when she heard the snap of a lock at the door. Another snap sounded.

Reese's widened eyes fixed on the old man's. He

jerked his head furiously, motioning that she should hide. She didn't want to leave him there in such a way, but what choice did she have?

As quickly as she could manage, Reese bolted for the nearby shelf. She used the lowest plank to boost herself up, propping her elbows on the one above it. With a bit of effort she hoisted herself onto the next flat surface. The boxes there were close to the edge; she had to lay just in front of them in order to fit in the space.

Boxes nudged against her from behind, threatening to toss her off the edge yet she didn't move, only waited as she heard footsteps treading across the room. And that's when she realized the person wasn't wearing any shoes either. Not unless they had soft soles. No – she would have heard them earlier, and she'd hear them now. This person had taken the time to remove their shoes.

"Time for you to get on outa' here, Gill," a voice said. Soft, high, and whispery. The woman at the counter. She heard a trail of squeaking next, and guessed it was the office chair wheels moving along the cement floor. Gill piped up too, grunting loudly as he moved. Reese took advantage, turned to face the boxes at her back and felt at them from side to side. Top to bottom. With one wrong move, she could easily fall back and onto the hard floor below, but she had to get behind the stocked items or she'd be seen.

With an extended arm, she felt the beginning of yet another box. The grunting sounds of the man were close to the door now. Reese forced herself to come to a stand in the cramped area, nearly teetering off the edge as she did. There, she felt a space above the second stack – an opportunity. She took it, hoisted herself over the large packages, sticking her toes between them for leverage. The cardboard was dry and rough against her cheek as she slid onto it, barely wedging herself between the stored items and the metal rack above.

The door clicked closed.

Snap went the locks, one after the next.

Reese pulled in a shallow breath.

"We couldn't have Gill in here spoiling things now, could we?"

A heightened wave of fear crept over Reese's skin at the sound of his voice. Donald's. It was his without doubt. *You wore it to all your public appearances.* The words played out in her head, a precise match to his tight tenor and faded twang. The woman. Had it really been Donald Turnsbro? A manic sounding giggle came next, traced with a hint of genuine humor. "I bet you're wondering how I knew you were afraid of the dark."

Reese tightened her lips and pulled in a silent breath.

"Ms. Taylor, tell us something about yourself that even your closest friends might not know," Donald said, his voice rising from a different spot in the room. Reese recognized the question from her pageant days. All of them had to answer it. "Well," Donald said, sounding exactly like a woman. "Y'all wanna know my deepest and darkest secrets, do ya?" He allowed for another small chuckle, one that sounded just like Reese's. "Y'all might as well know I am completely terrified of the dark. Just terrified. I avoid it at all costs. In fact, I have a lamp by my bed that I keep on until my eyes are driftin.'" He'd moved once again, was somewhere behind her now.

"Do you know how many times I watched you while you sat in that lamp's light?" he asked, his voice sounding more like a man's. "Do you, Reese Marie Taylor?" he shouted.

A shallow breath snuck silently from her lungs in a slow crawl. She wasn't sure how long she could hide from him. Or if anyone would come. Would Blake come looking for her? The thought caused her to shudder.

"You and I are more alike than you think," he went on to say, a layer of confidence laced in the words. "Your father is an accountant. Mine was too. Of course he wasn't so wealthy as your old man. We went to the same schools. Grew up in the same town. And when we want something, we get it. We get it even if it takes time. Even if other people want it too." He'd made his way down the aisle, was strolling around the end, approaching hers next.

"Another likeness: We both used to have a sister," he said.

Used to? She wondered if he lost a sister in the same tragic accident that took his parents.

"Yours was younger. Mine, older. She used to worry for me. *Why do you want to be like a woman,* she'd ask. Only I never wanted to be just any woman. I wanted to be you. Always you. And as you know, *we* get what we want. And now it's *my* turn." He had stopped. His voice now rising from directly in front of her. Was it coincidence, or had he noticed the disorganized spot in the boxes? Or perhaps he'd realized that she'd be somewhere near the old man when he'd come in.

"I'm not sad that I shot the wrong girl back at Pearland's event. Because what I really want is to figure you out more deeply. When I look at you, I see more than your face and your hair and your smile. I see the unique shape of your delicate skull – one that I want to get into. That I want to crack open somehow. I want to look at what's inside. Touch it. Feel it. Be with it. And then I want to do that with the rest of you. All of this will get me closer. More like Miss Reese. Marie. Taylor."

He still hadn't moved. Stayed just in that spot, his violent words drifting through the air like poisonous fumes. "I tried it with my sister," he said. "I had to get a little practice before our special night, you see. But it didn't excite me. There was no real mystery there. No urge to see what made her tick." He released a bored-sounding sigh as Reese fought back tears. Tears of hurt and disgust. Of sheer nausea and fear. She began to develop a plan. What she might do if he discovered her there. Climb higher? Make her way down the other side? She knew there had to be some door that led to the outside, but she lacked the space to even lift her chin.

"Had I shot you instead of that other girl, I'd have gone inside, locked us in, and done my work right there and then. I had a toolkit waiting just outside the bathrooms. A hammer. Small saws. But nothing like the equipment I have here.

"Ya see," he continued, "I've waited patiently for this moment. Dreamed of the day you'd come. It took longer than I guessed – back at home a week didn't go by that you weren't visiting the cosmetics department at the mall. But the time only helped me prepare. It's given me a chance to look forward to it. Originally, I'd hoped to let you off the first few times, hold out a bit longer. But I couldn't. Not when you came shuffling down the aisle this morning before the store even opened. It was an opportunity I couldn't pass up."

Reese clenched her eyes shut, silently cursing herself for stepping foot in the place early as she had. Yet Donald would have gotten to her either way. Was dressed up as a woman, for crying out loud. A disguise Reese hadn't seen through even while staring him in the face.

"They'll find me after I'm done, of course. And I won't even fight it. I don't care if I rot in prison the rest of my life. I'll spend every day of it reliving what I'm about to do now. And I'll be happy as a lark. No. As happy as Reese Taylor."

The sureness in his words heightened the fear she felt. The sheer terror seemed to rush through her blood, forcing her heart to pound painfully out of rhythm.

Suddenly Reese felt the boxes beneath her rumble and shake. It went still before more rumbles came. In quick and short lurches. Reese's eyes widened in horror as she realized what it was – him. He was climbing up the shelf now. His weight causing the items to jiggle and shift.

At once Reese held her breath, trapped it in her lungs while she waited. But waited for what? For him to find her?

Donald was panting now. Loud and labored. The

movements growing near. Reese knew that she'd be seen. If he climbed high enough, if he looked closely as he moved, he'd see her lying there, trapped in the small space.

With conscious effort, she forced her jagged breath out slowly, tuned in to the sound of his movements, and wiggled back, a bit further into the darkness.

Another lurch, the force of it jerking her toward the front of the box. In the shadowed space before her, Reese spotted the rounded tips of his fingers, reaching until they rested exactly on the edge of the box she lay on. If she reached out her hand, she could touch his long, painted nails. She considered loosening his grip on the box. Would it send him to the ground with a crash, or simply reveal her hiding spot. And what if Donald knew she was there already? If he jerked the box off its shelf, would Reese tumble down with it?

Paralyzed, she kept focus on the tips of Donald's fingers and prayed that she wouldn't be seen.

CHAPTER THIRTY

"Just what in the world is all this?" Blake grumbled as he pulled up to the department store. A cluster of people had gathered outside the very doors he'd dropped Reese at just short of an hour ago. He caught sight of a squad car pulled close to the building and decided to park next to it.

An officer stood among the confused-looking group. "What's going on out here?" Blake asked. "Are you the officer the Sheriff sent?"

The thin man lifted his chin, squinting from the sun. "Yes. There seems to be a bit of a problem. These folks can't get in here to work their shift. Most likely their boss hasn't shown up yet, what with the lights being out and all."

"I told you there was someone inside," an older lady hollered. Blake looked over the crowd, glancing at the woman's face; it was pinched with irritation. He moved closer to hear as the woman continued.

"Marie was in there. I saw her myself, and when I pounded on the door for her to let me in she strode right past. Few minutes after that the lights went out, and here we all are. Stuck out here and not getting paid."

"Marie's a weirdo," somebody muttered.

"What if that's her?" Blake turned to the officer. His paranoia was gaining merit, and it terrified him. "Donald Turnsbro. He's dressed up as a woman. He could be in there with my wife."

"No, sir. You don't understand. No customers are inside. They don't open for another minute yet."

"*Somebody* let her in," Blake insisted. "I saw it myself from the parking lot. She walked right through these doors."

A younger kid spoke up, flicking a long set of bangs from his face. "Gill does that sometimes. Let's people browse before we open."

Blake turned back to the officer, watched as he stuck a pinky in his ear and twisted it around, saying nothing.

An explosion threatened to erupt deep in his chest. "Listen, I know she's inside this building, and if you can't manage to open these doors somehow I'm going to bust out the glass and go in there myself!"

The officer pressed a hand to the back of one hip, sniffing while he lifted his chin once more. "Well then I'd have to arrest you, sir. You can't just go charging into places like that. Right now I'm waiting for back-up, and like it or not – you'll have to do the same."

Blake took a step toward him, proving he was greater in height no matter how high he lifted his chin. "My wife is under protection right now. From a crazy man dressing as a woman who is right here in this very city. The fact that these doors are locked and there's some weird lady in there with my wife leads me to believe she could be in danger. Now are you going to help me out or do I have to resort to my own means?"

The officer held out a hand and reached for the box at his belt. He stepped away to mumble something in the speaker.

"Pst," the angry woman said. "I have a way to get in through the warehouse if you want to check on your wife."

"Please," Blake said, following her lead.

"I'm not supposed to have this key, which is why I haven't gone in myself. They don't allow just anyone to go into the stockroom, but it's not like I'm gonna steal nothin'. I just hate waiting for people to check on the items I need so I do it myself, you know?"

Blake nodded absently, his pace increasing to speed her along.

"They weren't kidding," the woman continued, scurrying along the length of the building. "Marie's a real freak. I don't like being alone with her myself. And I wouldn't be surprised if she *was* a man."

They were in the shadows now, the dirty brick of the white building scraping Blake's arm as he moved. Was it crazy for him to be so concerned? What made him so sure that Reese was in danger? The information he'd gathered from the sheriff or the fact that Reese was stuck in some dark building with an employee dubbed only as a weirdo and a freak? It was both, along with the fact that Reese was being hunted by a crazy person.

There was reason enough for extreme measures.

Blake pulled in a deep breath. He'd had times where his mind had become a blur. Intense moments. Near misses. Times when there was a lot on the line. Now it was possible everything was on the line. His entire future – a woman he loved more than life itself. But his head wasn't blurred in the slightest. Instead he was focused. A sharp mind on protecting Reese at any and every cost.

Metal met metal as the woman shoved a key into the first lock, failing to make it move one way or the next. She muttered a curse under her breath and tried again, shifting to the lock below it. After smoothly flicking it to one side, she fumbled through her keys once more, shoved another into the upper lock, and clicked that one open as well. She turned to look at him warily. "You'll go straight through this room. Head to the north-west corner and you'll find a door leading to the department store."

"Thank you," Blake said, and pushed the door open to step inside. He spun around to close the door behind him, turned back to the darkened room, and was greeted with a great mass flying toward him. Instinctively, he thrust up his forearm to block his face, cringing as it was struck with a sharp blow.

Blake straightened up, working to see in the low light as the object came at him again. This time Blake reached out with his hand, grabbing the wrist holding the weapon. A hammer. A struggle ensued. The knobby hand with long nails gripping onto the handle while Blake worked to pry it from the firm grip.

"Reese," he shouted through the chaos.

The struggle ceased. The fingers loosening all at once. "How do you know Reese?"

If there'd been any mystery as to this person's gender, the sound of his voice worked to clear it. But the man's question gave away even more – it revealed that he knew who Reese was.

"She's my wife," Blake spat. "Now where is she?"

The news seemed to throw the guy off balance. Blake took advantage, ripping the hammer out of his grip and tossing it across the cement floor. He wrestled the guy to the ground next, cursing himself for not bringing his gun. Of all the days to leave it behind.

The man's wiry build shifted as Blake pinned him down like an angry calf, pressing a knee into his back. "Reese?" he called again. "If you touched her I'll kill you."

"Oh, I'm going to do a lot more than touch," the man said.

The blatant remark burned Blake to the core. He leaned into him, wrapped an arm beneath his neck, and tightened a headlock around his throat. "Tell me where she–" His words came to an abrupt stop as a sharp prick stabbed him in the arm. A heated sting flared up in the single spot, but was quickly replaced with a numbing sensation.

The tingling effect started at the place of the poke, then seeped over the rest of him at a rapid pace. His grip weakened. And he knew he was going. His mind along with his body. Into a deep sleep he couldn't escape. It was a desperate thought that caused him to rouse. A sliver of consciousness in his near-dream state. Reese needed his help. With that thought, Blake grabbed tight onto the only thing he could. The man's neck. He squeezed. Exerting every shred of strength he could gather, focused on choking the life out of him while he had the chance.

Yet his grip loosened.

His mind slipped.

And soon all was black.

CHAPTER THIRTY-ONE

Reese's eyes widened as she saw Blake drop into a lifeless heap. Part of him landed on Donald Turnsbro, who'd been trapped beneath. The other half – his head included – had dropped to the hard floor.

With an anxious thrum pounding at her chest, she surveyed the scene. Her eyes shifting from Blake to Donald, to the area around them. Had Blake been stabbed? From her perspective – which was no more than a silhouette – she'd seen Blake choking Donald just a moment ago. But then he'd groaned and loosened his grip and... *Oh, please say he hasn't been stabbed.*

She spotted it then – the small tube in a spot of light, a sharp needle gleaming at its tip. Inwardly Reese prayed that the contents of that syringe had only put Blake into a harmless sleep. It had been meant for her, she realized. So that Donald could have at her without a fight. In fact, he must've had it stashed somewhere on him as he'd neared her on the shelf only a moment ago. He'd been inches away from her when the doorknob rattled, causing Donald to climb back down in a rush.

Reese had followed suit, silently scaled the structure along the other side, hoping to escape once the door was open. Only then she'd heard the sound of Blake's voice.

Reese slipped silently behind the shelf, watching as Donald pried himself out from under Blake's muscular form. She peeked around the edge and spotted the door Blake had come through, the exit she'd been looking for all along.

Her gaze shot back to Donald as he pushed himself upright, wobbling slightly while glaring down at Blake's lifeless form. He cursed, rammed a foot into the side of Blake's ribs with stocking-covered toes, and then spit on him. The man straightened his skirt next before lifting his gaze. "Oh, Reese-ee," he sang. "You've been a very bad girl."

Reese lost sight of him when he rounded a corner, but kept her gaze on Blake, making sure Donald didn't cause him any harm.

Soon a loud engine roared from within the space. A series of paced, high-pitched beeps rung out next; the sound large equipment makes while backing up. Reese leaned far over, shocked to see Donald steering a pallet truck.

A dart of panic shot through her as she burst into a run toward Blake, her heart pounding out of place. He was nearly within her reach when Reese noticed something from the side of her view. Donald wasn't headed toward Blake at all. Instead, the giant wheels crept toward the outside door.

Donald killed the engine once the exit was blocked

off entirely. Reese sighed. It wasn't like she was going anywhere anyway. Not without Blake. And there was always the door she'd come through, she reminded herself.

A pair of nylon-covered feet hit the floor, causing Reese to shrink silently around the corner and hold her breath.

"So what's the story, Reese-ee pooh?"

Reese knew she should hide again, but she couldn't. Wouldn't leave Blake lying there unguarded.

"Did you really get *married*?" He spat the word. "Did you really think I was going to let you live? That I had just given up on you?"

Reese sunk to her knees before lowering her head. Between the dusty floor and the bottom shelf, she watched for any sign of Donald's feet. At last she spotted them. He was moving toward Blake.

In a panic, she scurried out of her hiding place toward the foot of the aisle and watched in horror as Donald bent down to retrieve his hammer. A gaping tear ran the length of his stockings as he hobbled back toward Blake.

Quickly Reese sifted through her options. Run toward Blake and do what she could to block Donald, or distract him altogether – make him think she was making a run for it.

Donald shook his head as he eyed Blake. "Tsk, tsk, tsk. Should have just stayed away, cowboy," he said. He gripped hold of the hammer, lifted it over his head, and Reese did the only thing she could do. Scream. Loud and alarming.

Donald's head shot up. His green eyes piercing through the low light. Once his focus was set on her, Reese spun around and shot toward the opposite door. The one he hadn't blocked off. A deep gasp sounded from Donald's direction, followed by the mounting thuds of his feet on the floor.

Reese ran. Ran toward the door like her life depended on it. Knowing full well that Blake's did. Aisle after aisle of products, packages, and boxes flew by in a shadowed blur. She screamed again, terrified by how quickly he was gaining on her. She'd hoped to throw him off her trail, make him think she'd gone straight for the door, but she was losing her lead all too fast.

As almost an afterthought, Reese reached out a hand, gripped hold of a sturdy post as she passed, and used the leverage to sling herself down a random aisle. *A weapon.* She needed something to defend herself with.

To her right, packaged linens filled the pallets. She glanced to her left – boxes. Reese hadn't had a chance to think about Donald's whereabouts, had assumed he was somewhere close behind her. So when she saw the dark shadow of his figure looming straight ahead, her eyes widened in shock and terror. He stood there waiting at the head of the aisle with a wide grin. A cat waiting for a mouse to fall into its trap.

The momentum she'd built nearly caused her to do just that, but Reese veered toward the shelves instead, hands ready to grab anything she could. The pole. She wrapped her fingers around it, hoping to pull the structure over, but failed to even make it budge.

At once her feet did the thinking. Climbing nimbly

up the shelves at a rapid pace. Soon she was crawling over the packages, and then making her way to the other side. And there's what she'd been hoping to see. Tools. Stacked in bundles along the shelves across the way. She'd have to climb down to get them.

She glanced around, her view limited by the items on the shelves. Had Donald climbed up the storage unit as well, or was he waiting somewhere below? She paused to listen, failing to hear anything but her own rapid breath. The silence frightened her, made her fear that he stood hovering over Blake with an ax or a sledgehammer. Or even a gun. Soon her feet were off again, this time bringing her to the edge of the unit where she climbed quickly down.

As soon as she hit the floor, Reese bolted for the garden tools. There were hoes, rakes, and shovels. She grabbed the closest of the three and ran toward Blake in a mad rush, praying she wasn't too late.

She gripped the grainy wooden handle with a sweaty palm, keeping the end of the metal shovel upright, knowing the pull of gravity would add to the blow if she had to strike. And there was Blake, his massive figure lying just the same, no Donald in sight.

Reese spun around as she moved closer to him, slowly walking backwards with her face toward the length of the walkway. White streaks of light crept across the quiet shelves. Her movements were all but soundless, and she knew Donald's were too.

Once she was close enough, Reese dropped to one knee, felt Blake's cheek with her palm, glad he was warm beneath her skin. She felt the heat of his breath against her fingers as he exhaled. Quickly she checked his belt, frowning when she caught no sign of his gun. If it came down to it, Reese could shoot to save her life. She'd always been a good shot. But did she have it in her to nail somebody in the head with a garden shovel?

She shivered, gripped hold of her weapon tighter, and then hoisted the thing up, wrenching it over her shoulder like an oversized bat. At first it threw her off balance, so she slid her hands down, moving her grip closer to the center. She looked over the stockroom, watching for any sign of life. Waiting. Guarding. She would not leave Blake's side.

A noise sounded in the distance, causing her gaze to shift to the outside door – the one Donald had covered with the machine on wheels. Someone was on the other side, jostling the handle with a vengeance. Pounding came next. Heavy fist-sized pounds. "Open up," a man said, his voice sounding tight and distant. He spoke again, announcing that he was a city officer. Excitement brewed within her. And hope. They'd come for her. Soon she and Blake would be saved.

"Help," she screamed. "Please! It's blocked. Come through the other door."

"They're not going to be able to get in," Donald assured her, his voice unwavering. He appeared at the foot of a distant aisle. Dust mites crept over his skin as he took a leisurely stroll along a streak of sunlight. "I've only now blocked off the other entrance. Like I told you. We – you and I – we get the things we want. Of course for you it's been constant. Immediate. You want something, you get it. Over and over. For me it's different. I've been waiting a very long time for what I want. Patiently. Quietly. Fantasizing of this moment."

He stopped walking, tilted his head while the shadows cast a dark, demon-like quality to his face. The hollows of his eyes grew deeper. The arc of his brows more severe. He was so disturbed. So sick. She squelched the instinctive side of her that wanted to pity him. The side that wondered what he'd endured in his lifetime to make him capable of such dark and evil deeds. *No.* There was no room for that.

She tightened her grip on the shovel, Blake's steady breath sounding just behind her. She knew he could do a much better job at this than her. Had Donald not had the stupid syringe up his sleeve this would all be over.

"Reese..." Donald sang as he took a step closer. "Put the shovel down."

Her eyes narrowed. Her lips clenched tight.

Donald floated a hand to his chest and batted his eyes, the movements smooth and easy. "Why, I'm just harmless little Reese Marie Taylor. I wouldn't so much as hurt a fly." His voice was high – his accent strong and mocking. "Ya know, I think everybody should have a dream. And that they should do whatever they can to make it come true. It's more than just wishin' and prayin' it'll happen. You have to chase it. Chase your dream, and one day you'll catch it." With his face half-hidden in the shadows, he smiled. A wide, Cheshire grin. "That was good advice you gave to the good ol' folks at Shadycrest Elementary, Reese-ee pooh. So good that even I took it. Like I said, I went to every public appearance. I've chased what I want. And now I'm about to catch it." Suddenly Donald lunged at her. A mass of short, curly hair, smeared lipstick, and sweat-coated skin.

The steel edge of the shovel cut through the air with a swoosh. Her grip was solid. Her shoulders tense. And her eyes clenched shut. The wooden handle rumbled against her palms as the shovel met resistance with a thick, fleshy thud.

Reese pried her eyes open in time to see Donald hit the floor with a muted thump. The shovel slipped from her grip as she dropped to her knees, stunned into numb silence. Voices sounded. It took her a moment to realize they were coming from right there in the room. They were asking if she was okay. Two men. In uniform. Reese nodded her head, watching as a team of paramedics rushed in. And as they worked, putting Blake on a gurney, and then Donald, Reese offered a prayer of thanks, hardly able to believe the ordeal was over at last.

CHAPTER THIRTY-TWO

A series of beeps sounded as Blake struggled to open his eyes. His lids were like lead. His body too. And his mind was a thick and hazy blur – until an image of Reese shot to the surface. His eyes flicked open. A white ceiling loomed overhead.

"Reese?" he shouted, kicking the covers from his feet. He was halfway off the bed before he heard her voice.

"Right here, Blake," she said. Her face came into view, calming the frantic pace of his pulse in an instant. "How are ya feelin'?"

His gaze held hers before his head rolled back, causing the room to spin. "Fine," he muttered, surveying the tubes strapped to his arm. "What's all this for?"

"Don't sit up just yet," she said, digging into her purse. She pulled out a bright red sucker and tore off the wrapper. Before he could protest Reese popped the thing into his mouth. "Eat this," she said. "It'll get your sugars up."

Blake brought his hand up to remove the cherry

flavored candy, but stopped short when he caught sight of her glare.

"You suck on that for at least five minutes." She eyed the tubes for a bit. "It'll probably kick in faster than what they've got running through these things."

He couldn't quite grasp onto her logic, which seemed to muddle his mind even more. Made him forget what he was even doing there. "What happened?" he finally asked.

Reese's eyes went wide and bright. "I hit him!" She reached for an icy mug by the side of his bed and proceeded to lift his head off the pillow like he was an invalid. "Drink," she demanded.

Blake glanced down at the flexible plastic straw, fighting a strong dose of nausea welling in his gut. He pulled the sucker from his mouth and forced down a few gulps, hoping the cold fluid would wake his senses. Had Reese just said she'd hit somebody?

"Hit *who*?" he asked.

"Donald Turnsbro, of course. I smacked him dead on the head with a garden shovel."

"*What?*" Blake shot up, pushing the mug from his face. "Are you kidding?" The nausea flared up again.

"Nope. Not kidding." Reese set down the mug and pressed a button on the controller by his bed. Once the upper half of the mattress met his back, she set both hands on his shoulders and pressed until he slouched into it. "I really did hit him. Can you believe it?"

If Blake could form words he'd say no. That he couldn't believe it at all. He was stunned.

Reese took the sucker from his hand, popped it in

her own mouth, and tucked it into her cheek. "You sure you're feelin' alright?"

"I'm fine. And did you say Donald's dead?" He worked to recall what had happened.

"No. Just, well he's gone now, but I smacked him so hard he hit the ground like a sack of potatoes."

The events came back to him in staggered bits and pieces. He'd entered the warehouse, fought with Donald Turnsbro, and then... "He stuck me with a needle," Blake blurted.

"I know. I'm so glad you're alright." She took the sucker out of her mouth, offered it to him once more, and grinned when he accepted. "Can you believe that I did that?" Her smile was wide. Contagious. He felt something like it forming at his own lips.

"No," he managed, realizing what she wanted from him. "I can't believe it."

A trace of delight whirled in her eyes. "I can't either. I've been dying to tell you. They said you'd be up and at 'em in no time. That you just needed some fluids in ya to speed things along, but it has felt like forever."

"So they've got him?"

Reese nodded proudly. She didn't appear to be wounded in the least. "And you're alright? Nothing's broken or hurt?"

She shook her head. "Well..." She lifted her foot onto the edge of his bed. "I did get this." A bandaid covered one spot on her shin, a hint of blood evident at the center. "I did this when all the lights went out, but that's it."

Reese went on to describe the events in great detail,

an entire play-by-play that made Blake's stomach crawl. He was sick at the thought of losing her. At the idea that she had been left alone to defend herself against Donald Turnsbro, but he could hardly dwell on it. Not with Reese standing there, her face lit up like the Fourth of July. All he could do as he looked at her was celebrate that she'd survived. That the good Lord had seen fit to help her through it when Blake couldn't.

"Come here," he said, tossing the sucker stick into the trash.

Her smile widened. "I *am* here."

"No. Closer."

"Like...how?" She dropped her foot before hoisting herself onto the edge of his bed, letting her legs dangle. "Like this?"

"More like..." Blake reached out to spin her toward him, pulling her against his chest.

The sound of her astonished laughter filled the room. "Stop that, Blake, you're gonna get us in trouble."

Before she could speak another word, Blake took hold of her face, pulling her in for a kiss. "Who cares?" he mumbled against her lips. The woman he held was a mystery. As strong and resilient as she was beautiful and kind. And he loved her.

Her lips parted in time for their next playful kiss, and Blake took advantage, relishing in the sweet, cherry taste on her lips. Just as their pace began to build, Reese pushed him away and sat up on the bed. She plopped onto the floor next, wordlessly walked to the door, and closed it. The curtain rings squeaked as she slid the fabric along the rod, further blocking the door.

She strode back to him then, the hypnotic sway of her hips making it hard to blink. Once at his side, Reese joined him on the bed, bringing her full and tempting lips to his. "Now," she purred, "where were we?"

EPILOGUE

"You know, I'm actually gonna miss this house," Reese said, gazing out the kitchen window one last time. She'd been fond of the old place since day one, and had only grown to love it more over time. It was dark beyond the glass, but the small bulb at the barn lit a glowing patch of falling snowflakes; the sight was nothing short of majestic.

"There are a few things I'll miss about it too," Blake said. "Being so close to Tucker and the barn, for one." His boots strolled over the floor, the steady sound stopping just behind her. His strong arms wrapped around her waist as he nudged his chest solidly against her back. "'Course we'll just be a mile down the road. One thing I won't miss is having the three stooges living beneath us." He pressed a longing kiss to the side of her throat.

Reese sighed and tuned into the sensation. "So did they finally decide who's moving up here with Tom?" she asked, working to gather a conscious thought.

"Naw. They'll have to fight it out. Until Shane's ready to move in, that is. Of course Gavin could always come back too. Guess we'll just have to wait and see."

Reese spun around to face him, enjoying the feel of his masculine arms around her. "I hope he does come back one day. He could find a nice girl out here. Settle down."

"Maybe we'll have to hook him up with a gal needing protection," he mumbled against her skin. He kissed her just beneath her earlobe and let out a low chuckle. "Worked for me."

"Mmm, hmm," Reese said with a laugh.

Blake laced his fingers through hers. "So, you ready to go home?"

"Yep." She pictured the newly built house. All their items had been moved, the new furniture delivered, they'd only returned to the ranch house to tidy up one last time. Now Reese could hardly wait to spend their first night in the new home.

Outside, a thick layer of pale grey clouds lightened the night sky while hiding the moon and stars completely. The Montana landscape seemed to change with each new season, and Reese could hardly wait to witness the beauty of it.

As she and Blake made their way to the new home, tiny flurries of snow danced and swirled in the headlights, their crystal-like flakes magical and bright. Reese leaned into Blake as he drove, resting her head on his shoulder. He dropped one hand from the wheel and smoothed it over Reese's hand where it rested on her tummy; she hadn't realized it was there.

"I can't believe it's really happening." He shook his head. "A baby. We're actually going to have a baby."

Reese smiled. "I know. Aren't you dying to know what it is?"

He shook his head. "I already know."

Reese pulled away from his shoulder. "You do not." She'd only just found out herself that very morning. "Is that why you were so fine with waitin' until tonight to see the pictures? Because you're secretly positive you already know?" She tilted her head until he met her gaze.

"Maybe." He shrugged.

"Man," Reese said. "Keepin' this to myself all day has been harder on me than it has you."

Blake smiled. "We're having a boy. I know it." Reese decided not to answer. He'd find out what they had in store soon enough.

As they pulled into the new driveway, a soft layer of powdery snow clung to the concrete. The porch glowed bright while a warm haze of lamplight lit the windows. "I can't believe this is actually our house," Reese said. "It's so beautiful."

"Sure is," Blake agreed. He pulled the truck into the garage and shut off the engine. "Don't move a muscle," he said, removing the key from the ignition.

"What kinda ideas do you got goin' through that head of yours?" Reese asked.

"Just wanting to carry my lovely wife over the threshold of our new home." With that, he climbed out of the truck, tucked his hands beneath her, and lifted her from the seat. After shutting the truck door with an elbow, Blake headed out the garage toward the front of the house.

"Why aren't we going in through the garage door?" He furrowed his brows. "'Cuz I'm carrying you over the threshold. Has to be the front door for that." She laughed. "I didn't know that was a rule." "It is."

Cool flakes of snow drifted onto her hair as they moved, some landing on her cheeks and arms as well. She giggled as Blake burrowed a kiss into her neck. "We're going to need a fire to keep us warm tonight," he breathed against her skin. Sounded good to her.

While propping the screen door with one foot, Blake pushed open the front door to their new place, revealing a sight that was fresh and familiar all at once. Reese had helped pick out everything from the carpet to the counters, had seen it all several times while moving in and decorating and getting things just right, but from this perspective it was entirely new. Blake was right – he'd needed to bring her in through the front.

Once he set her onto her feet, Reese gave him a kiss on the cheek and walked about the place, a wide smile on her face. "Well," she said, stepping over to the coat closet. "Are you ready to see?"

Blake strode to the couch and took a seat before leaning forward. He rested his elbows on his knees, ran a hand over his jaw, and smiled. "Ready."

Her heart sped up in delight, fluttering excitement at what she was about to share. She twisted the knob, pulled her purse from the hook in the closet, and dug out the photo she'd placed lovingly in a heart-shaped frame. She pressed it against her chest as she walked toward him.

"Okay. You said you were ready; right?"

Blake patted the seat next to him. "Uh-huh."

She exhaled, lowered herself onto the couch, and pulled the frame away from her and into Blake's view.

"I thought you said you had a picture." He tilted his head, narrowing his eyes as he neared it.

To Reese it was clear as day. "It *is* a picture. An ultrasound, anyway. See?" She pointed out the shape of a small body. "Here's the head, the back, legs and arms." Her heart sputtered as he inspected it further. "Do you see?"

Blake nodded absently. "Looks more like I'm seeing double."

Reese shot off the couch and cheered. "You're right!"

"I am?" He still looked confused.

"Yes. We're having twins." Just saying the words aloud made it seem more real. More exciting.

"You're kiddin' me."

She shook her head, dying to see if he'd be happy or freaked out or…

Suddenly he shot off the couch and wrapped his arms around her. "Twins? Really?" He kissed her cheek as he lifted her off the ground, spinning in place.

Just as Reese wrapped her arms around him in return, he stopped and set her down. "Oh, sorry. I've got to be more careful with you. It's just, you're not showing a whole lot yet."

Reese's eyes widened. "I am too."

But Blake shook his head in protest. "You should've seen Allie when she was pregnant." He put his arms out in front of him. "She was clear out to here."

That earned a him a playful swat on the arm. "You best not be saying that in front of her if you want to live."

Blake shook his head. "Naw. She already knows. It's 'cuz she's so short." He picked up the frame once more, eyes lit up as he stared at it. "Wait." He glanced up. "You said you knew if we were having a boy or a girl... How can you tell in this thing?"

That reminded her. "Oh yeah," she said, rushing over to her purse once more. "These right here." The next two pictures wouldn't take a whole lot of guess work. Each had a small arrow pointing to the identifying feature of the baby, along with the words *it's a...*

"Boy? It's a boy?" Blake looked at the next picture. "*Two* boys?"

Reese nodded anxiously, feeling as if everything was right with the world. Blake came in for a softer hug this time, a low chuckle rumbling in his throat. "Can't believe we're going to have twin boys."

"Me neither."

He started humming then, a soft country tune as he took her hand. They slow-danced in the center of the room as Reese thought back on her journey there. The case that had brought her to the ranch had been settled just a month ago. Donald Turnsbro was serving a life sentence for what he'd done to his sister alone. The words *no chance for parole* had been heaven to her ears.

And as Blake's hand slipped beneath the hem of her shirt, his fingers skimming over her back, Reese thought maybe it was time for a *taste* of heaven too.

With that thought, she gripped Blake's hand and led him down the hallway.

"I got you something," Blake said as he trailed after her.

She stopped at the doorway, spotting the new item at once. "The lamp. Where'd you get it?"

"I ordered it online. It's really cool." He stepped ahead of her and into the room. "See, it turns off and on at your touch. And it has different levels of brightness too."

The simple gift meant more to her than words could say. "Blake, that ... I love it." She hurried over to his side, tapped the gold base as he'd shown her, and smiled as it went from bright, to dim, and then dimmer still. With the next tap, the light went out completely.

She melted. Loving his thoughtful nature. Loving him. The light flicked back on, and Blake gave her a grin. "I bought one for the baby's room too," he said.

Reese pushed herself up on her toes and planted a kiss to his lips. She brought her hands to his chest next, smiling as she pressed him back onto the bed, and giggled as he fell back at her will.

Blake propped himself with his elbows and lifted a brow. "You're going to join me, right?"

She nodded her head slowly, and then reached out to give the lamp one, single tap. The light dimmed a notch, and Reese stepped out of her shoes. She gave the lamp another tap, the yellow glow dimmer still, and shimmied out of her levis next. It wasn't so brave, considering the maternity blouse she wore went to her thighs.

Reese reached for the lamp once more, but Blake spoke up. "No, no," he said, sitting up and scooting to the edge of the bed. He put his large hands on her hips and gave them a warm squeeze. "There are times I don't like the dark either. And this," he nodded to the buttons at the top of her blouse, "would be one of them." He pulled her onto the bed with him as their laughter filled the room.

The feel of his scruff on her neck caused a thrill to rush through her body. He teased her there for a while, filling her with longing and desire. At last his kiss was hers. His lips strong and persuasive one moment, gentle and caressing the next.

With a hint of a groan, Blake pulled away for a blink and gave her a mischievous smile. "Okay," he said, motioning to where she'd stood a moment ago. "Time to pick up where you left off."

A burst of confidence struck as she narrowed her eyes in return. "Okay," she said, climbing off the bed once more. And as Reese immersed herself in her time with Blake, a thought flittered through the back of her mind. Lamp-light dim, dark, or bright, none of it mattered anymore. With Blake Emerson in her life, Reese wasn't afraid. There was bound to be a few dark moments in store, but with twins on the way and her man by her side, Reese's future had never looked so bright.

READ SAMPLE CHAPTER OF GAVIN'S STORY BELOW

Dear Reader,

Thank you for taking the time to read Reese's Cowboy Kiss. As a reader myself, I dive into novels seeking an enjoyable getaway from the daily grind – I hope this story provided that for you! If you enjoyed the book, I could really use (and would sincerely appreciate) your review on Amazon and or Goodreads.

If you'd like to contact me or sign up to hear about my latest releases, please visit my webpage @kimberlykryey.com

Find me on Facebook for updates on new releases and sales: https://www.facebook.com/pages/Kimberly-Krey-Author-Page/106826456029568?ref=hl

And Twitter: https://twitter.com/KimberlyKrey

Complete your collection of The Sweet Montana Bride Series
by KIMBERLY KREY

(Entire collection on Amazon, Barnes & Noble, and CreateSpace now)

Reese's Cowboy Kiss
Blake's Story

Jade's Cowboy Crush
Gavin's Story
(Sample Chapter Included)

Cassie's Cowboy Crave
Shane's Story

Also, look for the new series, Second Chances, a companion to the Sweet Montana Bride Series.

Starting with

Rough Edges

Allie's Story, Volume One

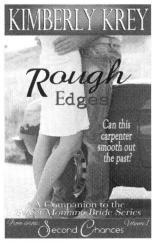

Allie's ex-husband might have left Montana in search of greener pastures, but his old high school friend, Braden Fox, is still running the woodshop just miles down the road. The handsome carpenter has been in love with

Allie since he can remember. Now, with Terrance out of the picture, will he finally have a chance? Or will bitterness and hurt from years back keep him from welcoming her into his heart? Find out in this newly released novel, Rough Edges, where Allie and the carpenter try to smooth out the past.

Available now on Amazon, Barnes & Noble, and CreateSpace

Next in the Second Chances Series, *Mending Hearts*. Logan and Candice have struggled over the years. With hardships ranging from their inability to conceive, to loved ones lost, the two have finally called it quits. Almost. Logan Emerson isn't ready to let go just yet. Perhaps with a little persistence and a lot of forgiving, the married couple can mend their broken hearts.

See Amazon.com, Barnes & Noble, and CreateSpace for availability

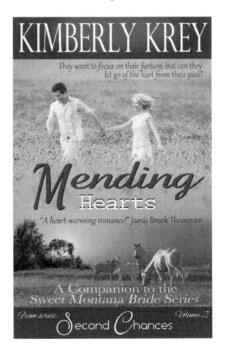

Also look for *Fresh Starts*. Bree has had her fair share of difficulties. The loss of her parents, a not-so-recent divorce, and the disruption of her life caused by a dangerous stalker who's serving jail time. When the determined criminal finishes his sentence, Bree is sent into hiding. And while she's doing all she can to steer clear of this frightening piece of her past, a new man enters the scene, determined to be part of her future.

See Amazon.com, Barnes & Noble, and CreateSpace for availability

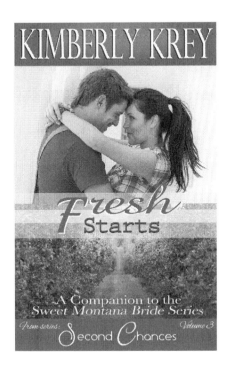

Sample chapter from Jade's Cowboy Crush: (Gavin's story)

CHAPTER ONE

Jade's phone buzzed, causing a smile to tug at her lips. She huddled closer to the glowing screen, anxious to read the message.

We've done enough texting. Time to talk face-to-face.

A quiet thrill rushed through her as she laughed out loud. "The nerve of this guy," she muttered, typing back to the unknown stranger.

Not going to happen. You could be psychotic for all I know.

"What'd he say now?" LeAnn hovered over Jade's shoulder, blocking the afternoon sunlight with her spikey hair.

"Nothing yet." Jade glanced at the time on her phone. "Crap. Our break's almost over." She looked up to see LeAnn checking behind her.

"I'm not even on break," her friend admitted, adjusting her apron, "but I've got to see where this leads."

Jade twisted each one of the small, silver studs in her left ear as she waited for an answer. Nothing said entertainment like flirting with a guy she'd never met. Or at least couldn't remember meeting. The guy swore he'd collected her number over a year ago, had marked it with four stars to ensure he wouldn't forget to call. Problem was, according to him, he'd had a girlfriend at the time.

Her phone vibrated, the screen glowing with his response.

You think you would give some psycho your number?

No. But that was just it. Jade didn't give out her number. And she rarely went to clubs. She sighed, sensing an end to their little game, and typed out her message.

I've got to get back to work.

The text earned a groan of disapproval from LeAnn. Jade stared intently at the phone, vaguely noting the sounds of cats rummaging through the dumpster across the alley.

WAIT! I really think we should meet. Why won't you do it? What are you... scared?

"Oooh," LeAnn said, "he's trying to bait you. Don't fall for it. You don't want to end up like Wanda with all those restraining orders."

Jade rolled her eyes and typed out a reply.

Not scared. Sane.

"Who else does Wanda have a restraining order against?" Jade asked once she sent the text. "I thought it was only Rhet."

LeAnn flicked her blue-streaked bangs out of her face. "The other guy is from last year sometime. Like, her ex, ex-boyfriend."

"I wouldn't be surprised if a hundred women had a

restraining order against Rhet," Jade said. "I feel like *I* need one for talking Wanda into breaking up with him." Jade meant it as a joke, but felt a level of truth in the words as she'd spoken them.

"Me too," LeAnn said. "That guy terrifies me. Glad we don't have to see his face around here anymore."

The phone buzzed again, bringing Jade's attention back to the matter at hand.

You may not remember me, but I definitely remember you. It's the reason I'm being so persistent.

LeAnn laughed. "What a load of crap."

"Totally." Jade was already texting back a reply.

Yeah, right. What number am I on your little list, friend? Ten? Eleven? Or have you been rejected by an even dozen?

It may not have been nice, but Jade was done playing along. Chances were, the two had never met at all and he'd only stumbled onto her number by accident. Another text showed up on the small screen.

Okay, your eyes are brown.

Jade fought back a smile. "Lucky guess."

The phone buzzed again.

I thought your hair was blond at first, but when we sat down at the table I realized it was red.

"Strawberry blond," Jade mumbled, a bit of recollection mingling just beyond her grasp.

When I finally got you to smile, I noticed the light freckles across your cheeks.

Jade felt herself blush. She hated those freckles.

"Maybe you two *did* meet," LeAnn said, hunching closer to the phone as it buzzed once again.

You were wearing green when we met, and for a reason I tried to drag out of you, you were sad that night.

"Whoa. This guy is good," LeAnn said. "Seriously. I'd meet up with him."

Jade's jaw dropped. "Two seconds ago you were talking about restraining orders." Never mind the fact that Jade had goose bumps rising all over her skin and a pool of warm, liquid sugar bathing her heart. His final text caused her to remember. She liked this guy. Was interested in him. And disappointed when he hadn't called. Too bad she'd sworn off men since then.

With a sad sort of resolve, Jade texted him back.

Well, sorry to break it to you, but I'm married.

In order to make her lie more convincing, she added to it.

Got hitched three months ago today.

The small screen glared at her – daring her to hit send. What was stopping her? The image of the guy; the strong, ruggedly handsome, not-your-typical-L.A. guy at the club. One who'd managed to cheer her up after a terrible day. There had been something about him that caused her to give out her number – an act she avoided at all costs.

"Married?" LeAnn shouted. "No! Don't send that. Just meet the guy somewhere. For a drink. Or a yoga class. The beach."

"He had a girlfriend at the time, LeAnn. And he was

hitting on me that whole night." Her thumb hovered over the word *send,* before pressing down on it.

LeAnn groaned. "Hitting on you? How? Did he try to make out with you?"

"No," Jade realized. "He just, didn't leave my side. He was sweet, actually. But still... single moms shouldn't date."

LeAnn came to a stand and pulled a pad of order slips from her apron pocket. "You can't let the advice of some radio shrink run your entire life." The flutter of pages flipping sounded as she thumbed the corner of the small pad.

"But she's right." Dr. Movay's voice echoed within Jade's mind as she repeated the woman's famous phrase. "Kids don't need the drama of a dating mama. Luke deserves better than that." She watched for something to show on the screen. Anything. And despite the conviction of her own words, a bitter sting of regret sunk into her chest. An ache for something that might have been.

"Wait a minute. Was this the guy you said reminded you of a country boy?"

Jade glanced up. "What?"

LeAnn nodded her head, a fresh spark of light in her crystal blue eyes. She hunched down as she spoke. "I remember. You came into work one day, high as a kite. It took me half-a-shift to drag it out of you, but you finally admitted that you'd met a guy." She looked away for a blink before staring back at her. "He had some cowboy-sounding name. You liked him. I remember because you never liked anyone."

Jade backed away, glancing down at the lifeless phone once more. "You better get in there before Angelo comes out. Tell him I'll be there in a sec."

LeAnn shook her head in disgust. "If you don't get

past that doctor's advice, you're going to be alone forever."

As the sound of LeAnn's footsteps grew softer, Jade couldn't help but wonder if that were true. Once the door had closed, she typed out one last text for the mysterious stranger.

Just out of curiosity, what is your name?

The heated thumps of her heart picked up a rapid pace as she watched the screen, waiting for any sign of life. At last it came. Just two words.

Gavin Emerson.

This ends the sample of Jade's Cowboy Crush.

ABOUT THE AUTHOR

Kimberly Krey lives in the Salt Lake Valley with her husband, four children, and two dogs. She has a great love for literature, family, and food.

Made in the USA
Middletown, DE
29 September 2019